One More Time

MORE SERIES BOOK ONE

S. VAN HORNE

Copyright

Dedication

In Memory of my OPG (Old Plain Grandma) if it wasn't for your mothering and your encouragement to read I wouldn't ever have been able to take this step. I know you're smiling down at me from heaven for finally following this dream.

I love you and miss you, tons and bunches.

(Sonya and her OPG - May of 2013)

P.S. Mari, Dante's yours.

One More Time

At twenty-five, Len Shields had it all, a promising medical career, a loving family, amazing friends, and her brother back from his time in the Navy. Everything was perfect—until the first letter . . .

At twenty-seven, Dante De Luca was finally finished with his time in the Navy and was starting his new career at Seal Security with his buddies from the service. Everything was finally settling into place for him—until the phone call . . .

Now the hunt is on to find a stalker that could shatter everything Len and Dante have been building . . . including the love they have for each other. When they both finally admit their feelings for each other, the worst happens . . . will they ever get their one more time?

Note From Author

I wanted to take a moment to explain how the phrase One More Time came about. If you know me personally, you will know that my husband and I say this to each other a lot. It started over sixteen years ago when we were just dating and now it's something we say to each other multiple times a day.

It first began when I was a little girl with my Daddy. He would look at me and say, "I love you first." I then would look at him and say, "I love you second." At that point we both would say as fast as we could, "I love you all the time." We were trying to beat each other. This is something we still do to this day and he now does with my daughter. Anyway, at one point after he beat me yet again on saying it faster; I stated to him, "I love you all the time plus one more than you love me."

Fast forward years later . . . one day I was reading the

paper when my husband (who was my boyfriend at the time) and I saw a story about SHMILY. If you're not familiar with this story, I encourage you to look up SHMILY Coins for the story. It really touched me and so I explained to my boyfriend that we needed a saying too.

It wasn't much after that, I want to say less than a week; when my boyfriend said, "I love you." I immediately thought of what my dad and I do and I said, "I love you too. But I love you one more time than you could ever love me." At that point, I stopped and spun around to face him with a huge smile on my face.

"That's it! Our saying! One More Time!" I exclaimed to him, and he smiled.

That's how the saying One More Time was born and has been going strong for years. My children say they love hearing it from us because it shows just how much their parents are in love and it's a great feeling to know that our love is affecting them in a good way.

So it's with this that I encourage you to find a saying for your loved one. It's never too late to do this. The More Series is about finding that one and making a statement in a saying. I really hope you enjoy this and find a saying that will change how you show the world what your love means.

Much Love,
Sonya

P.S. There are two characters in this book that's from another book. Mace and Coleman are from Mary B Moore's—Forever Mine. Make sure you go and check it out. Our characters will be visiting each other and working together. Also, they'll be vacationing together soon. So keep an eye out for that.

Now, on to Len and Dante . . .

One

Len

SCARED DOESN'T EVEN BEGIN TO describe what I'm feeling right now. Looking at my shaking hands holding the note that was left on my car windshield, I'm not sure what to think. I'm trying to figure out who would send it. I've never led a guy on. How could I when I'm still stuck on the one guy who thinks of me as his best friend's annoying little sister? Hearing those words spoken from him broke my heart, but what shattered it was when I'd heard him and my brother talk about becoming Navy Seals. Not only was I losing the one guy I had loved since I was twelve, I was losing my brother as well.

Don't get me wrong, I support my troops, but I was terrified that they were going to die in combat. I'm not dumb, and even back then, I knew being a Navy Seal was a big thing. I knew it meant secret dangerous missions without knowing if they were okay. To keep my mind off my fear and because I loved them more than words can describe, I did all

I could in supporting them. I sent care packages, wrote letters, and helped with charity events to raise funds. I also visited my brother when he was stateside, a difficult task with me being in school, then in college, and then during my residency to become a doctor. Now, as a second-year Emergency Room resident at Center Point Medical Center, I'm even more busy and have less time to myself.

It helps that my family moved back to Kansas City when I began college. Even Mamma Gio and Papa Tony followed along with the boys in tow. They said they were ready for a change and wanted to join their second family. Now, Neil is done with the Navy and has opened his own security business, which Dante ended up partnering with him.

Since his return, I've yet to see Dante. It's been nine long years since I've seen him, and I have no clue what I'm going to say when I'm finally face to face with him. I don't want it to be weird, but I know it will be. Ever since the day they left, I've had to re-evaluate my feelings constantly.

The chaste kiss he placed on my lips not only scared me, but had given me hope. It would've to any sixteen-year-old girl who'd just had her first kiss from her Prince Charming, the boy she'd been in love with her whole life. But then letters from my brother about the crazy crap they were pulling and the women Dante was screwing changed everything.

"Neil will be with you shortly, Len," Sara, my brother's receptionist, tells me as she walks back to her desk.

"Thank you, Sara." I take a seat, then look back at her and add, "We really need to set up that girls' night we keep talking about. I miss hanging with you guys."

"You're the one who's always busy at work. Call Ashley

and tell her your schedule. Then we'll see about getting you in the club and finally getting you a man. We both need a man. We really need to get laid!" she says and then rolls her eyes at the outburst that comes from Neil who is in the next room.

"What the hell are you talking about? I don't ever want to hear about my sister getting laid," Neil growls as he joins us.

I don't miss the heated look he shoots Sara. I start giggling because I know Neil wants her and she wants him; however, they are both so oblivious of each other's desire. I stand up with the letter in hand and walk over to him.

"Aw, there, there, care bear, that doesn't concern you. I'll do what I want, when I want. I'm twenty-five years old, not twelve. If I want to sleep with a man, I will," I say, giving Sara a mischievous wink.

She knows I'm a virgin, he doesn't and I don't plan on telling him. I just love teasing him.

"I don't want to hear that. I'll tell Pops if you don't stop. I swear to God I'm going to be in jail for murder."

"If you don't want to hear about things like that, then I suggest you cut out the eavesdropping." I end up laughing at the look of disgust on his face as he leads me to the conference room.

"It isn't eavesdropping if what was spoken was practically being yelled out," he growls at me. "Let's drop this conversation and you tell me what's going on. You never drop by during the day unless you're bringing lunch to me or you call first," he states as he sits.

A feeling of terror hits me as I remember why I'm here. Handing him the note, I take a seat as well. Neil and I are very close. He isn't going to take this threat well. I'm scared of what he's going to do or say.

Watching him read the note, I see the change come over his face immediately. He looks up at me, and I'm struck with what I see. His blue eyes that normally have a hint of green in them are now full-on green with fury tightening his jaw and his nostrils flare as he takes in a harsh breath. He picks up the phone off the conference room table and barks three words into the receiver, "Conference room. Now!"

DANTE

I stare down at the receiver in confusion before I hang it up in the cradle. Lucky isn't one to let his temper get the best of him. There's only been a handful of times I've seen this side of him. The only thing that can get him this worked up is when his family or one of the guys is being harmed or when we have a sensitive case we're working on. A sense of dread washes over me as I start to get up.

I turn towards the door and the overhead light gleams off the photos lining my bookcase. My eyes immediately go to the one picture I can't seem to avoid.

Len's beautiful smile makes me catch my breath. She's the one woman that I can't get out of my head. I'm looking forward to seeing her again at the party this weekend.

Over the years, I got letters and care packages from her. I wrote her back and sent her things I bought from places all over the world. She never sent a picture and when she came to visit Lucky, I'd make myself scarce because I knew that if I were to see her, I wouldn't be able to stop myself from making her mine. I didn't want her to be waiting back home not knowing if I was ever coming back. So, when they'd Skype, I'd go into the other room. I also couldn't chance Lucky knowing that I'd fallen for his kid sister.

It hit me when she was sixteen, however I wasn't sure what the feelings were until around four years ago. She was already such an amazing woman and she hadn't even finished growing yet.

I knew I'd run into Len, at some point, since I made the choice to move to Kansas City with Lucky and start Seal Security. I wasn't giving up the opportunity to work with my brothers and the guys from our troop even if that meant I couldn't avoid her.

We aren't your average private investigators. We specialize in security systems, bodyguard work, missing persons, and stalking. We work a lot with KCPD—Kansas City Police Department.

We also have our own motorcycle club that we started. Not one of those one percenters which are considered an outlaw MC because they don't follow the laws. We're just a bunch of guys who love to ride bikes, but also, we help with charity drives, special victims, and offer assistance around the community. Well, we haven't officially started, but that's what we're planning. Right now, we just ride together.

I head out of my office and down the hall to the conference room, listening to Sara talking on the phone to one of her girlfriends. It has to be Ashely because out of all the girls, those two are the closest.

"Yes, we need to have a girls' night, ASAP. We need to find some men. I need to get laid and we need to get Len laid too. She needs to give up that v-card already."

That stops me in my tracks. Holy shit, Len's still a virgin! That's going to make this weekend even harder when I see her. You'd think it would make me want her less, only, it just makes me want to claim her even more.

Shaking my head, I enter the conference room. The first thing I notice is the back of a small woman being comforted by Lucky.

He looks up at me and then leans down to whisper into her ear. The man is seriously hung up on Sara, so I know the gesture isn't sexual since that isn't her in his arms. Shifting slightly, he looks at me again.

"We have a problem."

He nods to a piece of paper on the table. As I'm picking it up, I shoot him an odd, sidelong glance.

"Squirt, go to the bathroom and wash up, okay? I'm going to fill Dante in on the situation. Come back when you're better. Don't worry about anything. We'll never let anything happen to you."

My head jerks up and I'm caught in a pair of blue eyes that literally take the breath from my lungs. The same eyes that have haunted me every day since I was eighteen. She's even more beautiful than the last time I saw her, and my body takes notice. I'm harder than I've been in ages. Holy shit, I think I just fell for my best friend's little sister in one glance. I'm in deep shit because it's at that moment that I realize those feelings from so long ago was me falling for her. She has totally changed and I didn't recognize her.

Her hair is a brighter blonde from what I remember and lies over her shoulders. She's in a light dress that hugs her curves just right. Her dress has a V neck that shows off her full breasts. I can just assume that the rest of her body, which I can't see because she's sitting down, is going to be just as hot. My gaze travels back up to her eyes where I can see the fear that's running deep in her soul.

"Hey, Dante, long time no see. I wish it was under better circumstances," Len says as she smiles at me sadly, then she looks back at Neil. "I'll be back in a second."

She stands up and walks towards the door. Damn, she has an ass that won't stop. Seeing the sway of her body has the air knocking out of my lungs, yet again. Her legs are tan and long, and I want them wrapped around my waist as I pound into her. She's wearing these fuck-me shoes that I can almost feel pressing into my back. There's no way I'm going to be able to stay away from her now. Lucky's going to kill me.

I glance back over at Lucky and see the anger raging through his body which has his fist clenching and his muscles pulling tight. I take a deep breath and pull my thoughts away from Len.

"What's up?"

"Look at the note. As I said, we've got a problem."

I skim through the note quickly, and what I read has me seeing red.

LEN,

DO YOU THINK YOU CAN FLIRT WITH ANY MAN THAT WALKS IN HERE, AFTER YOU HAVE GIVEN ME YOUR HEART? YOU BETTER THINK AGAIN. STOP FLIRTING WITH DR. JOHNSON, OR I'LL KILL HIM AND PUNISH YOU.

YOURS ALWAYS.

21

Oh, problem is not a big enough word to describe what I'm reading. What's in my hand calls the beast in me to come to the surface. All I see is blood, and it isn't mine. Shit's going to hit the fan, heads are going to roll, and someone is going to die a very slow and painful death. *Nobody* threatens my woman and lives.

Lucky must have seen the thirst for blood in my eyes because his facial expressions go from rage, to shock, to something I'm unable to distinguish. I know what he's seeing. I've been trying to hide it from him and the world for years. Now, it's time to let them all know that Len belongs to me. Damn the consequences, because no one can protect her better than the man who is willing to die or kill to keep her safe.

Two

Len

Thirteen years earlier...

I HATE THAT I'M STARTING a new school, so mad that I had to leave my friends for a new area. Pops said it's only until I graduate from high school. I'm only starting seventh grade, but since Neil's starting high school, he needed to make this move now. He was doing it for Mom.

Since Pops is a real estate agent, he can work anywhere. With Mom just getting her PhD in therapy, she was given the chance of a lifetime to work at Seattle Children's Center in the autism department. Plus, he said he'd always wanted to live near the ocean.

So, here we are, living in Oak Harbor, Washington, a small town on Whidbey Island. It's pretty, but I miss Kansas City, Missouri and can't wait until I go back to visit my grandparents.

Both my Pops, Anthony, and Mom, Constance, were born and raised in the good old heart of our country,

Missouri. They met in high school and said it was love at first sight. Mom was an only child and, right after her senior year, her parents were killed in a car crash. Mom and Pops married a few weeks after they buried her parents. They said they realized how short life could be and didn't want to wait any longer. Shortly after they were married, they discovered they were expecting my brother. A few years later, I was born.

I know the spelling of my name is weird for a girl, however, we're a huge football family. We love our Kansas City Chiefs. Pops always said he would name his kids after the Chiefs' greats. So Neil's named after Neil Smith, and I'm named after Len Dawson. It also doesn't hurt that our last name is Shields, like Will Shields. We have season tickets to the Chiefs and to our amazing baseball team, the KC Royals. Yes, all of us are die hard KC fans. But now, we're in Seahawk country.

What was Pops thinking?

Stepping out of the shower, I decide to wear my Chiefs jersey. As I look at myself in the mirror, I still cannot understand what's so *special* about me. My mom keeps saying that I'm beautiful, but I don't see what she sees.

My mother is stunning. She's five foot four, has blonde hair, blue eyes, and is fit. My Pops is very handsome too, for his age. He's tall at six foot three, has dark brown hair, green eyes that have a hint of blue in them, and is very built. Neil's a spitting image of Pops, which explains why he has girls hanging on him all the time. He hasn't even hit the height like our pops', but football has made him huge. Me, on the other hand, I'm the awkward one of the bunch. I have blonde hair that goes to the middle of my back, bright blue eyes that are framed by my glasses, braces that I hate, and a set of freckles on my tan skin. I'm plain average and the shortest of my family at five foot one.

I'm called a nerd because I love learning and plan on being a doctor. I'll attend UMKC, University of Missouri—Kansas City, once I graduate. My plan is to graduate from high school early so I can get my medical degree as soon as possible. Neil's smart, as well, but he seems more interested in football and women. I swear my brother is a walking, talking hormone, which I find disgusting.

The knock at the door shakes me out of my thoughts.

"Yeah?"

"Are you almost done, Squirt? You're not the only one starting a new school today. Since I'm the new quarterback, I need to make sure I make a damn good first impression, especially on the ladies. It takes a while to achieve the standard of perfection that'll bring out the sexiness the women will love!" Neil yells though the door.

"You're so sick, Neil. I don't understand how we're even related." Tightening the towel around me, I open the door and stomp past him.

"Ah, there, there, care bear. It will be all right, once you get done with puberty. On second thought . . ." he shakes his head. "I don't want to think about that and don't really want to talk with you about puberty," he tells me with a look of disgust on his face.

"Neil, I'm twelve and you're fourteen. You're going through puberty as well, and I'm not into boys. You know I'm focused on school."

"Squirt, please don't talk about boys with me. It's not

something I ever want to think about." He walks into the bathroom and shuts the door.

Shaking my head, I go into my room and get ready for the day ahead of me. Did I mention I hate starting a new school?

DANTE

"Dante, get your lazy butt up. Today's the first day of school," Mamma yells from downstairs.

Yawning, I slowly crawl out of bed. Damn, I'm sore. Coach has been busting our asses during practices. We're one of those schools that do their tryouts at the local football summer camp, and if you make the team, practices start three weeks before school starts. I head off to the shower thinking about how different this year's going to be. I'm a freshman in high school, running back on the varsity football team, and I have a new friend, Neil.

My *nonno* was in the Navy, a combat veteran who died during his last mission, leaving behind my *nonna* and my papa. She didn't want to move back to Italy so she stayed here. My papa met my mamma in Italy while visiting his *nonni*. It was love at first sight. They married that summer, moved back Oak Harbor, Washington, and started their family.

Over the years, we've visited Italy to look over the family winery that my parents own. Even though we have money, my parents have always made my brothers and I work for everything we have.

My papa, Anthony, who goes by Tony, is an accountant

for a big firm. My mamma, Giovanna, is a stay at home *madre*. They have three sons: the twins—Carlo and Nicoli—who are twelve and me, their eldest at fourteen. Mamma said, after the twins were born, she was done, even though she wanted a little girl. They're a handful and I agree, despite the fact that I'm very close to them.

We all have the traditional Italian look: dark skin, dark brown hair, dark brown eyes, and the straight long nose. All of us kids ended up taking after papa in height and build. He's around six foot four and solid muscle. The twins are five foot six, and I'm five foot eleven. Then, there's Mamma who's short compared to us at five foot one. She always grumbles that we haven't even hit our growth spurt yet.

Mamma hates that we're growing up so fast. She's commented a time or two to Papa that she doesn't like the looks we're getting from girls already. Papa laughs and tells her that it's going to be alright, that it's part of growing up.

"Get out of the shower already, Dante. You're not the only one starting school today!" Nicoli yells while he bangs on the bathroom door.

"What in the hell's wrong with your shower?" I yell, washing the soap off quickly.

"Carlo won't get out. He's taking a shit, and I don't want to smell that while showering."

"You're screwed because I'm not getting out of the shower for that reason. Coach busted my ass this week. So, I'm enjoying the hot water," I say, amused by what Carlo is doing to Nicoli.

"You're horrible, Dante!" he says, walking away.

I finish my shower, get dressed, and head out into the kitchen. I walk up to Mamma and kiss her on the cheek as I grab a piece of bacon she's making.

"Morning, Mamma. I can't stay for breakfast. I'm going to Neil's house so we can walk to school together. His *madre's* making us breakfast," I tell Mamma.

"Okay, sweetie. Give his *madre* my number. If you boys are going to be friends, then I think it's time the families got together. Also, you need to watch your mouth when you talk with your brothers. I heard you and Nicoli. Trust me, I'll be getting him next," she says in the sternest, but not really meaning it, voice. She knows we are our *padre's* sons. We get our cussing from him.

"Okay, I'll be more careful. Neil's going to come home with me, and then we'll go to his house to go over plays. Love you, Mamma," I yell over my shoulder.

I make it to Neil's a minute later. They live a block away. With him being the quarterback and me the running back and living this close, yeah, this year's going to be great. I ring his doorbell and wait. The door opens, and I see this short blonde-haired, blue-eyed girl with braces and glasses, smile at me.

"Can I help you?" She blinks up at me from behind her glasses.

"You must be Squirt. I'm Dante, I'm supposed to meet Neil," I introduce myself.

She's pretty in an awkward way, but I have a feeling she'll be a knock out when she gets older.

"Ugh, that name," she growls. "I'll kill him. My name's Len. L-E-N. Anyway, he isn't done getting ready. Why don't you come in and get some breakfast? He told us you were coming," she says, motioning me into the house.

"Okay, L-E-N, show me the way." I make sure to

enunciate her name, just like she did.

She growls again and shows me to the kitchen. "Mom, this is Dante." She makes the quick announcement, then walks to the table and begins eating.

"Mrs. Shields, thanks for having me. My mamma wants me to give you her number. She would like the families to get together and meet."

"Please, call me Connie. Mrs. Shields is my mother-in-law. I'd love her number. Neil should be down soon. Sit and eat," she says motioning to the empty seat.

I go to the table, make a plate, and sit down directly across from Len. She looks up and rolls her eyes at me. "You think you have enough food there, RB?"

"RB?"

"Gosh, Running Back, and you're supposed to play football?" She smirks.

"Squirt, leave him alone," Neil says walking in and patting me on the back. "Ignore her, we all do." He gives his mom a kiss on the cheek. "Mom, we're going to Dante's after school, then we're coming here to go over plays. Is that okay?"

"Yep, just don't forget you're supposed to walk your sister home today. I won't be back until late due to traffic. Pops will be bringing dinner home."

"Connie, I have brothers that can walk her home. They're in the same grade as she is, and they'll make sure she's safe. That is, if that's okay with you," I tell her as I look at Len and give her a smile.

"Mom!" Len cries, her face red. "I don't need protecting! I'm a red belt in Tae Kwon Do. I can protect myself," she says with a pinched face.

"Nonsense, Len. You *will* be walked home. Thank you for the offer, Dante. However, I'd like to speak to your parents first and make sure they are okay with it as well. For today, do you boys mind walking her home?"

"Are you okay with us walking her to my house first to introduce her to my parents and my brothers?" I ask Connie.

"Sure, that's fine with me. Just make sure she's back before her dad comes home. Thanks, boys. You guys have a great first day. I'm off to work." Mrs. Shields walks around giving kisses on cheeks and leaves.

Looking over at Neil, I get a big smile on my face, "This year will be epic!" We bump fist and finish our breakfast.

Len

Breathe, Len, just breathe.

I look up again from my breakfast at the hottest guy I've ever laid eyes on. He's breathtaking. When I opened the door, I thought I was going to faint, and then I figured out that he had to be my brother's new friend. Now, I have to walk to school and to his house before I can call my girls back in Missouri to tell them all about him.

"Ready, Squirt?" my brother asks.

"Yeah, let's go and get this over with."

"It won't be that bad, I promise you will meet some great people," Hot Stuff says as he stands up and walks his plate over to the sink.

"Whatever," I mumbled out quietly.

They walk me to school and say they'll meet me by the tree in the front at the end of the day. I head into my first class and take a seat. I feel someone poking me in the back.

"You know the Seahawks are better."

I turn around to see a set of twins looking back at me. They are cute and kind of look like the hottie from this morning.

"That's nice, but not true," I tell them with a smile.

"You must be new. I'm Nicoli and he's Carlo," he says, pointing at his twin.

"I'm Len. I'm from Missouri and can't wait until I move back."

Laughing, Carlo says, "We're from here and not sure if we ever want to move."

"I'm sorry that was very rude of me. I just miss my friends and family." I give them a strained smile.

"It's okay, Len. I'm sure we'd be the same way actually. What period is your lunch hour?" Nicoli asks as he starts to get his books situated for class.

"It says here that it's at twelve forty-five," I murmur while looking at my schedule.

"That's the same as ours. Look for us in the cafeteria, you can sit with us, and we can introduce you to some of our friends," Carlo offers up.

"Thanks. I think I'd like that." I give a real smile this time, and then turn around to get ready before class begins.

The day's long, and I haven't really met anyone since Nicoli and Carlo. Walking into the cafeteria, I look around and don't see the boys. I decide to find a table to sit by myself until they show up. I find one off in the corner by the doors that lead to the outside eating area, so I make my way to it. Sitting down, I'm pulling my lunch from my backpack when I'm startled by a voice from beside me.

"Excuse me, but you're sitting in the wrong spot and need to get your fat, ugly ass out of my chair."

I glance up and find a pretty red-head looking at me like I'm an alien.

"I'm sorry, but I don't see your name or picture on this spot. So, I'm not moving," I inform her, not liking her tone of voice.

"Look here, you little bitch, this is the *cool* table. Listen to her before we make your life hell," says the brunette girl next to her.

"Hey, watch it. No need to be mean." A voice sounds from behind them. "Oh, hey, Len, glad you found the table." Nicoli comes into view, smiling. "Guys, this is Len. Len this is the guys. Len will be part of us from now on." He makes his way over and sits next to me. Carlo takes my other side.

"What the hell? She's nobody worth hanging out with. She isn't pretty, and she's fat," the red-head states.

"Shut up, Katy, or you won't be allowed to hang out with us. Now, be nice or walk away," Carlo tells her with a look of disgust on his face.

"Don't talk to my girlfriend like that," a boy growls as he walks up behind Katy.

"Or what, John? You going to hit me? Try it." Carlo stands up and gets in John's face, daring him to make the first move.

"Guys, it's okay. I'll move. Please don't fight. It's not worth it." I grab my stuff and walk outside. I don't know what happens between Carlo and John after that because I finish eating, and then go to my next class.

For the rest of the day, I was called fat ass. Katy and her friends were in all of my classes, and they made sure I was called every name they could think of. I heard the twins got into a fight and then had to leave school. For a moment, I wondered if the fight was over what happened at lunch, and I felt even worse for them.

Standing by the tree, lost in thought, I feel something tap my shoulder. Screaming and turning around, I punch the person's gut and I'm overcome with guilt when I realize it's Dante.

"What in the hell, Len? That shit hurt." He glares at me with a pained expression while he rubs his stomach.

"Sorry, I didn't know it was you. I told you this morning, I'm a red belt. Don't sneak up on me." I look over to my brother who is laughing his ass off.

"I should've told you that she really was speaking the truth earlier. Sorry, man." He sobers up and looks at me noticing something is off. "Squirt, what's wrong?"

"Nothing. Can we just leave?" I start to walk away.

Neil catches up and stops me.

"No, what's wrong? Tell me or we won't go anywhere."

"Ugh, nothing! I just want to go home and call my posse. So, let's go already." I get out of his grip and storm off.

We get to the De Luca's house within minutes. Dante opens the door, and we hear yelling.

I look over at Neil and mouth, "*Oh crap.*"

He nods his head and the expression on his face shows the desire to turn and walk away from what's going on. I'm positive that I'm showing the exact same expression.

Dante glances at us and you can see the embarrassment

on his face, which doesn't seem to change how hot he is. He then turns and heads inside towards the yelling. Neil and I exchange another glance and follow him. We end up in the entrance of the kitchen and see the back of his mom and dad who, you can tell by their body language, are really upset at someone or something.

"Mamma. Papa. I have company with me. Would you like for me to take them to the living room?" Dante asks his parents.

"Hey, son, welcome home. Hello, Neil, nice to see you again," his dad says while trying to control his anger at whatever is going on.

His dad walks over and pats Dante on his back then turns towards us.

"Who do we have here, son?"

Neil looks back and forth between us all. He takes a deep breath. "Gio. Tony. Officially meet my little sister, Len."

"It's nice to meet you, Len," his dad says.

"Oh, Len, we've heard a lot about you. Please call me Gio and this lug nut, Tony. You're always welcome here," Gio says as she walks over and hugs me to death.

Movement to my left causes me to glance over and see the twins from school earlier standing up from the table.

"Holy shit! Papa! Mamma! This is the girl we were standing up for," Carlo exclaims.

"Mouths!" their mom yells out, anger from earlier still simmering under the surface.

"What do you mean standing up for?" yells my brother, looking at me.

"Um . . ." I murmur, wishing I was anywhere but here right now.

34

My brother can be a hot head when it comes to me. I was hoping he wouldn't find out about what happened, but the cat is out of the bag now.

"This is the girl you guys got into a fight over?" his dad asks.

"Okay, um . . . I don't know what happened because I ended up leaving the cafeteria, remember?"

"After you left we told them that it isn't right to bully people. Of course this led to John saying that he didn't care and said more things that weren't nice. Papa, you taught us to stand up for what we believe in. I didn't like that they were bullying her and honestly, what John was saying wasn't something that any woman should have to hear. We got in a fight with him over it. Did you have any other problems with them during the rest of the day?" Carlo asks me.

"Um, yes and no. Katy and her friends are mean, but nobody else said anything. I have a saying that I use all the time . . . it's one more time," I tell him and glance at Nicoli. "What it means is that whatever anyone says can't be worse than being one time more than that."

"So if I say you're awesome that makes me better?" Dante says with a sexy smirk that I want to slap off.

"No, that's when I'd say I know, and I'm one more time." I stick out my tongue, which pulls a laugh from him.

That sound causes me to feel something I don't understand. I decide quickly that it has to be my hormones messing with my mind. I need to get away from him so I can figure all this out.

"Well, I made it clear that I won't be friends with someone like that," Nicoli tells all of us.

"I agree with you, bro. Len, sorry we didn't get a chance

to talk more over lunch," says Carlo.

"Well, we wanted to introduce her to the twins and see if they'd walk her to and from school. With practice starting up, her *madre* wants her walked home to make sure she's safe. Neil and I have practice right after school, but the twins can get her home and back to practice before we can. So, I thought they'd be perfect. Connie said she'd be calling later to make sure it's alright," Dante says.

"Thanks for letting us know and for asking if it's okay. I'll talk with her *madre* and then with the twins. Now, your *padre* and I have a few more things to work out with the twins if you three would like to go into the living room," Gio states and turns back to the twins who both look down at their feet avoiding the glare coming from their mom.

"Um, Neil, can we head out? I'm supposed to be home when Pops gets there."

"Right and I'm sure you want to call your posse," he says, laughing. "Okay, Carlo and Nicoli, we'll see you in the morning when you get Squirt. Come on, Dante, we have plays to go over."

Back at the house, I make a call to the girls. I tell them all about my day, the twins, and the hottie who's now my brother's friend.

Three

Len

Four years later....

"SQUIRT, DID YOU MISS ME?" I turn around at Kansas City International and see my brother walking towards me. I run and jump into his arms.

"It's time for you to watch me walk across the stage, big brother!" I say, laughing as he whirls me around.

"I still can't believe you're graduating two years early. What the heck?" Putting me down, he smirks at me. "You know that makes you a huge nerd."

"You know you're the bigger nerd," I giggle and then before he can say it, I shout, "One more time!"

"Stop teasing your sister and give me some love," our grandma, or as everyone calls her OPG says, opening her arms up.

"Sorry, OPG, but she *is* a big nerd."

"Again, one more time, big brother."

My parents come and give me a big hug.

"Your Pops and I are so proud of you, Len. And we have a present for you," Mom says.

"Really? What is it?" I ask them, pulling away.

Right before the start of my freshman year, my grandpa passed away. I ended up moving back to Missouri to live with OPG so she wouldn't be alone. I've always been a grandma's girl. I named her OPG when I couldn't figure out why she was only called Grandma when other kids called theirs with two names like Grandma Allen or Grandma Tina. I asked her and she said, "I'm just Old Plain Grandma." So that's what I called her for years. I shortened it to OPG. At first I was the only one to call her it, but now everyone does.

Since it was just the two of us, I poured myself even more into my learning. I busted my butt for years to graduate high school early and now I start at UMKC in a month. I'm going to become the doctor I always wanted to be. Since my brother graduated three weeks ago, in Washington, my parents are moving back home to Kansas City. I'm beyond thrilled to have my family back home.

"Look behind us," my pops says, shaking me out of my thoughts.

They step aside, and I look up to see the De Luca family. I didn't get a chance to see them when I was in Washington for Neil and Dante's graduation. OPG and I drove up there, since she doesn't fly, and we got into town an hour before the ceremony started. Once Neil's name was called she was tired, so we drove back to my parents' house and took a nap. My parents woke me up when they got home telling us that the De Luca's gave Neil a trip to Italy with them for a graduation present. I was heartbroken that I wasn't going to see them and my brother before we had to leave, but I was excited for my brother.

Screaming, I run to the twins, who are still two of my best friends next to Ashley and Julia. Jumping into Nicoli's open arms, I hug him and give him a smacking kiss on the lips.

"I'm so glad you guys came to see me graduate! How long are you in town? You know the girls are going to shit bricks when they see you!"

I jump down and jump up into Carlo's arms, hugging and kissing him too.

After I moved back, the boys always came to visit me for two weeks during the summer breaks. At first, OPG wasn't too sure about them being under the same roof as me, but once she saw they didn't want in my pants and our relationship was that of siblings, she ended up adopting them into the family. We have pretty much combined our families so to speak, however the only one I haven't ever been able to view like a brother is Dante.

"We're so proud and excited for you, Len!" Mamma Gio exclaims, hugging me close. "We have some exciting news to share with you."

"What's your news?"

"Congrats, Len, I knew you were the smartest of the five," Papa Tony states then gives me a hug and a kiss on my cheek.

"Papa, that isn't nice. Just because we're going to wait two more years doesn't mean shit," Nicoli says, laughing

"Mouth, Nicoli!" Mamma Gio yells at him

"The news is that they're moving here as well. Dante's finishing up some stuff for the family, which is why he's not here. But he'll be here towards the end of the month. Exciting, huh?" Neil says, pulling me into his side then smiling down at me.

"Oh, my God! That's awesome! You will be in school with the girls!" I say, jumping up and down.

"Okay, enough. Where are we eating, Len? We're starving," Pops says, then grabs my hand and walks towards baggage claim.

I glance at the twins and we scream at the same time, "Gates N Sons!"

Graduation was awesome. My face was beet red, but it was so worth it. My family and the De Luca's were loud. Their excuse was, *you only graduate high school once.* I'm not looking forward to hearing how bad it'll be at my college graduation. OPG and I moved in last week with Mom and Pops. Once we got her house on the market, she ended up moving into the in-law suite. This makes me extremely happy having her so close to me, as I can't imagine my life without her. She's my rock.

Walking down the hallway to my room, I hear Neil on the phone. I come to a stop when I recognize Dante's voice. I was going to walk away because I didn't want to eavesdrop on my brother's conversation, but then again he shouldn't have had it on speaker phone if he didn't want people to overhear.

"So, three more days and I'm there, man. I'm so ready. What's the plan?" Dante's voice sounds through the speaker.

"Well, I have a party lined up for you. Women galore to

choose from. Are we going to share or just getting a girl each?"

"Let's play it by ear when we get there. The twins are coming too. I already told them. Just don't let Len know; I don't want her following us," Dante says.

I don't hear how my brother responds because there is roaring in my ears and the tears start. My heart hurts at the thought that he doesn't want me around. He hasn't seen me in four years. He doesn't know that I lost the braces, that I wear contacts instead of glasses, and I'm no longer fat.

I'm pulled out of my thoughts by what my brother says next. The words feel like they're going to choke the life out of me.

"Better let the twins know not to tell her, and she won't be following us around much. She starts college next week, and we're leaving for training soon. I talked to the recruiter. He said we report in about two weeks. Once you get here, we'll finish signing up. We need to break the news to our families. They aren't going to be happy, but we're going to be kick ass Navy Seals!"

I drop to my knees, slump against the wall, and let the tears pour down my face. How am I going to deal with my brother leaving to join the military, much less become a Navy Seal? I don't hear the rest of the conversation and have no clue how long I sit there. I'm so lost in my thoughts of possibly losing my brother and the guy that I have deep feelings for, that I don't hear Neil exit his room.

"Squirt, what's wrong?" Neil kneels before me, concern on his face.

"N . . . Navy Seals?" I stutter.

Understanding flashes over his face before he drops

41

down next to me.

"Aw, Squirt, I wish you hadn't heard that. Please know I'm doing this because I want to be a part of something bigger than me. I want to serve my country. I want to be a better person. I promise to be safe, and I'll always contact you when I can. Please don't say anything yet," he says, holding me close and rocking gently.

I can't say anything. All I can do is cry in my brother's arms.

DANTE

"For those of you staying, the weather in Kansas City is eighty-seven with a heat index of ninety-three degrees Fahrenheit. Thank you for flying with us today." The voice sounds through the planes intercom.

I've never been so happy to be anywhere as I unclick my belt and stretch. I've missed my family, and I feel bad for missing Len's graduation. Grabbing my bag, I walk off the plane and into the airport waiting area. I spot the twins who wave and scream my name.

"About time you got here," Papa says and pulls me into a hug.

"I'm tired and hungry. Let's get out of here."

I hug Mamma quickly before leaving the airport.

"Where are we going to eat? Can we go to that BBQ place you all couldn't stop talking about?" I ask Mamma as I climb into the car.

"Gates N Sons? That's where we were planning. The Shields' are meeting us there," Papa says as he backs out of the parking space.

"Great." I grin. "I can't wait to see Momma Connie, Pops, Neil, and Len. I have her graduation gift in my carry-on."

"Oh, Len won't be there. She has her introduction at UMKC. She may join us at some point, but if not, we'll see her at the house," Papa explains as he pulls onto the highway.

About forty-five minutes later, we're pulling into the restaurant. I get out of the car, and I hear my name being called out. I look up and spot Neil walking towards us.

"Glad you finally got your ugly ass here," he says then pulls me into a hug and claps me on my back.

"Neil, mouth," Mamma scolds as she hugs him.

I look behind Neil and see that his whole family, minus Len, is here, including his grandmother, whom I've never met. She doesn't fly and this is my first time here. The one time she was in Washington, for Neil's graduation, she left before I could have the honor of meeting her.

"Momma Connie, Pops. I'm glad to see you both."

I walk over and give them both hugs.

"It's good to see you too, son. Dante this is my mom, May. Mom, this is Dante," Pops tells the older woman next to him.

"Oh my, you are a good looking young man. It's nice to meet you." Len's grandmother looks me up and down.

"You too, ma'am."

"Don't call me that. I don't run a whore house. Ms. May will be just fine unless I tell you otherwise."

Laughing, Neil steps up alongside me and whispers, "We told you she is very picky on what she's called."

We head into the restaurant, and I notice that it's different than most. You order your food, you're handed your drink, then go to the next line. There, you get a tray with your food, and then you go and find a spot to sit. We're talking when I look over at the door and see this hot blonde walk in. She's wearing a little strapless dress that hits right above her knees. She has on high heels that make her smooth sun-kissed legs look miles long. I continue my upward journey and stop when I get to her face, seeing the most amazing smile. Her eyes are covered in sunglasses and her hair is hanging down in loose waves that kiss where her small but full breasts are. Damn, this girl's hot! She starts to walk our way and is met halfway by Nicoli and Carlo who both give her a kiss and a hug. I feel this tug in my chest at seeing this, but I don't understand why.

"Squirt, get over here and tell us about that introduction thing you went to."

I'm still trying to understand the slight jealousy that I feel when the twins finally let her go and move out of my way. I can see she took off her glasses. She looks right at me and my breath is gone. Holy shit, I feel that tug deep in my gut, and I'm not sure what it is. She has changed, and I barely recognize her.

"Dante, is that you? I'm so glad you're here. Sucks you had to miss my graduation," she starts walking over.

"Hey Len, good to see you too." I smile and force myself to get my shit together. "Oh, here's your present. I hope you like it. I didn't know what to get you." I reach into my pocket and pull out the small package.

"Thanks, Dante. You didn't have to get me anything," she says, smiling at me.

44

She stays where she is and opens her gift. She stills for a brief moment then looks up with tears in her eyes, and I'm scared for a second thinking she doesn't like the gift.

"This is beautiful. Thank you, Dante. Can you help me put it on?"

I nod and she turns. I stand and reach for the necklace so I can place it on her. It's fourteen karat gold and has her name on it.

"You're welcome," I say as I clip the chain. Turning, she gives me another hug, a kiss on my cheek, and then goes to sit between the twins.

"So, I got my class list . . ." I listen to her as she tells us all about her evening.

The music is blasting through the house as we make our way to the patio, beers in hand.

"Where are the twins?" Neil asks, taking a seat on the love seat.

"No clue. They found a girl and went into a room. You know how they are."

I let out a laugh before taking a sip of my beer.

"So, are you planning on getting a girl tonight?"

"That's the plan," I tell him, but honestly, I haven't been able to get Len off my mind since I saw her.

"We leave in a week. We telling everyone tomorrow?" I ask Neil trying to get my mind off of her.

"Um, about that. Squirt knows. When we were talking last week she overheard. She's taking it hard. She'll be writing to us. Promise me you'll be nice and write back. I

45

know you don't like her, but please do this for me."

"Who said I didn't like her?"

"You said you didn't want her following us around. That you thought she was annoying. So I assumed you didn't like her. Anyway, do I have your word?"

"Yeah, no worries."

"Cool, I'm off to find a girl. See ya later." He walks over to a red-head and starts to strike up a conversation with her.

I look out over the deck, lost in thought about a blue-eyed, blonde-haired beauty and what exactly these feelings I'm having for her are.

"I'm going to miss you so much. Call and write. Promise me," Mamma says crying into my shoulder.

"Mamma, I promise. Let me say goodbye to Papa and the others. I have to go." I pull away and go and tell my Papa, Nicoli, Carlo, Momma Connie, and Pops goodbye.

I save the best for last.

"Okay, Len. Be safe, do good in school, and you better write me. I want care packages, too. If I'm with your brother that means I'm stuck seeing his goodies and I don't want to share," I tell her with a laugh as I hug her goodbye.

I glance over, and I see that Neil is giving hugs to my family.

"You know I will. Make sure you write back," she says with tears running down her face.

God, she's so beautiful. Holding her like this feels right. I notice nobody is watching us, so I quickly place a chaste kiss on her lips. I feel a zap of lighting that goes straight to my dick, and I'm harder than I've ever been before. How the hell am I going to walk away from this? Startled, I pull back, look down at her, and see she has a look of bliss on her face. I know she feels it too, but I'm struck with fear of what could happen if I don't make it back from a mission. Also, she's only sixteen and our families are so intertwined. No matter how much I want to figure out these feelings that I'm having, I can't do that to her and so with that thought I turn and load onto the bus without another word.

Neil climbs on and looks over at me.

"You ready for the hardest thing we've ever done?" he asks with a smile on his face.

As I glance out the window, watching Len as we drive away, I answer him honestly, "Scared shitless, but excited as hell."

Four

Len

Present Day...

I WALK OUT OF THE conference room and take a deep breath as I pull the door shut. I take a brief moment to gather my thoughts and try to control the bombardment of feelings that assault me. Holy cow, if the note isn't bad enough, seeing Dante again after nine long years about did me in. Entering the bathroom, I lean on the sink and look into the mirror. I try to see the changes that have accrued over the years, but I still see the young girl that I saw back in high school. But what does he see? Does he still view me the same? Or, does he see the woman I have become?

Old feelings assault me: desire, want, need, and the memories of that chaste kiss he brushed across my lips the day they left. I want to ask him what that kiss meant, but I'm scared of his reaction. Will he want me like I want him? Or, will he brush off the kiss as nothing but a moment that should never have happened? I think about what I'm doing here, and my heart starts to race and my breathing starts to pick up.

Breathe, Len. In. Out. In. Out.

Just breathe.

I turn on the faucet and splash cold water on my face. After grabbing some paper towels from the dispenser, I gently pat my face dry. Tossing the towels in the trash, I take another deep breath, preparing myself to go back and face him again. Distracted, I make my way out of the bathroom and run smack into a wall. *Shit that hurt.* I slowly open my eyes and realize that wall was really a huge wall with arms. Those arms shoot out and manage to catch me before I can fall on my ass.

"Shit, I'm so sorry," I say, trying to remain upright. "I was distracted."

"It's okay, sugar. You can run into me anytime." A sexy, gruff voice sounds.

Damn, that's a sexy voice. I look up into a handsome, brown-haired, blue-eyed giant. He has to be six foot six because even in my heels, I barely come to his shoulders.

"I really am sorry. I'm normally not this clumsy. I didn't hurt you, did I?" I take a step back.

"No, you didn't." He chuckles. "Allow me to introduce myself, I'm James, or as the boys call me, Doc. And who might you be?" he says, taking me in.

"Oh, I'm Len. Nice to meet you." I stick out my hand for a handshake.

"Shit, you're Lucky's sister?" he exclaims with a shocked look on his face.

"Who's Lucky?"

"Lucky is Neil." He smiles at me. "We were in the Navy together and on the same Seal team. I was the doctor of the group, hence the name, Doc. Lucky mentioned you were a doctor as well."

"Oh, yeah, he's my brother. And, yes, I'm currently doing my residency to become an ER doctor."

"Well, it's finally nice to meet *the* Squirt," he teases.

"Ugh, that n—"

"Doc, Lucky's looking for you. I would strongly suggest you back away from Len before he sees you." The suggestion is growled from behind me.

Doc and I jump apart. I look down the hall and see Dante with a strange look on his face. It takes a second for me to register that he's pissed. What in the hell is that all about?

"Don't get your panties in a twist, Ghost. I was just meeting Len here. Conference room?" James asks and at Dante's nod, he walks toward the conference room. All the while, I'm trying to figure out what just happened.

"Dante, are you okay? And what's with Ghost?" I ask as I approach him.

"Ghost was my name in the Seals. The boys just won't stop calling me that. Neil and I never told anyone outside of our team those names," he says, pulling me into a side hug, as we follow James to the conference room. "We're going to fix this problem. Just hang in there."

I step out of his hold and enter the room. There, I see two others have joined us besides Doc. And, dear God, they're freaking hot, too. What the hell is going on here? Is my brother only hiring sex gods?

"So, Lucky?" I say to Neil as I sit next to him and bump

shoulders with him.

"What the hell?" He jumps back in his seat. "Who told you that? I never told you that because it isn't a name that I want my family to call me."

"Um, I kind of ran into Doc." I giggle and look over towards Doc and see him smiling at me.

"Feel free to do it again soon," Doc replies, giving me a wink.

"Who is this sexy ass woman, Lucky? And why did you call us in?" asks brown-haired god number one.

"Watch your mouth asshats," Neil barks. "You don't ever talk like that in front of her."

"What the hell, Lucky?" says bald god number two.

"This is Len, Neil's baby sister. Len, this is John, we call him Sin." Dante points to the brown-haired god. "And that's Justice, who we call Eagle." He points to bald god.

"You guys, it's nice to meet you." I smile at each man.

"Man, Lucky, I now know why you didn't bring your sister around when she visited," Sin says.

"No shit," Eagle says.

"Guys, enough, and don't talk or even think of my sister like that. That's the only warning you will get." Neil glares at each of them. "Next time it will be my fist in your face. Now, I'm going to pass this note over to you. Look it over. My sister found it on the window of her car this morning."

The boys are looking over it when I feel a gentle touch on my arm. I glance to my left and see Dante is looking at me.

Smiling he leans over and whispers, "We'll fix it."

I take a deep breath and nod. He and my brother will try their hardest to make this situation better.

"What in the hell? Do you know who wrote this to you?" Doc asks, diverting my attention away from Dante and back to the terrifying note.

"No. I normally park my car in my garage, but my opener wasn't working so I left it outside. I needed to go to work today to finish some reports, and when I got to my car I saw it on my window. Dr. Johnson works in the ER with me and is a really good friend outside of work too, so I'm not sure what the note is talking about. He's gay so it isn't like we have something going on," I explain and I shiver in fear.

"Has anyone asked you out recently that you've turned down? Anyone showing you a lot of unwanted attention?" Sin asks.

"None that isn't normal. I've been asked out before, but everyone knows I don't date guys I work with. I've made it very clear."

"Good girl." Dante looks at me with an approving look as he leans back in his chair, his arms crossed.

I look back at him, like he's nuts. When did he start getting all possessive about me? I know he's always had Neil's back when it came to guys saying or doing things to me, but right now, he's acting like I'm his woman. Part of me is pissed off by this, but there is a small part that has hope that he's finally seeing me the way I want him to.

"Okay, Dante call the twins." Neil interrupts our staring contest. "We need to check and see what's on her security system. We also need to find out why her opener wasn't working. We're more than likely going to have to not only get KCPD involved, but the hospital as well. There will need to be a protection detail for Dr. Johnson, and we need to make sure Squirt is protected at all times."

"Hell no!" I almost jump out of my chair. "Neil, I don't need to be protected every second. I work in the ER. I can't have a bodyguard following me around in the hospital. No." I shake my head, trying to get my point across. "It isn't going to work. Also, my house is protected. Remember, you did the security system? I'm a grown woman."

"It isn't negotiable." Neil answers, unmoved by my outburst.

"And how are you going to accomplish this in the ER? You're not allowed in the rooms with the patients, and there isn't enough space in the hallways. Also, there is security at the doors of the ER," I explain. Lord, you would think I was twelve again.

"Fine, not during work hours, but any other time. Understand?"

"You know you can be really annoying at times," I snap.

Yeah, I wanted their help, but I didn't want to be followed all the time.

"One more time, Squirt," Neil tells me with a smirk on his face.

"I'll take the first shift. I know you have a spare bedroom; which I hope you don't mind us using?" Dante asks.

"Ugh, fine! I need to go. I have to meet Mom and Mamma Gio for lunch. We're supposed to talk about the company party you all are hosting this weekend. Does that mean you're following me?" I huff at Dante.

"Yep, it sure does, Len. Neil, give me a call shortly and fill me in on the rest of the plan." He stands to follow me.

I walk up to Sara and give her a hug.

"So, plans with the girls, make them. Text me the info.

I'm off until Monday. It's Tuesday and the party is Saturday night. Let me know when and where," I tell her, and she smiles at me like she just won the biggest prize ever.

"Yay! Are we going to finally do it?" she asks and I know she's talking about finding a guy.

"Yes, I'm done and so ready," I say over my shoulder as I walk away.

Just as I reach the door, I hear Dante mutter something, but I can't make it out. This just makes me roll my eyes as I walk towards my car.

Whatever. It's none of his business what I do.

DANTE

"Let me get my motorcycle, and I'll follow you to Gates N Sons," I tell her as she climbs into her car.

"How did you know where we were going to eat at?" She cocks her head at me.

"It isn't very hard to guess. It's your favorite place and both our families will do anything to make you happy," I smile at her and know that I'm also one of them that would do anything.

"Whatever." She rolls her eyes at me and puts her keys in her ignition.

I hop on my black and red with chrome trim Road King custom Harley-Davidson, a gift to myself after that messed up mission we went on. I close my eyes, take a deep breath, and push the memory aside. I can't think about that now; I need to focus. Focus on Len and her situation.

Opening my eyes, I start my beauty and follow Len all

the way to the restaurant. Once there, I jump off my bike and hurry to her car before she gets out.

"Our moms aren't here yet, let's go get settled," I tell her as I open her door.

After our moms arrive, I sit back and listen to them talk about the party coming up.

I take the time to observe her. I can't believe how much she has changed over the years. Lucky is never going to forgive me for falling for his sister. But watching her, I know I can't let his feelings stop me from taking this step. It's time to tell Len how I truly feel about her. That I've fallen in love with her.

While I sit here and look at the most beautiful woman I've ever seen, I start to think about our future—Len loving me, marrying me, giving me children. God! Thinking of her growing big with my baby is such a turn on. I try to adjust myself without the moms and Len seeing me.

"Dante?" I hear her sweet voice call to me.

"Yes?"

"Can we stop by the hospital? I got a text, and they need me to go over a file," she asks, still looking down at her phone.

"Sure, but I stay with you and, if you're in a room, I'm right outside the door. Is that okay?" I ask her, still willing her to look up into my eyes.

"What's going on?" Momma Connie asks, alarmed. "Why are you following her around?"

"Nothing, I'm just practicing my body guarding skills." I give them a smile and hope it throws them off.

I don't think it's wise to tell the parents just yet.

"Oh, okay. Don't worry us like that," Mamma says,

relaxing once more.

"Sorry, Mamma," I say, kissing her cheek.

"Okay, I love you both. I'll swing by again on Friday afternoon. Bye, Mom. Bye, Mamma Gio," Len says as she kisses and hugs them goodbye.

After giving them both a kiss and a hug, I wave goodbye, and then follow Len out of the restaurant.

I walk Len to her car and open her door. I look into her eyes and want to kiss her so badly, but I know that will have to wait until we have the talk. Because I won't be able stop once I taste her sweet lips.

"I'll follow you, alright, Len?" I whisper as I kiss her by her ear. She shivers, and I smile at the knowledge that I've found her sweet spot.

"Okay, Dante," she answers breathlessly.

I walk over to my bike, throw my leg over, and start her up. Then, I watch Len and see that she's confused by my actions. I smile knowing I can throw my girl off guard.

After leaving the restaurant, we drive the short distance to the hospital. I follow the same procedure of rushing to her car and opening her door, and then follow her into the hospital. I watch her ass sway in front of me and visions of me grabbing it while pounding into her cause a rise from below my belt. Those thoughts are cut off when a man walks up and engulfs Len in a hug. My vision turns red but before I can step up to snatch her out of his arms, she releases him and turns to me.

"Dante, I'd like for you to meet my friend, and fellow doctor, Chris Johnson. Chris, this is Dante." She waves a hand towards me. "Chris, Andy, and I often hang out with each other after we end our shifts."

"Andy?" I'm about ready to lose my shit and tell her that isn't happening anymore when Chris answers for her and things start clicking into place.

"Andy is my fiancé." He smiles at me knowingly.

"Len, is this the Dr. Johnson from the note?" I ask and she nods.

"Note? What note are you talking about?" Chris glances at her with confusion etched on his face.

"I'll explain in the conference room. Let's go get these files done." She turns and walks over to a door that's marked: *Medical Staff Only*. "Dante, we'll be in here."

I'm leaning up against the wall outside the room Dr. Johnson and Len are in. I'm glad I know he's gay or I'd have a hard time with them behind closed doors alone. I pull out my phone and call Lucky to find out what the next plan of action is. As we talk, I watch people walk by and try to figure out if that son of a bitch, who is trying to hurt my woman, works here. I have every intention of ending his miserable existence, and he better hope that God has mercy on him, because he's going to need it.

When I enter Len's house, several hours after I dropped her off after she finished up her files at the hospital, I stop dead in my tracks. I turn hard the moment I see what she's wearing. Her ass is framed in black tight shorts that barely cover it. Her matching black tank molds her breasts and shows off her hourglass figure perfectly. She has her blonde hair in a ponytail with a few strands falling to frame her face, and she's holding a mixed drink in her hand. She's standing next to her couch, where the twins are sitting, laughing about something they're telling her. Jealousy and possessiveness wash over me and I instantly become pissed because the twins are seeing her dressed like that. I know they don't want her in the same way that I do, but the caveman inside of me wants to scream out that I'm the only one who should see her body like this. I take a step into the living room, and at the sound of my footsteps, she snaps her head in my direction.

"Dante, what's wrong?" she asks, concern etched on her beautiful face.

"What in the hell are you wearing, Len? Thing One and Thing Two, turn your heads. You don't get to look at her like that!" I yell.

"What the hell, Ghost? We've seen her in a bikini, so this isn't anything. Anyway, why's it any of your business? You know, she's our best friend," Nicoli answers, unafraid of my reaction.

I haven't told anyone of my feelings for Len. My brothers must've known for a while. They've always hinted that I liked her when we talked, but I just ignored the comments. They never asked, I never expounded. Damn, it looks like that conversation with the twins was going to be happening sooner rather than later.

"Yeah, and what's up with the nickname, Ghost?" Carlo questions.

"Whatever, I still wish you would go and change clothes, Len. As far as the nickname, it was a name I was given as a Seal. Neil and I felt it was best not to tell the families our code names because we didn't want you calling us that. I'm going to put my bag up," I say, walking towards the bedroom I'll be using; I'd had a good look at her house when I'd dropped her off earlier.

I'm shocked at how much her house resembles the one I've always envisioned sharing with her. It's a two-story house with six bedrooms, four bathrooms, huge kitchen, living room, den/library, full basement, pool, large backyard, huge privacy fence, and a three-car garage. It also has a nice-sized shed in the back. The basement was awesome. It's to be a game room that has a huge TV, surround sound, huge wrap couch that could sit fifteen easy, pool table, dart board, arcade game, also an Xbox and PlayStation. She got the game systems for the twins, she said. It also has a half kitchen that has a built-in bar. I can't wait for football season to start because I know where I'm going to be watching all the games.

The bedrooms are a nice size. She made one into a home office, another was an exercise room, Nicoli and Carlo each have their own room, a guest room, and then the master suite. Which has an amazing ensuite bathroom. I can't wait to take her in that huge ass shower. It has a bench that I can just see her bent over while I'm pounding her from behind.

Damn, I need to get my head together.

Walking back to the den, I stop short when I hear Len talking on the phone.

"Okay, so we're going to Stetsons Thursday night? That sounds like a plan. I don't know what I'm going to do with him being back. I don't know how to stop my feelings, especially when he's all alpha male on me. It makes me hot as hell. Oh, Julia, you should see who's working with Neil. I swear my brother is only hiring hot ass alpha men. I needed a new pair of panties after visiting him. I promise I'll tell you girls everything. I'll have to figure out who's supposed to be my bodyguard that day."

Okay, she has to be talking about me, right? God, I hope so. It would make it so much easier when she becomes mine and if she likes alpha males . . . damn, I can't wait until it's official. I'm not into BDSM, but I do like control in the bedroom.

"I don't know, Julia. I want to see where it goes, but I'm scared."

I make some noise, not wanting her to know I was eavesdropping on her conversation. I walk into the den with a plan in my mind. I'll be that man she's with Thursday night. Just wait and see.

"Hey, Julia, I've got to go." She glances up at me. "Dante just walked in. I'll see you then. Love you too, bitch."

"Where did the twins go?" I ask, walking up to her and pushing the stray locks that fell out of her ponytail behind her ear.

"Went to pick up dinner. I didn't feel like cooking. Want to go down and find a movie for the night? I just want to relax after today," she says, walking around me towards the basement door.

Damn, her ass looks good in those shorts. This is going to be a long night.

Five

Len

IT'S A WEDNESDAY AFTERNOON, AND I'm hanging out with Doc and Sin. Lord, these two are a trip. From what I pieced together, they grew up together and joined the Seals like Dante and Neil had. But these two are like little kids with dirty mouths.

"Hey, Len, come over here and put some of that oil on me. I like it when you rub my body like you did last night," Doc says wiggling his eyebrows.

"Doc, you're not lying either. Her hands were like heaven. The shapes she can make with a stick in her hand, God, I'm going to have fantasies about that for days," Sin says with a wink.

"Oh, just wait until I get the right oils. Then, you're both in for a treat," I tell them, laughing.

Standing up from the lounge I was on, I walk over to Doc and pick up the suntan oil.

"Turn over, Doc." I motion with my hand. "And I'll put

some oil on your back. You want me to rub that knot again?" I ask him as I open the bottle of oil.

"God, yes, please," Doc exclaims as he turns over.

"I'm next," Sin says, and turns over as well.

I start put oil on Doc's back and rub between his shoulder blades, digging in with my hands to get the knots out.

"You're going to be sore in the morning, but remember it'll be a good sore." My hands move to one shoulder, work out the kinks, and then move to the other.

"Right there." Doc moans. "I swear your hands are heaven sent. So good." He moans again, louder and longer. "Damn, don't stop. Sin, you're fucked. I'm never sharing." I swear by the sounds he's making that he's about to have an orgasm.

"Doc, we've shared before, and you're not keeping that sexy ass from me. Len, hurry up. I can't wait much longer," Sin says from his lounge chair, where he's still laying on his stomach waiting for me.

A loud roar comes from the doorway, startling me and causing me to snap my head towards it. Doc's head spins fast and Sin quickly twists and sits up from his lounge chair. There, we see Dante standing with his fist clenched, and his face red with rage.

"What in the hell are you guys talking about?" he roars. "Nobody better know how good Len is. I swear to God I'm going to kill two of my brothers." He pauses and takes two deep breaths. "Explain right now, and aren't you supposed to be protecting her? How in the fuck are you supposed to do that out in the open?" He turns to look at me, his face transforming a little, and I see lust in his eyes as he takes in my bikini.

Interesting.

"And what are you wearing? Go put on something over that bikini," Dante orders, then storms out onto the deck.

"I'm only massaging them, and I'm fine with what I'm wearing. There's also a ten-foot high privacy fence. How the hell are we not safe?" His high-handedness is a little too much and turning him into an ass. I have to force myself under control before I chuck the bottle of oil at his head. "Go back in the house and come back when you're done being an ass. Why do you do shit to piss me off and hurt my feelings? You're making me feel like I'm a slut, Dante," I spit out between clenched teeth before standing up.

As I walk over to Sin, I can feel Dante staring a hole into my back. My cheeks are flushed with heat and my heartbeat is rising from the rage I'm feeling from Dante's rudeness in front of Doc and Sin. I know my blood pressure is up which means I need to hurry and finish what I'm doing before the tears come.

I can see Doc out of the corner of my eye staring Dante down. Beneath my palms, I can feel Sin tensing.

"It'll be okay. Don't listen to that asshole, Len," Sin whispers to me as I finish with his back rub.

I look over towards Dante and drop my mask to show him exactly how his words affected me. His face softens, and he starts to approach me. I shake my head and rush into the house. First, I need to get control of my emotions before I can confront him.

Fifteen minutes later, I hear footsteps behind me. I tense expecting to hear him yell again for not putting something on over my bathing suit.

"Len, I'm sorry. I know you're not a slut. Please don't cry." He turns me towards him, but I keep my head down, refusing to look at him. "Come on, where is that beautiful smile? I just lost my cool hearing Doc moan and talking like that . . ." He takes a deep breath. "I thought the worst, and all I could think about was making sure they weren't taking advantage of you. Please, forgive me, Len."

"No different than Neil and you. I heard all about it every time I visited Neil, or when I scrolled through Facebook. I hear how the twins are, too. I'm not blind, Dante. Trust me to use my judgment. I didn't get this far in life without making the right choices. I may not be as experienced as you guys, but I'm not as innocent as you like to think," I tell him, looking at his chest, still unable to meet his gaze; I don't want him to see just how much he hurt me.

He grabs me and hugs me tight to him. "I know. I'm sorry, *mio tutto*."

"What's that mean?"

I pull him tighter and breathe him in. God, I love his smell. It's a mix of his cologne and the soap he uses. A year after he left, I sent him *Reaction* by *Kenneth Cole*. It makes me feel good knowing that he liked the cologne so much he kept using it. I thought of it after he sent me a bottle of perfume. To this day, I still wear it, *Angel n Demon* by *Givenchy*.

"I'll tell you soon. Did you get enough of a whiff?" His chest shakes beneath my nose.

I know he's laughing because I'm smelling him, but I don't care. In his arms, I feel safe, safer than I've ever felt before. I feel whole.

"I love that cologne," I step back reluctantly and look up

into his eyes. "I need to get into the shower. The guys and I are going to watch a movie after I cook dinner. I have a long day tomorrow, and Neil still hasn't said who is coming with the girls and me. I think it should be the twins. They'll have fun."

"I think it'll be Eagle. His girl's going out of town. So, he said he could go," he tells me.

"Okay, sounds good. I'll see you on Saturday, right?"

"Of course, Len. I'm going to have that talk with Doc now," he says, smiling at me like he's hiding something.

He turns and walks away leaving me to wonder what he's up to as I make my way to the shower.

Six

Len

STETSONS IS PACKED.

I'm so excited to spend time with the girls and relax, even if we have to have a bodyguard with us. Eagle's a nice guy. He's funny, but very reserved. He doesn't joke around the way Sin and Doc do. Sure, he's straightforward, but when the guys aren't around, he's very sweet and laid back. He said he just met this girl and is trying to be more respectful of the ladies. I think he's normally that way and just acts different with the guys.

"Drink up, bitches. It's time to get our dance on, and we know Ashley won't dance without a buzz. So down the shots and those drinks." Julia holds up her shot in the air and screams, "Here's to the night and all it brings. And, here's to the hottie who wants a fling!"

We crack up laughing and down the shot. I wave at the waitress, asking for another. I look over at Eagle and see him shaking his head, shoulders shaking with laughter. I'm glad he's here.

"Okay, so, hooker, what's going on? I mean, don't get me wrong, I'm all for drool-worthy bodyguards, but I know something's up," Ashley states as we wait for our next round.

"Oh, hell no, you can't start without me, you cocking cockstorm jockey suckers!" A male voice sounds behind me. Squealing with excitement, I turn and jump into Andy's open arms.

Out of the corner of my eye, I see Eagle tense up and start to come our way. I quickly let Andy go, step back, and introduce them to each other. Eagle shakes his hand, and then walks back to his spot to continue watching us.

"We wouldn't dream of it." I smile brightly at him. "How did you know we'd be here?"

"Chris told me that you were going to hang with the girls tonight. Since, he's meeting with Neil and won't be home until late . . . well, I figured I'd come and hang with you girls. Now, I need a drink!" Andy picks up a shot and raises it in the air, "A toast. We drink to those who love us, we drink to those who don't. We drink to those who fuck us, and fuck those who don't!"

We all slam our drinks back and shake our heads. Having Andy here really makes the night even better. He has a way of bringing joy out of a bad situation, and his love for his friends and family is fierce. I'm lucky to be a part of that circle.

"Okay, now talk." Julia pipes up looking pointedly at me.

As I tell them what has been going on, I see the fear creep into their eyes and the lines of worry etching their faces. They know I'm not the kind of girl to lead someone on, so this situation is very confusing and fearful for all of us. I haven't had anything else happen, but since that first letter, one of the guys have always been with me.

"Everyone knows you're not one to lead men on, so this whole situation is kind of scary. Did you talk to Chris?" Julia says, handing the waitress her empty glass and getting her new shot.

"We did fill Chris in on everything, because he's mentioned in the letter. The hospital has been notified, as well as the police. However, since we have no clue who it is, the police stated there isn't anything they can do about it. The guys have someone watching Chris, and of course, there's someone with me all the time now. Unfortunately, until something else happens there isn't anything anybody can do. They just told both of us to be careful and make sure we aren't alone."

"That's why he's hanging with Neil tonight. Going over what needs to be done and also talking about getting security placed in our home," Andy tells us, reaching for his beer.

"So, that's it then? We just sit back and wait until this guy either hurts Chris or comes after you?" Ashley questions while waving the waitress down for another drink.

"We don't know who it is, so technically, there really isn't anything *anyone* can do. The police do not have the manpower to have someone staking out in front of my house in hopes of catching this person placing another letter. They also stated that having former Seals guarding me is better anyway."

"That's true. What about the party for your brother's company? Is it safe to have it now that this is going on?" Julia asks me with worry clearly showing in her eyes.

"Yes, from what I understand the guys have everything

worked out with the hotel about security. Also, everyone will be there from family to former military buddies. I can't imagine this person trying something with that many people surrounding me," I explain.

"Well, when you put it that way, it does make sense. We'll also be there, and if we see anything weird we can always alert the guys." Ashley starts handing out the shots the waitress just dropped off at our table.

"Thanks. I'm so glad we're out tonight. I needed my posse." I look at all my friends surrounding me. "Okay, so raise your shots and let's toast. Here's to you and here's to me, and here's to all the men that lick us where we pee!"

The people close to our tables cheer and laugh at the toast, and we toss back our shots.

"Let's dance, bitches!" Ashley screams.

I turn to Andy and he jumps up, grabs my hand, and drags me to the dance floor. Whenever we all go out, he will take turns dancing with all of us. He's about six-feet-tall with brown hair and deep blue eyes. He's built and is a huge flirt. Chris knows this is just how he is and trusts him not to go too far.

Right when we get on the dance floor, we hear *Luke Bryan's; I See You* start playing. Great. Even the DJ knows when I can't get Dante out of my head. I start dancing and getting lost into the music.

I look up at my girls and see guys starting to make their way to us. It never fails. My girls tend to draw in the guys' when we go out. Julia's a petite brunette with a body that makes you want to hate her, and Ashley's a tall brunette with huge breasts and curves women would die for. Then, there's Sara, who's a fiery redheaded goddess with the perfect hour glass shape.

I know Sara likes my brother. I keep encouraging her to go for him, but she's scared he doesn't see her that way. I've known Ashley and Julia since pre-school and Sara, I met in med school. However, she graduated in accounting and business, which is why she's working at Seal Security.

It seems like Julia has a crush on Eagle because she keeps glancing his way when he isn't looking at her. The moment he turns to glance her way, she turns her head with a slight blush. The funny thing is, he's doing the same damn thing. I don't condone cheating and neither do my girls. They know he has a girl, so I'll have to keep an eye on how things develop between them. I know they're adults and can make their own choices, however, I know Julia wouldn't want to do something that would hurt others.

I take a brief look around, share a smile with the girls, close my eyes, and start dancing to *Florida Georgia Line's, This is How We Roll*. I love this song and I love my country music. I'm a huge Luke Bryan fan so it helps he sings in this song, but *Florida Georgia Line* have really made a name for themselves.

Suddenly, I feel two strong arms wrap around me. I stiffen, open my eyes, and see Sara staring right at me with a shocked look on her face. I take a deep breath preparing myself for telling off whoever it is that thinks they can just grab me, when a very familiar scent hits me. My breath stops for a brief moment. I glance over my shoulder and see Dante looking down at me with lust burning in his eyes. He has on a plain black shirt that's pulled tight across his chest. The delicious sight immediately gets me wet, and I know my lacey boy shorts are ruined.

His burning gaze hides nothing from me. It gives me the strength to let my mask down. I allow the lust, the love, and the want from deep in my soul pour from my eyes. There are so many reasons why I should be afraid and why it's wrong, but with the liquid courage I've got running through my veins right now, I can't stop it. I'm so tired of running from him and my feelings.

I feel him stiffen, and I know that he sees the desire running deep from within me. He lowers his mouth to my ear, "Damn, baby, you look fucking hot." His whisper sends shivers down my spine. "You have every man in here wanting to see what's under that sexy as hell dress you're wearing. It's taking everything in me not to bend you over that table to see what color your panties are. Tell me, baby. What color are they, Len? Tell me, *mio tutto.*"

"Blue . . . n . . . navy blue. My favorite color. And my bra matches," I whisper. "What does *mio tutto* mean, Dante?"

"It means my everything in Italian." He murmurs to me.

I'm shocked, but I'm so turned on. I swear if he ends up walking away after getting me so hot, I'm going to be pissed. I'll kill him, but I know I'll also be broken. I can't deal with another heartbreak like I did after our first kiss. I start to pull away. Maybe this isn't a good idea.

"No, Len, don't pull away. You're probably thinking this isn't a good thing. Your body language gives your thoughts away. We'll talk later about everything. Right now, let me enjoy you in my arms. Be mine, *mio tutto.*" He pulls me closer and starts dancing with me.

I hear him singing in my ear, and I'm shocked at the song he's chosen to whisper to me. Until my last breath, I'll never forget the words he sings to me.

Chase Rice, Ride is now my favorite song. I decide that when I get a chance that it's going to be his ringtone. I'm afraid to get my hopes up, but I pray he means what the lyrics are implying.

"I know you feel it, Len. I've felt it since I was eighteen, when I kissed you goodbye. I'm tired of fighting it. Tonight, I'll make you mine in every sense of the word. If that isn't what you want, stop me now. But your body's showing me that this is what you want. Tell me I'm not wrong. Tell me that I can have you," he says in my ear, and I can hear the desperation in his voice.

Turning around in his arms, I gaze into his eyes and I see the truth.

However, I'm struck with a memory of him on the phone with my brother all those years ago when he didn't want me following him around. Despite his words now, I need to know if he still sees me that way. It's something that needs to be answered before we go any further.

"Am I still that annoying little girl you thought I was?" I ask, trying to keep the tears at bay.

I watch his expressions go from confused, to shock, to understanding. He takes a deep breath and closes his eyes.

He leans his forehead against mine, and then opens his eyes dropping the mask that normally covers them.

"No, Len. I'm sorry you heard that. I haven't thought of you that way since I saw you walking into Gates N Sons after your college induction night. I'm so sorry, Len. I didn't mean it," he says, looking deep into my eyes.

I take a deep breath and then lean up to his ear.

"Take me home, Dante. Make me yours. I want you," I whisper as seductively as I can.

I take a step back; gazing into his eyes, showing him the desire that's swamping my body.

He grabs my hand. "Say goodbye to Andy and the girls. Tell them no calling you at all this weekend. You'll see them soon enough on Saturday. Until then, you will not be leaving the bed unless I say otherwise."

He meets Eagle's eyes and nods his head. Eagle looks at him, then at me, and a slow smile stretches across his face. He nods, letting Dante know he has the other girls covered.

"Bye, bitches! See you Saturday," I yell at Andy and the girls.

Smiles and cheers are coming from them, they know how much I love Dante. I just hope it's the same on his part. I also have to somehow find a way to tell him I'm a virgin.

This is going to be interesting.

DANTE

We walk out, I look over my shoulder and see my future. Marriage, babies, careers we love, and family surrounding us. For the first time ever, I feel free and that everything's finally coming together. I think back to yesterday and what happened . . .

I'd almost lost my shit when I'd overheard Sin's moans as I was walking through her house. After the talk with Len and she went upstairs, I walked out to the deck and punched him in the stomach. I told him and Doc that if I ever heard them talk to her like that again I wouldn't think twice about putting them in their place. They had laughed and said that they couldn't wait until I had a talk with Lucky about how much I wanted to bang Len.

Shit, I was scared to talk with him too.

I went into Seal Security after I left there to talk to Lucky about the note that came with the roses. I wanted to throw up when I saw what that sick fuck wrote on that note.

MY BEAUTIFUL LEN,

I MISS SEEING YOUR SMILING FACE. YOU'VE BEEN SO BUSY, I HAVEN'T HAD A CHANCE TO SAY HI. AS I LAY IN BED AT NIGHT, I WONDER WHAT IT WILL BE LIKE ONCE YOU'RE IN MY ARMS. IT WONT BE LONG NOW. UNTIL THEN, THINK OF ME LIKE I THINK OF YOU.

YOURS ALWAYS

The inquiry at the floral shop came up empty. The camera showed a homeless guy coming in with cash, a note, and information on what to get. We found the guy two blocks down, and all he could tell us is it was a guy in a black hoodie who offered him a hundred dollars if he would follow the directions on the paper. After he brought back the receipt showing he followed them he gave him the money and left.

We ended up putting more cameras out around the house to see if we could catch this guy in the act of sneaking around. We talked to the hospital about security and wanting more eyes on her. We were informed that due to HIPPA, some shit that's about privacy for the patients, there are places that cameras can't be placed. So, for now, all we can do is amp up more security and make sure she understands not to go anywhere alone. We talked with the hotel, where the party will be held, and they are aware of the situation. They understand there will be more security, and we'll need to access things that aren't normally available for guests. There isn't anything else we really can do until this fucker decides to play his cards and try something.

Once we got that sorted, I decided to come clean with Lucky. I was expecting him to kick my ass but was surprised when he cracked up laughing and said it was about damn time. He's known for years that I've wanted his sister. He respects me for fighting it due to our friendship, but he's thrilled and happy I was finally stepping up, especially since this sick fuck is out there.

He knows his sister is safe with me. Though he did say he was going to punch me because he warned his friends to stay away from his sister. He also said if I hurt her he would kill me and bury me where I wouldn't be found. He didn't get his name Lucky for nothing.

I got my nickname Ghost for a reason. I can enter a room, assess it fast, and kill without a sound being made. It's why I was in charge of our team.

I showed him the engagement ring that I'd bought in Dubai during one of our downtimes between missions.

"When did you buy this, Dante?" he asked as he looked at the ring and its matching band.

It's a combined two-karat diamond ring and band set. It has a square diamond at the center and two-round diamonds on each side of the center diamond, then baguettes on each side of them. The band has baguettes, a round diamond on each side then another row of baguettes on each side of them. It's white and yellow fourteen-karat gold. I can't wait to see it on her finger.

"I got it when we were in Dubai the first time," I reply looking at the ring in his hand.

"That was four years ago. Why did you get it then?"

"Nine years ago I felt a pull towards her that I couldn't understand. As time went on, I knew I would claim her one day, or I at least hoped I would. I couldn't do it while we were in the Navy. I wouldn't do that to her knowing that I might not come back home. When I saw that ring, I just knew it was her, and that one day she would wear it on her finger. From that moment on, I didn't look or sleep with another woman," I explained.

Lucky stared at me with a stunned expression on his face.

"In my just in case letter, I wrote about the ring and gave instructions on it needing to go to her after she read her letter. I should've talked with you about this a long time ago. I just didn't know how and didn't want it to ruin the friendship we had. I can't wait anymore Lucky. I need her like the air I breathe." I exhale, then I take back the ring and put it in its case.

He studies me for a while, and I try to read his face.

"Do you think this is too fast?"

He takes a deep breath, looks at the box, and then meets my stare.

"Personally, I don't think it's going too fast, seeing how you've both known each other for over thirteen years. I think that's something you both should probably discuss when you talk about getting together. For what it's worth, I *give my blessing. I know you'll take good care of her. I also know she feels the same. When I first realized it, I wanted to beat the hell out of you. But as the years went on, I knew you were right for her. Take good care of her, man. She's special, I know I don't have to tell you that." He gets up and gives me a hug.*

"Now, you have to talk to the moms and dads, as well as the twins. Good luck with that." He laughs.

"Shit, any advice? I'm going to talk with them Friday when I take her to talk to the moms about the party," I question as I start to get nervous.

He laughs, shakes his head, and walks away. Damn him, I hope they agree to this. If they agree, I'll be asking her on Saturday. I know this is moving fast, but after wasting nine years, yeah, that wasn't going to happen anymore.

Our Moms' aren't going to be able to give her the wedding they want. They'll have three months from Saturday to plan that shit. Yeah, that isn't going to be a good conversation either. I can see them trying to stop that and make it a long engagement. I'll have to make it up to them by allowing them to go full out for a party later. Maybe, they can do it for our one year anniversary. I'll have to think of something . . .

I snap back to the present when I spot my truck. Pulling her along with me, I pick her up, and sit her inside. Then, I lean over her and put on her seatbelt.

"Baby, once we get to your house, you better be ready. It's going to be a long night," I tell her as I shut her door.

I run to my side, adjusting myself as I go. God, I'm ready

for her. I know the first time I have to be gentle. I'm not sure how gentle I can be, but I'll do it for her.

I rush to her house, our breathing the only sound you can hear. I can tell she isn't doing any better than I am. Fifteen minutes later, I'm pulling into her driveway. I reach out the window and punch the code on her garage door. After pulling into her garage, I turn to her and take a deep breath.

"I need you to stay here. Let me shut the door and check the system. I'll come and get you when all is clear. Lock the door until you see me," I tell her, kissing her forehead.

I jump down from the truck and make sure I watch the garage door as it shuts. I walk into the side door and pull my gun and check the system. Fuck, it looks like there were two attempts not even an hour ago on entering. I wonder for a brief moment why I wasn't notified of this. I pull out my phone and see I have five missed calls from Lucky.

I silently type in the code and wait for the all clear to show on the monitor. Then, I enter the code to alarm the system for staying. I slowly make my way through the house, checking the rooms. Next, I throw the switch to check the backyard. We have a night vision system where it stays dark outside when the switch is on, yet the screen by the back door shows everything clearly as if it's light outside. I don't see anyone there. As I walk back to the garage, I pull my phone and text Lucky.

Me: *Did you get the two attempts that were made at Len's house? Please, tell me you were able to catch the fucker who was attempting to break in.*

Lucky: *Yes, all was checked. I tried to call Eagle and* *you but figured after five failed attempts that you both couldn't hear your phones at the club. Face was hidden on the camera. We missed him by five minutes. Did you check everything?*

Me: *Yes, all is clear. I'm here now. Might be busy, so make sure whoever is watching the system knows that I might be indisposed.*

Lucky: *Just because I gave you permission to be with my sister doesn't mean you can tell me what you're doing to her, you sick fuck. I still owe you an ass kicking.*

Me: *Keep it up, and I'll tell you details. Now, I'm off to get Len out of my truck. Later, asshat.*

Lucky: *You're going to be hurting after the ass kicking that's coming your way. Later, fucker.*

A burst of laughter escapes me at his comment, and I put away my phone. I walk over to her side of the truck and tap on the window. She unlocks the door and opens it.

"That took a while. Is everything okay?" she asks with a worried look on her face.

Even with her worrying, she's still the most beautiful woman in the world.

"Yeah, *mio tutto*, everything's fine. Come here. Let's get you inside and upstairs," I say, reaching for her.

I pull her out of the car and set her down to grab my bag from behind her seat. I shut the door, turn around, and pick her back up. She wraps around me like a monkey, and I carry her into the house.

"I can walk you know," she says with a smile.

"I know, but I want to carry you into the house. I don't want you out of my arms. Do you want to talk first, or do you want to go into the bedroom?" I ask.

"We should talk, but can we do it in the bedroom?" she says, looking into my eyes.

She runs her fingers through my hair, something I've seen her do with her hair when she's nervous. I wonder if it's because she hasn't told me she's a virgin.

"Yeah, just keep your hands to yourself. I know how you get when you drink. You can't keep your hands off of me," I say, trying to get her mind off her nerves.

"You're so full of shit." She laughs as I carry her upstairs.

Dropping her on her bed, I walk over to her dresser.

"Okay, let's talk this out. What do you want to know? What are you feeling?" I take a deep breath and wait.

Each second that passes more agonizing than the one before.

Seven

Len

I SCOOT TO THE EDGE of the bed and take a deep breath, unsure if I should tell him I've crushed on him since I was twelve. I remember how he used to see me, however, if I want to start this right, I have to tell him everything.

"I've had a crush on you since the day I first saw you. I slowly fell in love with you over the years. You were my first kiss, and that day gave me hope. I didn't do anything until I was eighteen. It was my junior year in college, and I'd just got back from visiting Neil. While I was there, I overheard him talking to a girl about a threesome you guys had. She kept going on and on about you and him. I came back and kissed the first boy who asked me out. We dated for eight months. We had oral sex and, when he wanted to further it, I knew I had to end it. I couldn't give him the one thing that I wanted to give to the man I love.

"I went on dates after that and only had oral sex with one other guy in medical school. We decided to start a relationship shortly after we started our residency. We dated for over a year. When we broke up, it was awkward because we had to continue with our residency together. He ended up moving to a different state when his fiancé's, now wife's, family was killed in a car crash. She was also a first year resident who went to school with us. I'm still friends with her."

I take another deep breath.

"Anyway, that's why I won't date people at work. I always knew it wouldn't go far, and I didn't want any awkwardness. I love my job, so I've dated here and there through friends.

"That means that if this is something we're going to do, you need to understand I haven't ever been with someone. I don't have the experience you have. I don't know what to do past the foreplay stage. I also want to know what this will mean afterwards. What are you wanting after tonight? Is this just a fling or are you wanting me to be with you? I need to know what I'm getting into. I don't want to think it's something longer when you're just looking to sleep with me because you just want to know what it's like to get into my pants."

I look up into his eyes when I'm done and see a mixture of feelings; rage, love, lust, desire, and possessiveness. He takes a deep breath and pulls off his shoes, then his belt. He unsnaps his pants and then takes off his shirt. My mouth drops open. Across his chest is the words *famiglia è tutto*. Also, both nipples are pierced and his biceps are covered in tattoos. There's a tribal type tattoo above his heart. It wraps around what looks like a heart with a key hole and inside is the color of my eyes . . . light sky blue. He slowly walks towards me.

"Len, let me make this clear, I never want to hear about you with another guy. Nothing more needs to be said about that. As I answer your questions and tell you my feelings and thoughts can you just nod if you understand?"

I nod.

"Good girl. Now, I started falling for you the moment you walked into Gates N Sons. But I already told you that. I didn't tell you that I already gave you my heart four years ago. I realized that you were it for me. I haven't been with anyone since that day. I stayed away all these years because of my friendship with your brother. I also knew I couldn't be what you needed. I couldn't leave you behind. But now, I'm home.

"I plan on being everything you need, everything you want, and everything you desire. So, to answer your question, no it isn't me just wanting to know what it's like to be inside your pants, like you said. *This* is me telling you that I'll be the first and the last man in them."

I suck in a shocked breath at what he just explained. He hasn't been with anyone in four years?

"That means you will never have another boyfriend or date another man. I'm going to be your boyfriend, your lover, your best friend, your protector and very, very soon your husband and the father of our children."

By now, he's standing between my legs and his fingers are running down my neck towards my breast.

"And, *mio tutto*, I'm so glad that you're inexperienced. That's a good thing for many reasons. One being that I won't have to kill anyone, and for another, because you will learn what I like in the bedroom as we explore what you like as well," he says to me as he starts pushing the straps of my sundress down.

I'm trying to process what he just said, but I can't really think because I'm in a fog of Dante.

"Are you ready? I don't know if I can hold back much longer. You ready to belong to me and no other?" he asks as he continues to trace my collarbone.

"Yes, I'm ready, *amore*," I answer him.

A smile starts to break on his face and I can't help but smile back. It then dawns on me that I'm finally getting the man of my dreams.

"I like it when you call me *amore*. I'll always remember the first time you called me that. There's one more thing I need to say before we go any further. Stand up."

I stand up, and my dress falls to the floor and puddles at my feet. I step out of it and kick it aside. I hear a sharp breath and look up at Dante's face. His face has transformed, and I see the deep desire in his eyes as he takes in my strapless bra and boy shorts. There isn't much to them, but their lace material and navy blue color.

"Are you okay?" I reach out for him.

"Fuck! Damn, Len, you're testing my patience. You look fucking amazing. Are all your panties like this and with matching bras?" he asks, taking in my body again.

"Um . . . yes. I buy them online. I spend a lot of money on them, but I like nice bras and panties," I tell him looking away because it's embarrassing how much money I spend on them.

He hooks his finger under my chin and turns my face to him. Leaning in close to my lips, he whispers against them. "I love them. Next time you order, I'll be helping you pick some stuff out, yeah?"

Nodding my head, I start to lean in. He eases back and looks into my eyes.

"I have something to tell you. First, I want to say this so you know it before anything else. I've never said them to anyone outside of my family and closest friends," he tells me as he tries to get his thoughts together. He looks nervous.

"Look into my eyes, Len. Are you ready?"

Nodding my head, I can see love shining brightly in his eyes. It makes my breath catch. If he says he loves me I know I'll lose all sense of thoughts and have tears pouring down. I won't be able to stop myself since those words are what I have desired to hear from him since I was sixteen.

"Len, I love you with everything in me. I love you more than anyone I have ever loved. I'll love you until my last dying breath. I love you one more time then whatever you think you can feel for me. So know that I love you, one more time. That's our saying. Do you understand, *mio tutto*?"

My tears fall as I look at the man I love more than anything.

Anytime we would call each other names we would say, one more time, meaning that, no matter what that person said, if they said they were awesome we would say that as saying we were one more time better than them, or they were worse than what they said to us. I'm shocked that he used those words as a way to express the love he feels for me.

"I see you remember and understand. Now, look into my heart. What do you see?" he whispers and wipes my tears away.

I glance at his tattoo and see it really is my eye color. I also see that in the tribal design are the words, *TI'mo, Len.*

89

Un'altra volta.

I know *TI'mo, Len* means *I love you, Len* in Italian.

"*TI'mo, Len. Un'altra volta.* It means, *I love you, Len, one more time.* I got that done about four years ago. I don't understand how your brother or mine never figured it out, but they didn't. If they did, they never said anything. I figured if I never got to see you again, I knew you would see this. That my family would tell you what it means, and you would know I loved you," he tells me, looking earnestly into my eyes.

I have a small tattoo that's on my hip bone, too. I haven't told anyone I got it. It's a small flower with swirls that spell his name. I got it a week after he left for training.

I start sobbing. I know we could've lost both Neil and him during this last mission. He gently picks me up, starts rubbing my back, murmuring in my ear, and calms me down by rocking me.

"*Mio tutto*, I'm here. I won't be anywhere else. As a matter of fact, I think this is the perfect house. I know we talked before about houses and we had the same idea. It'll be perfect for our children," he tells me, smiling down into my eyes.

"However, the twins are losing their rooms. I'm sure they won't be happy about it. Are you okay now, Len?" He pulls me back to look at me.

I nod and lay my head on his shoulder trying to take in everything he has said.

"Yeah, I just got upset at what happened with Neil, the guys, and you. Anyway, I've dreamt about this for years. It's a little overwhelming," I confess.

He smiles at me and places his forehead against mine.

"Kiss me, Dante. Make love to me, claim me, and make me yours," I whisper.

I plunge my hands into his hair.

His lips claim mine fiercely. He pulls my bottom lip with his teeth, making me moan. Growling, he licks, seeking entrance. I open and his tongue plunges into my mouth. Holy shit, this is the best kiss I've ever had, and his taste is something I'm officially addicted to. I'm starting to get lightheaded, and I'm not sure if it's from the kiss or because I need air. All I know is if I'm like this after a kiss, I know I'm not going to live through us finally having sex.

Eight

DANTE

I KNEW IT WOULD ONLY take one taste of her to become addicted. That's why I waited until now to claim the kiss I've dreamed of for years. God, just from her kiss, I'm so hard and leaking. I don't know how much longer I can hold off.

"I need to taste you. I need to have my mouth devouring your pussy. I need to taste the sweetness that I'm going to be enjoying every damn day for the rest of my life."

I'm not sure what I'm saying to her.

I take off her bra, lay her down, and my mouth finds the most perfect nipple on the most perfect breast I've ever laid eyes on. Refusing to let them go, even for a second, I slowly start taking off the rest of my clothes.

I reach down and grab her panties and shred them. I trace her hip bone slowly, moving my hand between her legs and stopping the moment I feel bare skin. I finally release her nipple which causes her to moan at the loss and look down at where my hand is resting between her legs.

"You're bare."

Her cheeks start turning red, and I assume she's embarrassed.

"I wax. I don't like having hair down there. Sorry," she says shyly, and I laugh.

"Don't be sorry. It's fucking sexy, and I can't wait to kiss those lips," I say, staring into her eyes.

Shit, this is going to go fast. I haven't felt like I was going to come so quickly since I was a teenager.

She wraps her hands around my neck to pull me down for a kiss. "Then kiss me."

"*Mio tutto*, I'll always want to kiss these lips, but the lips I want my mouth on aren't on your beautiful face." I look up at her and smirk at her blush.

I give her a peck on the lips and start kissing my way down her neck to her breast. I take my time giving both breasts equal amounts of attention. She's making sexy as fuck sounds, and I know it's time to get my dessert. Slowly making my way down her stomach, I kiss and lick her smooth, soft skin. I get to a tattoo and look closely. I see a white rose and swirls. I trace the swirls, and it takes a second for me to realize it's my name. I hold my breath and look up into her eyes.

"Len?"

"I got it the week after you left for training. I knew I loved you then, and I wanted your name on me. Nobody's seen it, but the tattooist, my girls, my doctor, and a few . . . um . . . yeah."

"*Mio tutto*, you have no clue how happy that makes me. Seeing my name on your body, damn, that's fucking hot and sexy as hell," I kiss and lick where the tattoo is.

I love the tattoo. It's like having my mark on her permanently, and I wish it was in a spot that people could see. However, my ring on her finger will work just as well.

Laying down between her legs, I spread her and put her legs on my shoulders. I pull apart her lips and slowly lick her from entrance to clit while watching her face. Her head rolls back, and she moans.

Her spicy-sweet flavor bursts across my tongue. Holy shit, she's now my favorite meal.

"Len, you taste fucking amazing. I knew I would be addicted to you but I didn't know just how addicting it was going to be. I'm never going to get enough," I moan as I head back for more.

I devour her. I need her wet enough to take me, but I'm tempted to never leave this area. I need to get her as close to coming as possible. I slowly slip in a finger and break through her virginity. I still for a moment giving her a second to adjust and search for that spot I know is going to set her off. Finding it, I start moving my fingers back and forth.

"Oh God, Dante. So good." Her moans are hot and getting me harder.

I slide in another finger and start preparing her for my cock by scissoring my fingers back and forth.

"You're tight. You need to come on my tongue. I need to feel you squeezing my fingers tight like you're going to do with my cock. Give it to me, Len," I growl against her clit.

She's moaning and twisting on the bed. I gently ease in a third finger as I flatten my tongue and press on her clit. She detonates, and I eagerly drink up her juices like they're my last meal. I continue to pump my fingers in and out of her while my eyes peruse my way up her body. When I get to her face, it's flushed from her climax, but she's getting close again. I can see it in her eyes and in the way she's tightening up.

"I need you to let me know when you're almost there," I tell her, sweeping my tongue around her clit.

"Dante, I'm almost there. Don't stop," she tells me and grabs my biceps.

"Don't worry, I don't plan on it." I promise, rubbing her clit with my thumb.

"Oh, God, yes! Yes! Yes! I'm coming!" she cries.

I remove my fingers, keeping my thumb on her clit. Using my other hand, I line myself up and slam into her knowing this will be the easiest way. Fuck, she's so fucking tight. I keep my eyes on her face to see how her pain is. She tenses up and winces for a brief moment, and a tear slowly makes its way down her face which makes me bend down to kiss it away.

"Dante, *amore*, you have to move. I feel so damn full," she moans then she's wiggling under me.

"Are you sure you're okay? I don't want to hurt you."

"Dante, I swear to God, if you don't move, I'll hit you. It was a slight pinch, and now I'm fine." She's looking into my eyes, and I see there is no sign of pain clouding them.

"Okay, you tell me if it hurts."

I put my weight on my elbows, move my hands to frame her face. I gaze into her eyes as I start to slide out.

I knew it would be like this, heaven. I don't know if I'm going to be able to last much longer. Feeling such heat and wet velvet walls, it feels so good. Knowing that it's Len, only makes it even better.

"Fuck, *mio tutto*, you feel so good. I'm trying hard to

hold back."

"Dante, I'm so close. Don't stop. Please, don't hold back. Make me come."

She lifts her head and bites my shoulder while she digs her nails in my back.

That does it. Hearing her say that and feeling the sting of pain from her teeth and nails, I know I can't hold back.

"Hold on, Len."

I pull out and slam into her. She throws her head back and screams as I start to pound into her. The look of ecstasy on her face makes me fall deeper in love. I can feel her starting to tighten around my cock.

"I want you to come on my cock. I need to feel it," I tell her as I pull her hair and look deep in her eyes.

"Oh God, that's it . . . don't stop . . . I'm going to come. Yes, I want . . . Oh, God . . . don't stop . . . I'm going . . . to . . . oh, shit . . . Dante!" she yells.

Her back arches, and I can feel her soaking my cock. She's so damn tight that it's hard to move in her as she's squeezing me trying to milk every last drop out of me.

Seeing her face and hearing her moans has me pushing deeper into her and nudging her cervix. My balls tighten, lightning shooting down my spine. I realize that I don't have a condom on, and the thought that I can get her pregnant at this exact moment has me coming even more into her.

I drop down and nuzzle her neck. She twines her arms around me and keeps her legs wrapped around my waist. We lay there, trying to regain our breath. I slowly raise up, needing to see that she's really okay. She's flushed and has that just-fucked look. Damn, I want her again, but I know she can't take it. I think about going to start a bath for her so she won't be too sore.

I spot tears sliding down her face, and my first thought is that I took her too hard.

"Are you okay, Len? I didn't hurt or scare you, did I?" I ask.

"I'm so happy, and I love you so much. I'm sore, yeah, but I'm so glad it was you. And, no you didn't hurt or scare me," she says, smiling at me.

I lean down and kiss her gently.

"I need to get a bath started for you. I'm going to pull out. It's going to hurt. So, I just wanted to warn you. I'm sorry, *mio tutto.*"

I slowly pull out and we both wince, me at the loss and her at the tenderness. The blood on my cock makes me want to hit my chest like a caveman; knowing that I'm the only man to ever have her. I go into the bathroom and start the bath. Getting two washcloths, I clean myself, then go into her room and clean her up too before tossing the washcloths in the hamper. I pick her up, and carry her into the bathroom, sitting her down on the edge of the tub. Hopping into the bath, I sit her between my legs and grab the sponge, slowly washing her as she leans on my chest.

"I love you, Len. Thank you for allowing me to be your first. I can't wait to spend forever with you, baby. One more time," I whisper into her ear while I wash her stomach. The thought of her possibly being pregnant comes to mind.

"I love you, too, Dante. One more time," she says as she puts her hand on mine.

Len

I gradually wake up and feel as if I'm tied down to the bed. I'm trying to figure out why I can't move as the night slowly comes back to me. Opening my eyes, I feel a huge arm wrapped around my waist. I turn my head and see two big brown eyes staring at me.

"Morning, *mio tutto*. How are you feeling?"

"Morning. I'm good. I need to use the restroom," I tell him.

I start to pull away so I can go and brush my teeth because I know he's going to want a kiss.

"No, you can't get up until you tell me good morning properly," he tells me while he holds me to the bed and climbs over me.

He gazes down at me and starts to move his mouth to mine. I turn my head.

"I need to brush my teeth first, Dante. I have morning breath."

"Len, I don't give a fuck. Kiss me."

He grabs my head and turns me to face him, claiming my mouth and kissing me breathless.

He starts to nibble my lower lip and pulls away slightly. I open my eyes and look at him and see the happiness shining brightly back at me. I'm speechless that I can put that look on his face.

"That's how I expect you to tell me good morning every day for the rest of my life."

He bends down slowly and starts kissing me again. I can feel his hardness rub against me as he claims my mouth in a way I know nobody else will ever do.

"*Amore*, we don't have time. I need to shower and get

ready to go see our moms. You know this," I tell him after I turn my head to break the kiss. I look at the clock and see we only have an hour before we have to leave.

"Ugh, fine. Go take your shower. I'll start the coffee and breakfast. If I join you in the shower, we won't leave the house," he jokingly says then gives me a hard peck and climbs out of bed.

Holy crap, my man is hot! I watch him walk over to the dresser and dig through his bag. I start to feel tingly between my legs. I want him again. I don't know if I'll ever get enough of him. His back is to me as he pulls on his jeans that hug his ass just right. I watch as he slowly gets dressed.

"Len, you better get that sexy as sin body in the shower before I end up calling our moms and telling them that we won't make it because I have other plans with my woman," he tells me with his back still turned.

"Shit!" I jump up and run into the bathroom. I lock the door as he laughs at me. Damn him and his sexiness.

As I wash for the day, I start to think of what I need to get done. Then it hits me, we're going to Mom's house, together, after we just became a couple. I've just had sex for the first time. How's this going to play out? Is he going to tell them? Does he want to keep it a secret? I know he told Neil, but what about the parents and the twins?

I slide down the side of the shower and try to breathe deeply. I don't know how to ask him these things. Yeah, I've been in a couple relationships, but this is different because of our families being so intertwined together. I guess I'll just have to wait and see how he acts and go from there.

I finish my shower, get dressed, and head downstairs. I smell the scent of bacon, coffee, and pancakes. I stop in the doorway of the kitchen to a sight that I can't wait to see more often. I don't know what it is, but watching a man cook is a major turn on for me. Seeing Dante in my kitchen and seeing him cook like he belongs there does something to me. Is this normal?

"Come here, *mio tutto*. I feel you staring at me," he orders without turning around.

I walk up behind him and wrap my arms around his middle and put my forehead between his shoulders. I love that he's still taller than me when I'm wearing heels.

He grabs my hands and squeezes before returning to cooking. "Hungry? I've made breakfast. Why don't you set the table and I'll bring it to you?"

"Um . . . I'm not really a breakfast eater. I should have told you. Normally, I just have coffee," I tell him then I walk to get dishes to set a place for him at the table.

He stops me and gives me a hard kiss on the lips.

"Not anymore, Len. Breakfast every day. I need you healthy. We need to discuss the fact that we didn't use a condom last night," he says with a grin growing on his face.

Knowing he wants to take care of me has me melting. This guy's going to be the death of me. The only problem is I can't eat if I'm not hungry. We'll have to come to some sort of compromise. I can't do breakfast in the mornings.

"How about I eat a small bit of eggs and two pieces of bacon? Oh, and a cup of coffee. I honestly can't eat a big breakfast this early, Dante."

I can see he's getting ready to argue with me.

"Dante, I mean it and will not move on this. I will not change who I am. I agree I should eat breakfast, but this big of one isn't good for me. I'll eat a little bit, but that's it. If you

101

don't agree then I won't eat anything. Deal?" I tell him, looking him straight in the eyes.

He sighs before kissing me, and walking away. I smile, touchdown! I won this battle!

"Now, let's discuss this no use of condoms. Was this on purpose?" I question, I sit down with my coffee.

He makes both of us a plate and then takes a seat next to me. I can see him picking his words carefully, and I'm struck with a deep fear of what he might say next.

"It didn't really hit me until I realized I didn't put on a condom. I won't lie about the fact that it made me happy when I realized that it could've happened last night. We both are in our mid to late twenties, we've known each other for years, and that's why I'm not worried about it looking rushed or that you might be pregnant. I honestly feel like we shouldn't wait, we should start our lives together now," He calmly explains.

I take a few minutes to absorb the words he just spoke. On one hand, I'm pissed he didn't think about protection, but on the other, I'm a grown woman and know how to tell a man to put on a condom before we have sex. His explanation makes sense in the way that we've known each other for over thirteen years now. It really wouldn't look weird to move things along . . . wait . . . does that mean what I think it means?

"Are you talking about moving in together, Dante?"

"Fuck yes! I already told you how much I love the house and that it would fit our future children. Did you think I was just saying these things so I could fuck you and move on?" he growls, and I can see the anger building in his eyes.

"I don't know, Dante! It would've been fucking nice if

you just said that to begin with!" I exclaim while I throw my hands in the air.

"Fine, do you want me to move in? One day become my wife? And do you want to make babies with me, Len?"

"Yes! I've always wanted that, Dante!" I scream.

"Fine, I'm glad that's worked out. Now, let's eat, *mio tutto,*" he calmly states and starts eating.

I sit in stunned silence at what just happened. I take a moment and realize that I was just coerced into Dante not only moving in, but also him actively trying to get me pregnant, and at some point I'll become his wife. I shake my head and think that the fight I claimed victory with earlier doesn't compare to the fight he'd just won. I take a breath and decide that now isn't the time to really get into this. I'll bring it up again later when we have more time to go through it all.

Fifteen minutes later, we pull up to my parents' house, and I start to get nervous. I'm not sure how to act. I glance at Dante as he turns the truck off. I don't know if his parents are here yet, if they aren't, then they will be here quickly as they live right next door.

Years ago, the parents decided to buy a huge piece of land together and build two separate houses on it. Since the houses are next to each other, they often just walk or drive the golf cart since it's about three acres between them.

"*Mio tutto,* I'm going to run over to my parents' house. Both of our dads are there. I'm going to pack a big bag to bring back when we leave. We can figure out a good time to move me in once the party is over. Go ahead inside," he states.

He hops out of the truck and walks over to open my door to help me out.

"Len, one more time."

He kisses me, turns me to the front door, and pats my butt.

I walk up to the front door and look over my shoulder as I enter my parents' house. I see him smile and walk away.

I find the Moms in the den with drinks on the table. I walk over to them, tell them hello and give them kisses.

"Hey, so let's get everything finalized," I tell them while I try to act normal.

Deep down, I'm going nuts trying to figure out how to act and what to say. I don't know how the families are going to react about us being together.

Nine

DANTE

I'D CALLED MY PAPA WHILE Len was in the shower and asked him to get Pops and the twins over to his house so I could talk to all four of them together. He'd asked if everything was okay and I'd assured him that what I had to talk about was a good thing. He then asked what was going on with Len.

I'm assuming he knows something's up, which means we're going to have to fill them all in on the stalker. I told him that I'd call Lucky and have him meet us there, too. With the party coming up, we could use the extra eyes.

On my way to my parents' house, I try to think of how I'm going to break the news to them. I'm thinking of just pulling out the ring and telling them straight out. I don't think there's an easy way to break the news. I know Papa's going to be happy. He loves Len as if she were his daughter. It's Pops and Carlo I'm more worried about. Oh and her OPG; that old woman scares me.

I get to the door and take a deep breath. As I enter, I can hear them talking in the other room. I go to my room real quick, place my bag on the bed, take out the ring and walk into the den. They all look up at my entrance and get quiet.

"So, I see we're all here. Thanks for coming on such short notice," I tell them as I sit on the couch next to Lucky.

"Son, what's going on? You look nervous and kind of jittery," Papa says to me while he sits back in his chair.

"This is going to be epic," Lucky chimes in, laughing.

"Holy shit, you're going for it." Nicoli bursts out in laughter.

"No, you're not good enough. Not going to happen," Carlo fumes.

"What's going on? Going for what?" Pops asks, looking at all of us with confusion.

"Okay, just let me talk please. Before anyone else goes off or says anything, let me explain everything and then once I'm done you all can ask questions. I've waited years for this conversation," I tell them all, looking each one in the eye.

"Okay, son, go ahead and tell us what's going on," Papa says.

I pull out the box, open it and grab the two rings. I place them on the table and look up at Papa and Pops. Confusion are on their faces as they take in the rings on the table then look at me. It takes me a minute to realize that they were thinking this was a talk about what was going on with Len, which it is, but I wanted to get this over with first.

"I want to marry Len. I love her. I've loved her for nine years. I bought that ring four years ago with her in mind. I can't wait anymore. I need you to understand that I've never said anything to anyone about my feelings for her. I talked with her last night and laid it out on the line. We're together now, but I need to know that everyone in this room, besides the Moms and OPG, are on board and okay with Len and I getting married," I tell them.

I stare at Pops and then look over at the twins. Nicoli's smiling and nodding his head, but Carlo looks like he wants to knock me the fuck out. I don't know why he's acting this way. I know he loves Len, but it's only as a sister. Now, I'm wondering if his feelings are different. I don't give a fuck if they are. I won't step down for him. I won't step down for nobody when it comes to Len.

Papa's starting to grin as it dawns on him. Pops on the other hand has a mix of emotions flickering across his face. I'm not sure how I'm going to handle it if he denies me. I know he's protective of Len and this is his only baby girl, so I know it's important to get his blessing. If he says no, then I'll prove my worth to earn it from him. However, I'll still be asking her and she'll still be mine.

I hear a cough and look back at Papa.

"I've known for a while that you wanted her. I'm proud that you've finally taken the step and gone after what will make you both happy. I've seen the way she looks at you and it's the same way. I'm also proud that you came to us. So, with that said, don't hurt her," he tells me. He moves to embrace me in a big hug.

"I'm cool with it. I've known too. I know you'll be what she needs you to be. And now, she'll officially be my sister. This is awesome," Nicoli says holding his fist.

Two down.

"Carlo? Go ahead and get it off your chest," I say to him and get ready for the showdown.

I want to hear what he has to say before Pops speaks. I need him to see that I'll fight for her and for him to see the passion I feel for his little girl.

"You're not good enough for Len. I love her like a sister and I don't think anyone's ever good enough for her. I refuse for her to be treated like a piece of trash. She deserves to be treated with love and passion. Have you ever treated a woman you were sleeping with that way? No, you haven't. How do we know you'll treat Len the way she's meant to be treated? Explain it to me. Try and change my mind," Carlo says.

I take a deep breath and I let my guard down and let him see the emotions play across my face. I understand what he's saying, but he has no clue what I've been going through all these years, how I've loved her so deep that for the past four years I've laid awake at night just wishing I was back here to see her one more time. How I've wanted to claim her and make her mine. I decide to take my shirt off and show him the tattoo that's above my heart.

"Carlo, what do you think?" I ask him as I stand so all can see.

He takes a look at my chest then into my eyes and I see he's getting it, he then turns to everyone in the room.

"It says, *I love you, Len, one more time.* When did you get that? I can tell it's not new because it's slightly faded," he tells everyone.

"I got it four years ago, right before Lucky and I went on a mission. He had no clue that I got it done," I explain.

"That's where you went. I was wondering why you left for as long as you did. I just thought you needed some time to gather your thoughts about our mission," Lucky tells me while he studies the tattoo.

"Carlo, I love her with everything in me. I tried to wait as long as I could so she could follow her dreams. I didn't want her to give that up while I was in the Navy. I didn't want to chance leaving her a widow. I decided when I got out that, if she was still single, then I would let my feelings be known. I can't give her up. I won't give her up. Please believe that she'll be treated like she's the most precious treasure on this earth, next to our children. I need your blessing in this too," I tell him as I move to stand in front of him.

He looks at me for a long time. I'm beginning to think he's going to tell me to screw off. But he wraps his arms around me.

"Don't hurt her," he says quietly in my ear.

"Okay, now that I've heard all that, I'm going to say a few things," Pops says from behind me.

I turn around and put my shirt back on before sitting down and taking a deep breath.

"All right, Pops, let's hear it," I tell him, preparing for the talk of my life.

"Len's my little girl. The day she was born I knew that I would have to face this day at some point. In the beginning, I said that I would make sure that it didn't happen and that I would hand pick the person she'd marry. I realized that that would never work. She's too stubborn for that. I knew I wanted someone who was going to love her as much as a man could. I wanted her to have the love that her mother and I share. To see that she's happy and never lacking anything in her life. I want her to be protected and safe. I never thought that I would get that with the person who loved her, but I know that with you; I will. I couldn't ask for a better person than you. I give you my blessing. Just know that, you hurt my baby girl, your Seal skills will mean nothing. Because I'll kill you," He stands and comes over to pat me on the back.

I stand and hug him with a smile on my face. I'm finally going to make Len mine. Now, I've to announce it to the mothers and OPG. Maybe it will be better to have them surprised, or have Pops and Papa tell them. I'm going to have to think about this.

"So, when are you asking her? Also what's going on? I know this wasn't everything. You've been having Len followed," Papa asks me while we all take our seats again. I pick up the rings and place them back in the box and in my pocket.

"I'm going to ask her tomorrow at the party. Now, as far as what's going on, we're going to need help. Len's in trouble. Lucky, why don't you start this conversation?" I suggest as I sit back.

"So, here's what's you need to know . . ."

$\mathcal{L}en$

"Okay, I think that's everything. So, what's going on with Dante and you? Don't think we didn't see that kiss out there when he dropped you off," Mom says.

"We're a couple now. Is that okay with you guys?" I ask both moms.

I'm so scared of how they are going to react, that I start to shake and then mess with my hair.

"Who asked who and don't leave a thing out," Mamma Gio demands, taking a sip of her OJ.

"Well, he kind of just told me it was happening. He has a tattoo on his chest that he got four years ago. Then, we kind of kissed, decided we loved each other, and that we're going to be together. Wait, now that I really think about it, he did give me a choice but didn't. He pretty much coerced me this morning into him moving in with me, marrying him and having kids," I tell them.

"Is that what you're wanting?" Mom asks.

"Honestly, yes but I still have to talk to him about this coercion he did on me this morning," I smile at Mom.

Both moms jump up, scream, clap and hug each other.

"I knew my boy took after his daddy. He pretty much did the same damn thing to me. I'm so happy and totally approve. So, Connie, if I know my boy . . . wedding plans need to start ASAP!" Mamma Gio exclaims as she comes and pulls me into a huge hug. "I'll finally get to call you my daughter!"

"What's going on in here?" OPG asks while she walks into the room.

She's looking at me like she's seeing me for the first time as she approaches me and wraps me in a hug.

"It's about time that man told you his feelings. Are you happy, Len? Is this what you want?" OPG asks looking up at me.

"Yes, I love him. I'm happy to finally have him. I hope you're okay with this, OPG," I ask, kissing her forehead.

"Of course I am. He's a good man. You know I don't like in-laws, but I accept him. I know he'll treat you right and he'll protect you. That's all I've ever wanted for you, Len. Also, he's handsome to boot. I think I'm going to start calling him sexy sailor," she snickers at me.

111

Oh Lord, I can't wait to see his face when she says that to him. This will be epic beyond belief. I hope she does it in front of everyone tomorrow.

"Okay, let's get the boys over hear for lunch. Then we have an afternoon at the spa," Mamma Gio says. Her phone is in her hand, probably texting her husband.

Ten

DANTE

IT HAS BEEN SUCH A long day. After planning what needs to be done to protect Len, we headed over to Lucky's parents' house.

I walked in and had both Moms running to hug me. After I figured out what was going on, I dragged them outside and showed them the ring. They screamed and jumped up and down. I told them I wanted to ask Len to marry me tomorrow. I also said they would only have three months to plan a wedding, that I wasn't waiting any longer than that. I explained my plan for my proposal, and they were all for it. They knew the perfect time to do it during the party, and they'd cue me at that moment.

OPG walked out at that point, and I knew that I needed to get her blessing. As I looked at OPG measuring me up, I asked the Moms to leave us. I needed show OPG the rings, in private. As she looked at them, I held my breath; I needed her blessing.

"So, you think you're good enough for my granddaughter? I don't like in-laws, so what can you say to change my mind?" she asked me.

"Ms. May, I love her. I promise to make her happy and give her everything her heart desires. I'll never hurt her on purpose, and I'll treat her like she's everything in this world. It would mean the world to me if you would give me your blessing," I told her.

She took a moment to look into my eyes, and I hoped she was finally seeing that I was telling the truth. When she smiled, then started laughing, and handed me the box, I felt a weight lift from my shoulders. I finally breathed a sigh of relief.

"I gave my blessing the day I saw you look at my Len like she was so perfect. You have my blessing on one condition, you call me OPG," she stated and hugged me.

I was shocked at this request; it's a big thing. Len's mom doesn't even call her Mom. OPG doesn't let in-laws call her anything but by her first name.

We walked back into the house, and I jogged right up to Len. I grabbed her and pulled her tight to me and gave her a soft kiss. I gazed into her eyes and smiled. I turned to everyone and saw they all were grinning and had happiness shinning from their eyes for us.

"Everyone, I would like to let you know that this woman is the one that I love with all that I am," I told them as I gave her a small squeeze.

They cheered and gave their congratulations then we started eating lunch.

The girls ended up going to the spa after lunch, while the men lounged and talked.

Now, I'm holding my woman's hand and driving back to the house. I'm ready to get my baby to bed and prepare for tomorrow. The day the world finds out that she's mine.

Len

I slowly wake up and realize that, yet again, I'm pinned to the bed. I love knowing he can't get enough of me. After we made love well into the morning, I fell asleep quickly from the busy day we had.

Slowly turning over, I see Dante's still sleeping. I decide to let him sleep in. I need to go to the bathroom and get some coffee, anyway. I'm able to slip out of bed and quietly make my way to the bathroom.

After emptying my bladder, brushing my teeth, and getting dressed in my sleepwear that I didn't get to wear last night, I head downstairs and make coffee. As I scurry around the kitchen, I hear a knock on the door.

I'm startled for a second and slowly go towards the window. Peeking out, I can see it's a flower delivery, and I think about what to do for a second. I glance back out the window and recognize the man. He delivers the flowers to the hospital.

"Hey Dave, can you leave the flowers on the porch? I have my hands full."

"Sure, Len. I hope you have a great day."

He places the flowers on the porch and then leaves. Once everything's clear I unarm the alarm and bring in the flowers.

I shut the door and put the alarm back on. Walking into

the kitchen, I sit the flowers on the table. Dante's crazy. I can't believe he bought me flowers. I know they aren't my favorite, but still I'm in shock that he did this. Spotting a note, I open it as I sip on my coffee.

Next thing, I'm being wrapped in two big arms that are trying to soothe me.

"*Mio tutto*, you're going to make yourself sick," Dante states.

"Flowers, note, picture . . . oh, my God!" That's all I can get out before he's guiding me to the living room.

DANTE

Gradually opening my eyes, I know immediately Len isn't in bed with me. Damn it! This is something I'll have to explain really quick—that I want to wake up with her next to me, every morning. That before getting out of bed, I want a morning kiss and to show her how much I love her.

The smell of coffee reaches me, and I know she's been up for a while. Stretching, I slowly get out of bed and then make my way into the bathroom to relieve myself and brush my teeth. Once back in the bedroom, I'm pulling on my boxers when I hear screaming.

I rush down the stairs into the kitchen. There, I see flowers sitting on the counter. Fuck, I know what's going on, and I dread having to see what that fucking guy sent her today. I also don't want to tell her that we stopped a delivery before.

Grabbing her and holding her close, I try to calm her down and whisper into her ear.

"*Mio tutto* you're going to make yourself sick," I explain.

"Flowers, note, picture . . . oh, my God!" she screams.

I turn her towards the living room and sit down on the couch. I pull her onto my lap and rub my hands up and down her back. She slowly calms down.

After getting her screams to finally stop, I know I'm going to have to go and see what that fucker sent. I also need to get my phone from upstairs. I take a minute figuring out the best plan to get her out of the room while I survey everything. I decide a bath with some candles is the key to getting her out of the room. I quickly attempt to get her mind off of the situation at hand. I don't want her worrying about everything.

"Len, I'm going to take you upstairs and get a bath started. I want you to try to relax, and I need to get the guys here. So when you get out, you better dress in something ugly. I don't want to kill them for looking at my woman," I state.

"Dante, you're a crazy bastard, you know that? Anyway, I think a soak might be just what I need. Thanks for suggesting that, *amore*," she says with a sad smile on her face.

I hate seeing it there. This should be a good day for us. The day she'll become my fiancée, now, we have to deal with this. I'll make it better. For her, I'll do anything.

I stand up and carry her upstairs into the master bath. I sit her down on the counter and then start running the water. I see she has a lot of different things to add to it. I don't know what would be good.

"Len, what do you want in the water? You have too much shit to pick from."

"I'll do it. Move out of my way and go do what you need to do. I can't let this get to me. The moms and I have a lot of things to get done," she tells me this and starts pushing me out of the way.

Damn it, I don't know if I can think knowing she's naked and in the bath. I watch her bend over and grab some peach type shit off the shelf and pours a little in the water. I instantly love the smell that fills the room. Too bad it won't change the taste of her skin. I do love the taste of her skin the way it is and when she's sweaty from our fucking.

"Okay, *mio tutto*, I'll be downstairs. Yell if you need me, all right? I love you, Len. One more time," I tell her and pull her to me before she can jump in the tub.

I crash my mouth to hers as I rub my hands up and down her body. Fuck, I don't have time for this. I need to get my head together. Her life's more important.

"I love you, too, Dante. Now, go and get that finished. We don't have time for you to be messing with me today," she tells me with a giggle as she turns away and steps into the tub.

"Fine!" I tell her with a pout, again, trying to get her mind off of what waits for me downstairs.

She laughs and I smile, loving that sound.

Bending down, I plant a hard kiss on her lips and head into the bedroom to throw on my jeans and a t-shirt. I grab my phone and text the group.

Me: *Hey, I need all of you, dipshits, here ASAP! Len got a delivery of flowers today. Pops. Papa. Stay with the Moms.*

Sin: *Son of a bitch.*

Lucky: *You have got to be kidding me. We need a plan of action for tonight. I think we need the Moms to know so they can keep an eye out too.*

Eagle: *Doc and I are on our way. We agree with telling the Moms. The more in our inner circle who knows the better. Should we tell OPG, too?*

Thing One: *NOOOOOOOO!!! OPG will lose her shit. Len is everything to her. What do you think, Pops? Heading there now.*

Thing Two: *Fuck, I'm stuck at work. I can't leave until my backup arrives. Carlo, call me when you get there. Put it on speaker so I can hear everything. As soon as I can leave, I'll be on my way. Is Len making breakfast?!?!?!*

Pops: *We'll stay with the Moms. Call us as well. They're getting ready to go to the hotel to oversee the set up. I agree about not telling my mom. Not yet anyway, and we'll bring breakfast to the house. We can pick up Len that way you will have more time to plan and talk. Carlo, you will come with us to help out with watching. So, Dante, you do the conference calling.*

Thing One: *Shit, okay, heading to your house then, Pops.*

Me: *I'll let Len know. See you all soon.*

I poke my head in the bathroom and see Len relaxing with country music playing softly. My girl and her country music. I enjoy all kinds of music, but she listens mostly to country. Guess I'm going to end up learning more country than I do now.

"Len, the parents and Carlo are going to come and pick you up. They're heading to the hotel and thought you might like to go so you can help set up for the party tonight," I tell her softly so I don't scare her.

She jerks a little and opens her eyes.

"Shit, I better hurry. I still need to cook breakfast for everyone." She starts to grab her razor and some puffy thing.

"No need, they're bringing breakfast. You have plenty of time to get ready. I'm going downstairs now,"

"Leave so I can finish getting ready," she tells me with a bright smile.

Laughing, I wink and walk away. How the hell did I get so lucky? If I get this for the next seventy years, I'll die happy.

I walk into the kitchen and grab the note and the picture off the counter. First, I look over the picture.

Holy fuck! It's a five by seven collage of Len in different location. The one at the very end is a picture of her from yesterday when we were standing in front of her mom's house. My neck in the picture has a red slash across it.

I sit it down on the counter and pick up the note. After reading it, I'm now livid. I'm ready to kill someone.

MY BEAUTIFUL LEN,

I'M DONE WITH YOU FLIRTING WITH EVERYONE WHO WALKS IN YOUR PATH. I WARNED YOU WHAT WOULD HAPPEN. PUNISHMENT IS COMING. I'LL SEE YOU SOON.

YOURS ALWAYS

I set the note down next to the pictures and walk over to the sink. My hand grips the edge tightly, forcing myself not to pick up the cup next to it and throw it against the wall. I haven't been this pissed in years. Don't get me wrong, the other notes that were sent to her infuriated me as well. But, seeing that picture just made it reach a whole new level.

"Son of a fucking bitch! He followed you guys to Mom's house!" Lucky screams.

I was so lost in thought of how to get this guy that I didn't hear him enter the house and turn off the alarm. He was always the only one who could sneak up on me.

I turn around just as everyone else is starting to walk into the house and Len comes down the stairs. She's in yoga pants and a tank top that fits her perfectly. Her hair's in a ponytail, and she has no makeup on, and a huge bag hangs off her shoulder.

"Hey guys," she says with a dull smile on her face as she watches Lucky look over the note.

"Squirt, we'll get this taken care of. So don't worry. What are the plans for the day so we know when to show up? Also, are the girls coming?" he asks.

I sense this is his roundabout way of asking about Sara and trying to get Len's mind off everything.

The smiles around the room indicate he isn't fooling anyone. We all know he wants her. After we get this shit taken care of, I'll have a talk with him to find out what exactly is his fucking hold up with her. She's just as crazy about him.

"Well, my amazing big brother, you'll need to be there no later than four p.m. The party starts at six. We want you there to make sure it's to your liking since this is technically your welcome home 'slash' congrats on opening Seal Security, and to answer your other question, yes, all the girls will be there," Len lays it out to him.

Just then, Pops walks in with Papa, the Moms and Carlo. They're carrying tons of food. My mouth waters as the smell of freshly baked biscuits flows through the air.

"All right, let's eat before anything else," Pops says, walking to the dining room.

We all follow and start to dig in. I take a minute to let everything soak in and realize that it's going to be a long day.

Eleven

Len

I'M LOST IN THOUGHT AS I ride to the hotel. I've put on my mask. After Grandpa died, I learned how to hide my feelings from most people. OPG, Dante, and Sara are the only few who could always see through the mask. I know the reason OPG and Dante can, is because it's the deep connection we have. Sara hasn't had a good life, but I believe she understands the hiding behind a mask because she also hides her feelings.

While I was in the tub, I kept thinking about the picture that had Dante's neck cut. I can't have him getting hurt. So, I decided that I needed to go and hide until this ends. I packed the most important items I needed to get me through until I decide to come back. I wrote a note telling them that I'm hiding and not to find me. That I needed time to think. I figured I could sneak out of the hotel in the morning and go.

"Whatever you're thinking, Len, it isn't going to work," OPG whispers into my ear.

I snap my head to her, looking into her eyes. She's everything to me. I talk to her daily. She shares so many things with me that she doesn't share with anyone else. My favorite thing to do with her is to sit at her feet with my head in her lap while she strokes my hair and talks. I have to find a way to contact her while I'm in hiding without them finding out.

"OPG, I've no clue what you're talking about," I whisper back.

"Everyone assumes that I don't know something's going on with you. I can see something is happening. Promise me that you will wait until you know all the details, and that no matter what, you'll tell me you're okay," she demands.

"You know I can't live without you. Of course I'll be okay. You don't need to worry about that," I tell her as tears start to form.

"I love you, tons and bunches, Len," she says as she kisses my forehead.

"I love you, tons and bunches, too, OPG," I whisper and snuggle up to her.

I need to get this plan together and fast.

I glance around the hall; seeing that we're pretty much done with the set up. Food is catered from two different BBQ places, Gates N Sons and Arthur Bryant's. The bar is set up with bartenders getting things ready for the night. The tables are all around the edge of the dance area. The band we hired is getting set up on the stage. We also hired a DJ to play during the band's breaks between sets and when they finish for the night. There are streamers, balloons, and banners everywhere. I'm happy with the look of everything.

Arms wrap around my waist and make me jump. Instantly, I smell Dante. His head goes right into my neck, and he places a soft kiss right by my ear.

"Hey *mio tutto*, I missed you today," he whispers to me while pulling me closer.

"I missed you, too. What do you think of the hall?" I ask him breathless.

"It looks fantastic. The Moms and you did an amazing job with everything. Thanks for doing this. It means so much to all of us," he tells me then he turns me in his arms.

I smile up at him, and I feel so safe. I know he's going to be upset when he finds me gone in the morning, but I have to protect him. He went through so much with the Navy that I don't want this on his shoulders, too. I just hope he understands and we can work things out once it's finished.

Standing on my toes, I give him a soft kiss on the lips. He decides this isn't enough, so he grabs the back of my neck and pulls me into a deeper kiss. Everything melts, and its only Dante and me. I love these kinds of kisses.

"I know I said I'm okay with you and my baby girl, but that doesn't mean I want to see you mauling her, son," I hear a voice say.

Jerking back, I glance over and see Pops standing with his arms crossed. I look into his eyes, and see the slight humor there. I smile at him and wiggle out of Dante's arms, heading for my pops. He opens his arms, pulls me into his chest, and hugs me tightly.

"Pops, don't worry. You will always be one of my favorite guys," I tell him and stand on my toes to give him a big, smacking kiss on his cheek.

"I know, Len, but you keep giving me those wet cheek kisses, I just might have to demote you to the in-law and promote him to your spot," he tells me as he cringes and tries to wipe his cheek.

"Never going to happen. I need to go get ready. People are starting to show up. Love you, Pops!" I say turning to go to the corner to grab my bag.

I start to walk to the door and feel someone grab my hand. Looking behind me, Dante's standing there, smiling at me with a look of lust in his eyes. He's going to be disappointed when I tell him we can't have sex. I need a quick shower, and then I need to get dressed. It's going to take me at least an hour to get ready.

"I'm walking you up there. I need you. We have no clue how long we have until this party is finally finished," Dante tells me and starts to pull me towards our room.

"Dante, it isn't happening. As it is I'm going to be an hour late!" I explain.

I bust out laughing at how he's having problems opening the door because he's so eager and can't concentrate.

"Oh, it's so happening, Len," he says as he pulls me through the door and locks it.

He takes me into a fierce kiss as he picks me up and pushes me into the door. Thoughts of me getting ready fly out the window as he devours my mouth.

He lets go finally to pull off my shirt and bra. He sits me down on the ground and starts to strip himself.

"Len, get those pants off. We're going to need to get you some more of those. It shows off that amazing ass of yours, but I just don't know if I liked the way the guys were watching you walk. Maybe we need to keep these for house only," he says in a very serious tone.

I'm laughing at him and his possessiveness. I know those guys are giving him shit because they all know how much I'm in love with Dante. He starts to unsnap his jeans, and all laughter leaves me as a fresh rush of desire floods my body.

He slowly starts to push his jeans down, and I see he's decided to go commando today because he pops out of his jeans the moment they become undone. He grabs his cock with one hand and starts to stroke himself. Damn that's hot. I swear he's going to be the death of me. I see some pre-come leak, and I lick my lips. I want to taste him. I still haven't done that, and I really need to see what he tastes like.

"You like what you see, *mio tutto*? You want to taste me? I really want to see those perfect, pink lips wrapped around me," he says and starts to stroke faster.

Nodding, I walk towards him as he finishes stepping out of his jeans. His hand stops stroking his cock, which makes me stop and whimper and gaze into his eyes.

"Stop. You still haven't finished undressing. Take off your pants, baby. Then kneel before me, but don't touch. I'll tell you when you can," he orders, his voice husky.

I rush through his demands, getting my pants off and slowly kneeling before him. I glance up into his eyes and see a flash of something I've never seen before. Pride and determination are there along with desire and love. Despite the feelings that shines from his eyes, his face is controlled and calm. Interesting.

"Good girl. I'm in charge, and I'll tell you what I want. Hands behind your back and open your mouth for me. Don't move your hands or I'll punish you," he says with a sly grin on his face.

He takes his hand off his cock and swipes his finger in the pre-come and then slowly rubs that finger on my tongue.

"Suck," he demands.

Slowly, I close my lips around his finger and a burst of salty sweet is on my tongue. I'm addicted. I now get what he meant when he said he was addicted to my taste. I love it and want more. I suck him harder.

He slowly pulls his finger from my mouth and grabs his cock again and steps forward. He's holding himself towards my lips. I open them and wait for him to enter my mouth. He slowly rubs the head around my lips. I stick my tongue out and lick the head. His moans are low and long.

Gently, he puts the tip into my mouth and moves his hands into my hair. I didn't even notice that he took out my messy bun. I close my lips around the head of his cock and carefully swirl my tongue around the tip. He throws his head back and moans loudly. I love hearing it and it's making me wetter with each moan he makes. I circle my tongue again and start to move down his cock. His hands tighten on my head, stopping me, but not hurting me.

"No, Len. Let me do it. I won't hurt you. I promise. Do you trust what I just said?" he asks.

Nodding with him still in my mouth, I grab my hands behind my back tighter so I won't reach out for him. I know he's going to want me to deep throat him.

"Good girl. Open your mouth wider and flatten your tongue. That's good, baby. Shit, your mouth is warm and so wet," he's moaning, next, he's slowly working his way in and out of my mouth.

He isn't going too deep yet, so, I suck a little stronger, trying to let him know I'm ready for him. He looks down at me and takes a deep breath.

"You want me to go deep, don't you, Len? Take a deep breath and open your throat, baby. That's it . . . damn . . . fucking, yes, do it again . . . fuck, so good!"

He moans out when I swallow tightly around the head of his cock.

His dirty talking is getting me so wet. I don't know how much more I can take. He starts to pick up speed and with each thrust, I swallow. I really want him to come in my mouth. I never swallowed a guy before, but I want to do this for him. I need to do this.

"Shit, so good. Holy shit, that's amazing. It's never been this good before. Fuck, I need inside you. Now." He moans as he pulls out and picks me up into his arms.

My back slams against the wall, and he enters me in one thrust. I yell out at the invasion and the stretching. He's big, and I'm still trying to get used to him. It doesn't hurt, but it makes me feel so full.

"Fuck yeah, *mio tutto*, you feel amazing. I can feel just how slick you are. Did sucking me off get you wet? So fucking good," he whispers into my ear.

I clench at his words. His words alone have the power to undo me. He stays still, allowing me a minute to get used to his size. Wrapping my arms around his neck and my legs tightly around his waist, I slowly start to relax. My need for him grows more with every second, I can't wait anymore. Slowly turning my head into his neck, I kiss up to his ear and nip the lobe lightly.

"Fuck me, Dante. Fuck me against this wall. I need it

129

now, *Amore*," I whisper.

He jerks his head back slightly, then looks into my eyes. I can see I've shocked him with my talk. Next, there's a flash of something fierce. It looks like I've woken the beast. I'm eager to feel this. The past few nights, he's taken me slowly and sweetly, but I could tell he was holding back because I was new to all this. I'm tired of him doing that. I need him to know I trust him completely, and I know he wouldn't hurt me.

"You want me to fuck you? You want me to drill deep and mark you as mine? You ready for that, *mio tutto*?" he says through clenched teeth and flaring nostrils.

"Fuck me, Dante. Don't hold back," I tell him in a very clear and strong voice.

He looks at me and then nods once. He gets this very cocky grin on his face and with the sexiest voice ever says, "Hold on, Len. You're mine!"

He pulls back and I hold on tighter. He slams into me and my back pushes up against the wall. My head snaps back, and I cry out in pleasure. He stops and gazes upon my face. I lock my eyes onto his and, I guess he likes what he sees, because next thing I know he's pushing into me again, over and over. I grab his shoulders and dig my nails into his flesh. I feel his hands grabbing my hips hard enough to leave bruises, but I don't care. This feels amazing!

It's like he's claiming me and making it known that I'm his and nobody else's. I wouldn't be shocked if the room next to us could hear our cries and moans along with the banging of my back against the wall.

I feel myself getting close to the edge. I'm going to come, and I know it's going to be stronger than any other one I've ever felt. Right before I fall over the edge, I hear him whisper in my ear, "That's right, come on my cock. I need to feel it. I need to feel you tighten around me. Come now, Len."

I throw my head back and come around him. I'm feeling light-headed and seeing stars. I barely understand what he's saying as he slams into me twice more then I feel him come inside me.

"Fuck, Len, you feel amazing. That's it . . . yes . . ." he roars and stills his movements.

I slowly gain my breath and we come down from our high. I glance up from his chest where my head is laying down, and I smile at the love shining from his eyes.

"*Mio tutto*, you surprise me. Let's get in the shower so we can get ready to go downstairs," he says while he holds me close and walks into the shower still deep inside me.

"Sounds good. We need to do that more often," I say with a sly grin as he sits me in the shower and starts the water.

"Sounds like a deal. One more time," he says placing a soft kiss on my lips.

"One more time," I whisper against his lips right before I deepen the kiss, knowing it'll lead to shower sex.

Looks like we're going to be more than fashionably late.

Twelve

DANTE

AS I SIT AT THE table by the dance floor, I watch Len dance with her posse. She's having so much fun, and she deserves it. I gaze around and take in everyone who's here at our party.

I see some friends Len and Lucky went to school with when they lived here, the guys from our unit; some of their family and friends came to town too for the party. I also see people we work with from KCPD. They're all dancing, talking, and having fun.

The food's amazing. The bartenders are keeping everyone's drinks filled and the band and DJ are keeping the dance floor hopping. I gaze back at Len, thinking about what we just did in the hotel room.

When she said those words, I was shocked to say the least. I was so happy that Lucky was downstairs and not in his room next to us. I know he'd kill me right now if he'd heard what we were doing. I glance back over at him and catch him watching Sara dance with Len. Shaking my head, I make my way to his side.

"Man, why are you waiting? We all know you're both crazy about each other. Fucking stop already and go claim what you want to be yours," I tell him.

"Not that simple, man. I know something happened to her, and she won't talk about it. She says it isn't anything and that she isn't ready to trust anyone with whatever it is. If she can't trust me, then how can she open up and accept what I want to give her?" he asks while his eyes are locked on her.

I follow his stare and see Sara laughing at Len who's trying to teach her some country line dance. I had a feeling something was going on with her, but always respected her space and didn't invade. But hearing my best friend's longing and need for her makes me want to go over and demand answers. I turn back to Lucky.

"What do you need me to do, brother? I'm here and you know I'll help in any way I can."

"I know, thanks. I'm going to wait until this shit with Len's done. Then she'll have no choice but to tell me because I'm seriously debating to just take her and keep her locked the fuck up until she tells me what is going on," he replies with a sly smile on his face.

"Sounds like a plan. I'll make sure Len is distracted so she can't interfere," I tell him, laughing and shaking my head because we both know he wouldn't ever do that shit.

Momma Connie appears and gives Lucky a big hug and kiss and then shows me the same affection.

"You ready to do this? I think this is a perfect time for a speech! Get the rest of the boys and go stand by the stage. I'm going to let Len know it's time," she tells us.

I watch her lean in and whisper into Len's ear. She smiles at her mom and then points to the doors. Her mom smiles, nods, and walks over to Doc. I watch Len talk to the girls for a few more minutes before she turns and walks towards the door. I start to follow, but am stopped short when a big man steps in front of me. I gaze up and see Doc.

"Hey, you ready to get this over with? I don't like speeches, you know that, so let's get this shit done. Connie said Len's going to go to the bathroom, the twins are out there in the lobby waiting for their dates, and then she'll be back and make the announcement. Let's get to the stage," he says patting me on the back and heads toward the stage.

I glance around, I notice that the twins are missing. I take a moment and realize that you can't get to the bathrooms without passing through the lobby so I'm sure they will spot her. I relax knowing they'll be with her and head to the stage.

Right when I get to the side, I feel hands wrap around my waist from behind. I start to relax, but realize it isn't Len. I jerk out of the arms, and I turn to see who it is. A beautiful blonde-haired woman is standing there smiling at me. I smile back politely because I don't want to be rude but for the life of me I have no clue who she is.

"Hey, Dante, I heard you were back, and I had to come and say hello," she states like I'd know who she is.

"Hi, I'm sorry, I don't know who you are. This is a private event; how did you get in?"

"Oh, friends of Neil and Len brought me. I went to school with Neil before he moved to Washington. I'm Stephanie, you don't remember me?" she asks.

"I'm sorry, but I'm drawing a blank. I'd love to chat

more but I'm getting ready to make a big speech," I say trying to blow her off.

"Oh, we got together before you left for the Navy. Remember the party? I was hoping that if you're still single we can maybe have a drink or dinner? I'd like to get to know you better," she smiles and drops her head but I don't miss the way her cheeks turn red from embarrassment.

I take her all in, and she's a very beautiful woman, however, she doesn't even hold a candle to Len. I turn back towards the door and glance back at Stephanie.

"Look, that's a great offer, however, I'm in a very serious relationship."

"Okay, well, it's great seeing you again, Dante." She turns and walks off to a table full of people who, I'm assuming, are the friends from school.

I turn back to the stage and take a deep breath. I'm starting to shake and my hands are getting sweaty because I'm about to ask her to marry me in front of over two hundred people. I hate speeches as well, but I can't wait to get this done. I've been waiting for years.

I turn back when I hear the door open, I watch as the twins enter the room. Each has a girl on their arm. I glance behind them trying to spot Len. I don't see her. My heart starts to pound and I hear ringing in my ears. I rush up to them.

"Hey, where's Len?" I ask them.

"I've no clue. Last I saw she was on the dance floor. Carlo and I went outside to meet our dates. We haven't seen her since then," Nicoli says then he looks over at Carlo.

"You didn't walk her to the bathroom? Shit!" I run to the door.

I hear footsteps pounding behind me, but I don't look back. I run to the bathroom and pound on the door and open it screaming her name. I'm met with silence. I rush in looking into the stalls. The bathroom is empty. I turn and race past the guys, who are all standing around the door. I hurry up to the front desk, grabbing my phone from my pocket and pull up a picture of Len.

"Did you see this girl leave the hotel?" I say, holding out my phone to the guy at the desk.

"No, sir, I haven't seen her since she came downstairs with you for the gathering. I did leave the desk for about thirty minutes due to an emergency call from a room upstairs," he states.

"What kind of emergency?" I growl out.

"I'm sorry, sir, I'm not allowed to divulge that information," he explains.

"Yes, you damn well will! We already talked to your manager about this. I'm Dante with Seal Security. We need to know what kind of emergency! A woman's life is at stake!" I roar.

"Oh, you're with Seal Security? I need to see some identification before I can announce anything," he states.

I jerk my wallet out and slam it open onto the counter showing my information and next to it my PI license that shows the name of the company.

"Now talk!"

"Okay, I got a call about an emergency and had to rush to take care of it. Which was weird, because nothing was wrong with the room. The guy told me the pipes had burst, so I had to run up there and figure out what was going on. Once I got in, I looked through the suite and saw there was no issue with the pipes," he tells me.

"Fuck! He got her!" I scream and fall to my knees.

I'm lost in thoughts of what just happened. I can't believe I've failed her. I'll find her, and I'll kill him. He can't take her from me. I won't let it happen. The girls come running out from the party as I stand up and start dialing the number to Detective Walters so we can start moving forward on finding her.

I'm coming, Len. I'll make this right. Stay strong, mio tutto. I'm coming for you.

Thirteen

Len

Thirty minutes earlier...

THE GIRLS AND I ARE laughing hard at Sara's attempt at line dancing. For someone who is amazingly beautiful, she can't dance worth shit. At least she's trying, unlike someone else who isn't.

I glance over my shoulder and see Dante talking to my brother, whose eyes are locked on Sara. His expression is fierce and he can't tear his eyes from her. Sara's trying to ignore it, but she keeps glancing out of the corner of her eye towards him. I don't get it really. When I met her in college, she was very quiet and shy. She's come out of her shell a lot since, but still hides behind her mask. I'm hoping she'll finally come out with it. I know she doesn't want to tell us, thinking we would shoulder it, but she doesn't understand that that's what family does.

Spotting Mom walking towards me, I know it's time to do the announcements. I'd asked Mom to let me do it because I wanted to let everyone know how happy I was to have my brother back. I'd missed him terribly and I was so proud of what he and the boys had accomplished. Plus, I want to show everyone here that Dante's mine.

"Len, it's time for the announcement. Neil and Dante are getting the guys to the stage," she tells me in my ear.

"Okay, Mom, I just need to go to the bathroom really quick. I'll be right there," I tell her pointing to the door.

She nods at me and turns to walk away. I tell the girls I'm going to the bathroom and head that way.

Exiting the stall, I almost run into my friend Stacy from high school.

"Hey, Len, long time no see. How's everything?" she asks.

"Things are going great for once. Remember that guy I used to talk about? The one who was a brother to the boys that used to come visit during the summer?" she nods at me so I continue, "Well, we're finally together."

"Wait, the guy that was with your brother a second ago?"

"Yeah, why?" I question staring at her.

She starts fidgeting and looks over at the door like she doesn't want to have this conversation.

"Stacy, what's up?"

"Shit. Okay, my friend Stephanie said she knew Dante from back in the day and that she always had a thing for him from their night together. She was going to go talk to him and see if he wanted to pick up where they left off. When I was getting ready to head into the bathroom I saw her with her arms wrapped around him, and he was relaxed in her hold. I'm so sorry, Len," she whispers the last words out.

I smile slightly and nod my head at her trying to hold my

emotions in. She gives my arm a gentle squeeze and walks out of the door. I gather my thoughts and decide that I need to go and confront him about this information before I stand up and say something stupid during my speech.

I freshen up my makeup quickly and do a once over, deciding that's the best I'm going to get.

Right when I'm ready to head out, I take one more glance in the mirror, and I see someone in a dark hoodie behind me. It takes me a moment to realize that it isn't a woman that's standing there. I glance at the door and try to determine if I have enough time to reach it before he gets to me.

There's a movement out of the corner of my eye and I swing my gaze back to the man behind me to see him shake his head no. Fuck it, I can scream and hopefully get the attention of someone in the lobby.

I open my mouth but he strikes very fast covering my mouth with a cloth. I grab his arm getting ready to flip him off of me—hey I didn't take Tae Kwon Do for nothing—when I smell something really sweet and realize the cloth is covered in chloroform.

I start to feel the effects of the drug within seconds. I'm still struggling with him in hopes that it'll make enough noise to notify someone that something is wrong. My vision starts to blur, but I glance back into the mirror and see eyes I have seen before.

That's when everything goes black . . .

DANTE

The video from the front desk doesn't show the hallway where the bathrooms are. Also, the camera right outside the exit door at the end of the hall was covered. We went through the room Len and I are in and found a note laid out on the bed. Her stuff was gone too.

The note threw us all off. I don't believe it at all. KCPD said they have to go through all the details before they do anything. We've shown them everything, but still they have to follow protocol. We have protocol we have to follow as security, but it isn't as in depth as the police. Lucky and Sin are currently at the office working on things.

I'm sitting on the bed looking at the copy of the note that was left behind.

I know you're going to be upset when you see this, but I hope you understand why I had to. I'm leaving for a while. I decided that this isn't the life I really wanted. I'm off to find that life. I'll be in contact here and there to let you know that I'm okay. Don't worry about me. I promise I'm okay and have everything I need to restart my life.

Yours Always,

Len

Something about it doesn't seem right. Honestly the whole thing screams that it isn't Len, even if it is her handwriting. But there's something I'm missing in the note that I'm not catching. We've all looked it over and still nothing.

"Mr. Shields, we got everything we need. We'll go over it all and will be in touch with the family once we figure out what we're going to do. Please, contact us if anyone hears from Ms. Shields," Detective Walters says.

There's a knock on the door, and I run to open it up, hoping its Len. Seeing it's a girl from the party earlier just deflates me.

"Hey, I heard that Len's missing, and I think I need to tell you that I probably was the last to see her," she starts fidgeting.

"Please, come in and take a seat. Any information you can share would be grateful," I step back and wave her in.

She sits down and explains everything that was said in the bathroom. When she finishes I see red and want to scream out. She glances at me, and then looks down at her shoes.

"Stephanie filled me in on what you said to her, and now I feel awful. I hope it wasn't what I said that caused her to leave," she whispers out.

"Ma'am, I'm Detective Edmonds, and this is my partner Detective Walters. Is there anything that you left out or can think of that you might not think important?"

"No, I just feel horrible for what happened."

"Well, here's our card. If you think of anything else, please get in touch. Thank you for coming and telling us this information," Edmonds hands her a card.

Eagle walks Stacy to the door and then closes it and turns to face me.

"So that changes a lot of things. Ms. King might be right and Len just stepped away after her altercation in the bathroom. We'll give it about forty-eight hours and then see if we can go from there. Right now everything's stating she walked away due to the bathroom situation," Detective Edmonds states as he gathers everything up.

"No, you don't understand. My daughter wouldn't ever do something like that. Something isn't right here. You have to do something," Pops pleads.

"Sir, we have to follow protocol and this is what it's saying to do. We'll be in touch and remember to contact us if things change," Walters states as he walks out the door with Edmonds right behind him.

"Len wouldn't do this. What are we going to do, Tony? Our daughter wouldn't ever just walk away," Momma Connie says, holding on to Pops.

"I'll find her. I don't care how long it takes me. I'll find her alive and bring her back to where she belongs. I promise on everything that I am. I'll find her," I tell the whole room.

I decide there's nothing left for me to do here, so, I pack up the room and kiss everyone goodbye. It's time to get to my office and see what Lucky and Sin have found. I'll stop at nothing to find her. Even if that means doing things that wouldn't be looked kindly upon by the law. Nothing will stop me . . . nothing!

Len

I have a massive headache when I wake up. My first thought is I shouldn't have drank that much last night at the party. I'm definitely going to have to relax today since I have to go to work tomorrow.

Slowly stretching, I realize quickly that I'm not in my bed. The sheets aren't as soft as mine. I don't know where the fuck I am.

Opening my eyes and sitting up steadily, I glance around

the room and it's huge! I realize that it's a basement. It's set up like a studio apartment, except it's missing a kitchen. There are no doors or walls separating the rooms. It's just one big huge loft-like area. It's pretty nice, actually. The bedroom area's done in soft blues and whites. There's a queen-size bed, from what I can tell since I'm still on the bed. There are nightstands on each side with a blue lamp on each one. On one of them is a bottle of water and what appears to be two pills and a note. There's also a picture behind the water but I can't make out the image. Deciding to check that out in a second, I glance over to the other nightstand and see a dresser right next to it.

Across from the bedroom area is an open bathroom. It has a toilet and a claw tub with a shower attached to it. There's a shelf next to the tub that has shower items on it. A towel rack is next to it as well. There's a mirror above the sink that's by the toilet. It's pretty plain.

In front of me is a living room set up. There's a couch, two chairs, a coffee table, two end tables with blue lamps on each, and a TV on the wall across the couch. Behind the couch, there's a dining room table and a small fridge in the corner. That's pretty much it.

There are windows around the room, but they are very small. Just big enough to let in some light. Then, I notice there's one door next to the TV. I don't know what to make of this room. I don't remember how I got here. Something isn't sitting right with me. I need to think back to what happened, but my mind is still fuzzy from drinking.

Reaching to the nightstand I grab the glass of water and the pills. I glance at the medication and see it's Motrin. Dante must have left them for me. I swallow them then put the glass back and grab the note. I briefly read the note, freezing in fear as the night comes back to me.

MY LEN,

I KNOW YOU'RE PROBABLY WONDERING WHERE YOU ARE. IT'S OKAY. YOU'RE SAFE NOW. I LEFT THESE FOR YOU BECAUSE I KNOW YOU'RE GOING TO HAVE A HEADACHE. THERE'S SOME FOOD AND WATER IN THE FRIDGE AS WELL. THERE ARE CLOTHES IN THE DRESSER FOR YOU. I ALSO BOUGHT YOUR FAVORITE SHOWER SUPPLIES. I HAD TO GO TO WORK. I'LL BE HOME AFTER MY SHIFT ENDS. WE'LL TALK THEN, MY LOVE.

YOURS ALWAYS

I put the note back on the table. I reach around the bottle and pick up the frame that is behind it. Still with my head fuzzy I look down at the image and try to focus on what I'm seeing. The picture is of me from college smiling and carefree. My arm is around someone and it takes me a moment to try to focus on who it is. I realize who it is and then I remember now who I saw right before I blacked out. It was Dr. Steven Adams who went to school with me, and we started our residency together. He asked me out twice; once in college and once after Dex and I broke up. I said no both times.

It wasn't that he was ugly. He was just not my type. He's kind of on the short side and has a quirky personality. He was nice, but just didn't know how to socialize with people. I tried being his friend, but he just didn't seem to understand how friendships worked.

Shortly after our residency started, he went to another part of the hospital. I don't work with him due to that reason. He works mostly with cancer patients. We don't get many of them in the ER. Those we do we send upstairs to the cancer floor. I only see him here and there when walking around the hospital.

I gaze back at the photo in my hand and can tell that he photoshopped himself into the picture. I place it back on the nightstand and slowly crawl out of bed. I glance down and realize I'm still in my clothes from yesterday. I'm glad for that. I walk over to the door, hoping it's not locked, but I know it will be. I jiggle the door handle and, yep, it's locked. There's a small box on the wall by the door with a call button. I press it. Nothing happens. I'm assuming it's an intercom system. Moving around the room, I open the fridge; inside is a few small bottles of water and some containers that have food in them, I'm guessing. Closing the door, I glance up at one of the corners and see a camera.

Shit, he can see me from anywhere in the room, except the bathroom area, from what I can tell, unless it's one of those cameras that move. But it doesn't look like it.

I walk over to the end table and try to pick up the lamp. I'm thinking I can attack him using this. I can't lift it. I squint and kneel down closer, I can see it's bolted down. I start inspecting all the furniture better and see everything is bolted into place. I run over to the dresser trying to pull out the drawer all the way out and it stops short of falling out of its tracks. I realize I'm trapped.

I sit back down on the bed and try to think of a plan on how I'm going to get out of here. There's no phone, so calling someone is out of the question. I can't scream because I don't know how close he lives to someone. I start to freak out when I remember my black belt. That's what I need to do. I'll have to overpower him and get out of the house.

With that thought in place, I go to the dresser and decide I need to take a bath and get on something that I can run in. I grab a pair of yoga pants, tank top, and t-shirt from the open drawer. I open the top one and find socks, bras and underwear. I glance at the tag and realize that they're my exact size. They all look brand new, too. I slowly close the dresser and walk over to the tub and start the water.

As I get cleaned up, I realize that Steven has been planning this for a while. He knew what size I was and bought all this stuff with me in mind. I'm hoping that I can still get away.

After I'm clean and dressed, I go and look into the other drawers. The last two just has jeans, blouses, and sundresses in them. I notice that there aren't any shoes. I wonder how long he's planning on keeping me in this room.

I walk back over to the TV and turn it on. I stop on the news station, hoping to find something on there about me going missing. I sit down on the couch and watch.

About two hours later, I realize that my hopes of being on TV for missing persons isn't going to happen. Laying my head back, I try to think of what I'm going to do once I get out of this room. I'm going to have to figure out where I'm at first and then try to find the nearest police station. This is a nightmare that I'm not sure how I'm going to get through. I start to doze off with thoughts of how I'm going to explain to the police that I was kidnapped and how I got out.

I awaken to a tickle on the side of my neck. I quickly remember where I'm and jerk off the couch and get in a fighting stance. I look around and see Steven standing behind the couch where I was sleeping. I look over to the door and see it's closed. I run over and try to open it. It's locked. I hear Steven give a chuckle and I look back at him.

"Love, it won't open for you. I'm the only one who has the key. Do you think I would leave it unlocked? Now, why don't you sit down so we can talk and figure out what punishment you're going to get for not following my rules?" he asks as he walks around and sits in one of the chairs.

"No, let me out, Steven! I don't know what's going on here. I want to go home now. If you let me go, I promise not tell anyone about what's going on and who took me," I tell him as I try to reason and assess the situation.

"No, now, sit, Len, or you're going to be sorry for not listening. Oh, and I guess I should tell you this now, if you're thinking you can overpower me, think again. I'm a second degree black belt master. Now sit!" He shouts the last part at me, causing me to jump. "Len, I know everything about you, my love."

Shit! I know I'm no match for that. I should have continued my training, but I'd figured black belt would be enough for me to know how to defend myself in any situation. I never thought that I would be in this type of predicament. I mean, honestly, who would think they would be? I slowly walk over to the other chair across from him and sit down.

"Good girl. Now, let's talk about what you did wrong. You kept flirting with other men in front of me, you kissed another man that wasn't me, and I'm sure you gave him what belonged to me as well. Didn't you, little Len? Well, that means for the next three months, you're going to have to

149

make it up to me. I won't touch you until then. I thought about doing it, but decided that we need to be married first. It's the only way to do things. I mean, Mother has been on my case about finally giving her grandchildren, but she taught me I had to marry the woman first. She'll be so happy to know I finally got her. Now then, let's start with dinner. As you can see, I brought dinner from your favorite BBQ joint. Show me your gratitude and be the good housewife I know you're going to be, love," he tells me with a sinister smile spreading on his face.

I realize that he's nuts. I'm not sure how this is going to work out.

"Go fuck yourself!" I tell him.

Rage comes over his face as he stands up and walks towards me. I don't back down. I know I can defend myself if I need to. He pulls something from his pocket and reaches for my hair, jerking me up. I feel a pinch in my arm before I can reach up to hit him. I start to feel my body relax.

"I wish you wouldn't have done that, little Len. You will regret that when you wake back up," I hear him say as darkness takes hold of me once more.

Fourteen

DANTE

IT'S BEEN A WEEK SINCE Len went missing. Nobody has had any contact with her and no activity on any of her credit cards. We've searched everything trying to find her, and nothing's coming up. The police are finally starting to work with us and has put out a missing person's report on her. Pops, Momma Connie, OPG, and Lucky have all done interviews with the news and have a reward out for her safe return. I'm beginning to wonder if she's really gone for good.

We're working currently on all the hospital staff that Len works with. We're scouring their records and doing a little more research that a normal background check doesn't check for. So far we've come up with nothing.

We also reached out to Mace and Coleman to get their teams searching as well. Mace and Coleman served with us overseas and have resources that we don't have when it comes to situations like this.

A knock on my door startles me.

"Come in."

The door opens and Julia walks in with a piece of paper in her hand. She smiles sadly at me and walks over and hands it to me.

"This is a list of everyone that I can think of that might have something against Len. I honestly don't think many people have a problem with her but I'm really wanting to help find her," she whispers to me.

I take a look at Julia and notice she has bags under her eyes. I also see she has lost weight a bit, and that she isn't as put together as she normally is. She isn't taking Len missing well, and it's understandable. They've been friends since kindergarten and went through everything together. I stand up and walk over to her and give her a big hug. She immediately starts sobbing and her knees buckle under her. I hold her tighter so she doesn't fall and let her continue grieving out her pain.

"Thank you, Julia. It will help out a lot. You didn't have to do that, but I'm grateful you did. I'm trying to get her back where she belongs. I promise you we're doing everything we can. The only thing I need from you is to tell me if you see or hear anything strange at the hospital, all right?" I tell her as I rub her back and rock her back and forth.

"O . . . Okay." She stutters out and holds me tighter.

"What the fucks going on?" I hear from my door.

I glance over and see Eagle glaring at Julia and me. I slowly pat her back and push her gently away.

"Julia just brought a list of people for us to look into. She started crying and I needed to make sure she was okay," I tell him calmly.

"Come here, princess," he tells her as his face transforms

from fierce to soft and loving.

She runs and jumps into his arms and starts sobbing again. He holds her close, whispers into her ear, and picks her up. She wraps her legs around his waist and her arms around his neck. All I can think is huh as he walks her out my door and down the hall. Seeing them together makes a pain stab at my heart, and it reminds me of what I'm missing. I reach into my front left pocket and rub the metal that I've carried with me since that day. I push the thoughts and emotions away before they can swarm me.

I go back to my desk and look down at the paper on my desk. Well, this is a start that will help. I guess I need to get Sin and Lucky together, go to the hospital, and interview everyone on this list. It's going to be a long day.

We're down to two people on the list. Nobody's standing out as being involved in this fucked up mess. I lean back while Sin and Eagle go and get the last two on the list. We've been doing this for a week now. That means Len has been gone for two weeks. I just want my baby back and I'll stop at nothing to achieve that goal.

There's a knock on the door and Sin walks in one of the last two interviews left.

"Hey, Dante, this is Dr. Steven Adams. He went to school and did part of his residency with Len. Dr. Adams, this is Dante," Sin makes the introductions.

"Thanks for coming in, Dr. Adams. Please, have a seat. We're just seeing if you know, saw, or heard anything that will help us find where Len is." I shake his hand and then guide him to the chair.

"Please, call me, Steven. I don't know how much help I can give you. I haven't had any contact with Len. I moved to a different floor to finish my residency. I work up in the cancer ward. I don't get down to the ER very often. She was really nice to me and it bothers me that something happened to her," he explains.

Something seems off, but I'm not sure if it's anything Len related.

I make eye contact with Sin, and he nods that he senses something as well.

"We just want to know if you've seen someone watching her or something out of the ordinary. Has someone been saying anything or acting weird before or after she went missing? Even if it doesn't seem like much it might be what's needed to find her and get her back safely," Sin says while watching him from the side of the room.

"Not that I can remember. Like I said, I stay mostly up on the cancer ward. I don't talk to many people outside of work related stuff. I keep to myself and concentrate on what I'm supposed to be doing. So, I'm not sure just how much help I can be to you," he tells us.

He's starting to get uncomfortable and starts to fidget with his lab coat. I take a minute to study him, and I'm not getting anything from him that shows he has a part in this. So, I decide to stop the interview and let him get back to work.

"It's okay. Thanks for taking time to talk to us. Do you mind taking my card? If you think, hear, or see anything, please contact us."

"Of course. It's sad that this happened to Len. Like I

said, she was always nice to me. I'll call if anything comes up or if I remember anything." He takes the card and walks out the door.

He comes across as a loner. Like a guy who just doesn't know how to talk to others so he keeps to himself.

"What do you think?" Sin asks sitting down next to me.

"To me he seemed fine, little out there. Almost like he wasn't sure how to talk about anything other than work. But, he didn't throw any bells to make me think he's hiding something."

"And his answers didn't raise any flags either," he states.

"Shit!" I scream and grab my hair.

"I know, man. I really hope Lucky's got something. If not, we'll figure out what the next plan of action needs to be," Sin sighs next to me.

"Agreed. Let's get our shit together and get out of here," I tell him while gathering all the notes we took from the people we talked to.

"How are you holding up, Dante?" I hear from the door and glance up and see Chris standing there.

"The best I can. How are Andy and you?" I ask.

He shrugs his shoulders, and I stare into his eyes. He has bags, and it seems like he isn't as put together as he normally is.

"Any updates?" he murmurs.

I shake my head and take a deep breath.

"I just wanted to come and check in. Nothing has changed on our end. Keep us updated please. Also, let the girls know that Andy's wanting to get together when they feel up to it." At my nod he turns and walks away.

I put my head in my hands and try to control the

emotions swirling in me. Seeing our family and friends suffer is hard to deal with.

"Hey, guys, I got one guy and one girl that we need to look into. I can tell you though that Eagle and I don't think either of them had anything to do with it. They seemed off so I want to check it out. Did you two get anything?" Lucky asks as he walks into our room.

"Not a thing. Nobody we saw today showed any signs of anything. Let's get back to the office and go over these records. Also, Andrew, the hospital administrator, gave us the info to get into the video feed and what days Len worked for the past three months. We can go through them and see if we spot anything," Sin tells us.

I walk up to Lucky and really take a look at him. He's close with his sister and it's killing him knowing she has been missing for two weeks. He hasn't shaved and appears like he has been hitting the gym more than usual. When something's bothering him he's always went to work out the thought process. So, seeing that he's gained a lot more muscle lately tells me this is hitting him hard. I give him a brief hug and pull back to glance into his eyes.

"We'll find her, Lucky. No matter how long it takes, we'll find her! And she'll be alive. I know you're thinking, what are the odds of that, but stop. I'd feel it if she was taken from this world. If she was gone, I'd be dead, because deep down, I know my heart would feel when she took her last breath. And, if you reach deep enough you will feel it too," I whisper to him as I absently rub my pocket.

He studies me for a moment before nodding his head.

"Thanks, man. I needed to hear that. Okay, let's get the hell out of here and find my sister," he says and walks out the door.

I truly meant what I'd said to him. I know she's alive. I know I would feel if she were gone. My soul would feel it and my heart would stop beating.

Fifteen

Len

Three months later...

I'M LYING IN BED, LOOKING up at the ceiling, and trying to calm my stomach down. I can't wait for this to be done. It should be almost over with. I can't stand throwing up or feeling like I'm going to puke.

Lord, please make this go away. I can't handle this feeling. Please, just calm my stomach down. I've already thrown up today. Just take it away. After everything I've been going through please help me get through this.

I pray and hope that God's listening. I close my eyes and continue to take deep breaths. I have some country music playing on the TV. I think of the past three months and what's happened. How I've changed my way of thinking, about what still needs to be done, and how I'd made a deal with the person who kidnapped me so I can keep the one thing in the world that means the most to me.

I think back to seven weeks ago when I figured out what

was wrong with me...

I woke up puking yet again this morning. That makes three weeks. Steven has tried to make me eat with him whenever he's home. I refuse to do it. I only eat when he's not here. I know it isn't smart if I want to get out of here, but I just can't do it.

I've been here now for five weeks. Five fucking weeks! He's kept me locked away in this damn basement. Every time I try to get the upper hand, I'm given a shot and it knocks me out. I thought I was getting sick from whatever it was he was giving me, but that can't be it either. He hasn't given me a shot in a week now, and if it was that then I would be done with the detox that would come from it.

I'm still throwing up off and on all day long, so I wonder if I'm getting sick. That's possible and makes me wonder what it could be. There are a few options, like the flu. However, I seem fine when I'm done getting sick.

Wait!

No!

No, it can't be!

I haven't had a period yet. I thought the lack of my menstrual cycle was due to stress, but I should've started by now. No, this can't be happening. I can't be pregnant right now. Please, don't let this be true because I'm afraid of what Steven would do if I was.

The door opens, and I look over and see Steve walking in. He's carrying a bag. I'm sure it's food or something that he wants me to do with him. Lately, he's been bringing movies, games, and books wanting to spend time with me. I refuse to do it.

"Lovely, I need you to drink some water. I've noticed you've been sick for a while. I'm going to run some tests. Please, don't fight with me today. I really don't want to have to sedate you again," he tells me while he sits the bag down.

I don't have the energy to fight him today. So, I sit up slowly and take a bottle of water off the nightstand and drink it down. I watch him as he puts items in the fridge. I think again how I never noticed just how crazy he was. He started calling me lovely last week, and I hate it.

He's also been telling me how he knew we were meant to be together, that when I was nice to him in school, he knew that I would be the one for him. He's been watching me since then. He's shown me album after album of pictures he's taken of me. He's even Photoshopped a few to add himself to the pictures. I think he truly believes that we've been a couple this whole time. It's unreal just how much he thinks I'm his.

I'm very thankful that he hasn't raped me. He said that he was waiting for our wedding night. I remember screaming and yelling at him that I would never marry him. He then took a deep breath, stuck me again with a needle, and it was lights out. Then, the next day he said it again which ended up with me being sedated again.

Finally, I realized that I wasn't getting anywhere fighting with him, and that's when I decided to just not speak to him. It was for the best because I knew that if I opened my mouth it would only end with me being drugged. So for now, I'll keep quiet and bide my time until I can get away.

"I'm going to draw some blood and then you're going to

take this test," he says, snapping me out of my thoughts.

I look away as he draws my blood. I'm wondering how he's going to get away with testing the blood at the hospital. Then again, it wouldn't be hard to get it tested being a doctor. He could always just do it himself.

After he finishes drawing the blood, he hands me a white stick. I look down at it and instantly recognize it as a pregnancy test. Panic hits me full force knowing it's going to be positive. I'm scared of how he's going to react to the test. For a second, I want to refuse, but he's already drawn my blood and could test it that way.

"Will you please look away while I take it?" I whisper to him.

He nods and walks over to the dining table and sits down, facing away from me. I walk over to the bathroom and take the test. I wash up and sit the test down in front of him. Then, I walk back to the bed and lie down. I'm so scared of what's going to happen now.

I wish I was home taking this test with Dante. I wonder how he would've reacted while waiting for the results. Would he have held me and whispered words of love? Would he be pacing the floor? I try to imagine his face when he sees the results. I imagine his face would be full of love and amazement knowing I was carrying our child. I imagine he would be calling everyone to tell them he was going to be a dad. I could see him getting protective and not letting me do anything. I feel tears sliding down the side of my face as I think of all the things he would be doing or saying.

I'm pulled from my thoughts when Steven takes a deep breath.

"So, this will have to be fixed, Len," he says as he turns and looks at me with rage on his face.

"What are you going to do?" I ask.

"Why, termination, of course. We can't have a bastard baby, now can we. So, I'll get what we'll need to perform this here. I can take care of you like no other. Now, why don't you get some rest while I make a list," he says, getting his things together.

No! I can't let him take this baby from me! I have to think of something. I need to protect this baby. I need to figure out what can I do to make him change his mind and let me keep this baby. I'm running through everything in my head, and I realize I'm going to have to give him something that will change his mind. Something that I don't want to do, but will do because this is my child.

"Steven, please don't do this. Please, I'll do anything! I love this child and will be devastated if you do this. I'll start eating, playing games . . . watching movies with you. I'll stay and no longer fight . . . I'll even marry you! Please don't take my baby!" I tell him with tears rolling down my face and placing my hands protectively over my stomach.

"I can't have a bastard's child in my home, Len. It isn't going to happen! I'm the only one that should be the father of any child you have!" he roars.

"Please, don't. I'll do anything. Just don't kill my baby. Let me have the baby, and you can take it to the hospital saying you found him. If you do that, I promise to marry you and behave. Please, if you do this then how will I know you won't end up killing me or any children we have after we're married? Anyone who kills children are monsters in my eyes. Is that what you want me to think? That you're a monster? Do this for me, and show me you really are a good person. Please, just please don't do it." I'm sobbing, trying to think of anything that will change his mind.

I keep praying in my head that God will step in and not let this happen. I don't know if I can live if he does this to me. I need him to give me this.

I watch as he looks me over. I can see him thinking through what I just said. He turns his head and closes his eyes. I wonder what he's thinking. Just when I think he isn't going to change his mind, he opens his eyes and looks at me.

"You will marry me tomorrow under your new name. I know someone who has no clue who you are and will marry us. I made sure they were ordained and I got all the paperwork taken care of. You will do whatever I want and ask no questions. You will give birth here and I'll take it to the hospital. After you're done healing, I'll finally take you as a husband should. I refuse to sleep with you as long as that thing is still inside you. However, remember this, if you go back on your word at any time, I'll kill that thing. Do you understand, Linda?" He says, looking me in the eye showing me he means business.

"Linda?"

"Your new name's Linda Adams. That's what I'll call you from now on. Now, do we have a deal?"

"Yes, we have a deal," I whisper.

"Good, now get some rest. I'll be back later with all we'll need tomorrow. I look forward to seeing you this evening, Linda," he says, picking up his bag and leaving the room.

I realize that I just agreed to be here for at least six more months. I also agreed to marry the devil to save my unborn child. I just pray that once I get out of here, Dante *forgives me for the choices I just made. If he doesn't . . . I have no clue how I'll survive it.*

I'm snapped out of my thoughts when I feel another round of nausea hit me.

"Little one, our family is going to miss so much." I gently rub my stomach and think about what my family would be doing at this moment. "Let me tell you all about them. Your Daddy is very sweet and loving, but don't let that fool you though, he's a controlling man too. In a good way . . . a sweet, tender, loving way that only your father can be. Like that one time, I was giving a friend of ours a back rub . . ." I chuckle at the memory, as I continue to tell my child all about the family that I pray one day will be very involved in their life once again.

Dante

I have a pounding headache again from pouring over the papers on my desk for the hundredth time. It has been three months and still nothing. KCPD has given up searching for her saying that it has been too long and the chances of her still being alive are very slim. But her family and I haven't given up hope though.

Lucky and I go over everything daily, and we've watched the hospital security footage so many times trying to find anything that stands out. The only thing that broke in the case was the note that was left wasn't from Len. It was forged, as if someone had samples of her writing and placed a blank paper over the letters to trace them into a note. We also realized that the *Yours Always* is something the stalker used. Other than that nothing else is coming up. It's pissing me off.

"Hey bro, how you holding up?" I snap my head up and see Eagle walking into my office.

"As good as I can be. What's going on with you?"

"We need to talk and I'm going to say something you might not like. But, I think Lucky and you need to take a step back and maybe let us look into it. You're both too close to the case and it can lead to mistakes or something being overlooked. You know we have your back and will come to you with anything we find. Take a few days off and reprogram your brains. Come back fresh and maybe work on a different case. If we still haven't found anything, then come back to the case and see it with fresh eyes. It's what most do in situations like this," he tells me.

I take a deep breath and look over at him. I know he's trying to help. I feel like I lost myself when she was taken and I don't know how to get it back. Maybe he's right and this is what we need to get Len back. I just don't know if I can do it.

"What if I were in your shoes? Ghost, you know you'd be telling me the same thing and making sure I stick to it. Think it over, and we'll meet tomorrow in the conference room around nine in the morning. I already told the same things to Lucky, too. It's eight forty-five at night. Go home, Dante, and think about what I just said." He stands up, pats me on the shoulder and walks out the door.

I sit back and look out the window. I hadn't even realized it was night time already. I haven't really been able to sleep. It's crazy how quickly I'd adjusted to sleeping in bed with her and now I can't even step in the bedroom. I've been sleeping in the guestroom and Lucky has taken up the other room. We decided we needed to stay at the house just in case she showed up.

Taking a deep breath, I grab the files, my laptop, and put them in my bag. I turn off the lights and head to the house, thinking about what Eagle said. I decide I need to talk to Lucky about this.

I'm sitting downstairs with the TV on when I hear Lucky walk through the door. Looking down at my watch, I see it's one in the morning which means he's been at the gym since he left the office around nine last night.

"Hey man, I got your message. What's up?" he asks as he comes down the stairs.

Looking over at him, I see that he's really bulked up. Lucky's always been in shape, but he's huge now. He's also grown a beard which is odd because he's always so particular about being clean shaved.

"Eagle said he talked to you. I want to know your thoughts about what he said. I'm thinking he's right. We need to pass this off to them and take a step back. As much as it kills me to say that, I know that I would be telling them the same if it were them." I hold my breath because I know he isn't going to like hearing it a second time.

"Yeah, I know, but I just don't know if I can step back. If I do it's like I'm telling everyone I gave up. That Len doesn't matter to me anymore. I can't do that. She's my baby sister, and I didn't protect her. I have to do something to help find her! I just don't know what the fuck to do!" He grabs his hair viciously.

"I know, man, that's what I'm feeling too. So how can we

do this, but still have a hand in it? Maybe we should hand it off, but tell them that they have to report daily to us even if that means them saying nothing new?" I say into my hands.

"Yeah, I guess that's what's going to have to happen. I don't like it one bit but if it gets Len back, I guess we need to try it. I trust them so I know they will handle this with more care than anyone else. I keep hoping whoever has her will fuck up and we'll catch his ass." He grabs two beers, comes over to the couch, hands one to me and takes a seat.

"I'm lost, man. I just don't know what to do. I feel like my heart and soul is gone. I can't sleep, eat, or even concentrate on anything, but finding her. Lucky, I don't know how to live without her," I say, my throat closing up with a knot and tears in my eyes.

"I know it's the same with me and my family. OPG isn't doing well. She's sick and we're trying to keep her from the stress. She keeps saying that Len is okay and not to worry. I'm beginning to wonder if she knows something, however, I don't want to stress her out with questioning her. Something has to break, Dante, or we're going to lose it worse than we already are," he whispers with tears falling down his face.

"How are the girls doing?" I ask, since he keeps in contact with them daily.

"Julia and Ashley are doing okay. They keep asking people about her or if they have seen her. They're just trying to keep it together for my family. Sara's withdrawn. She won't talk to anyone about Len at all. She stares off in space all the time and she won't hangout with anyone anymore. I think Len was her rock and now that she's gone, Sara doesn't know what to do. Once this shit's over and Len's home, I'm going to make sure she knows she's mine! I realize me holding off or being scared because she's friends with Len was the stupidest thing ever. I won't make that mistake again." He downs the rest of his beer. "Dante, are you still wanting to be with my sister after this? What if she was raped? Are you going to be able to stand by her side through whatever she might need to get through this?"

"Nothing will ever stop me from being with Len. I don't care what happened to her, Neil. She's mine, and I'll do whatever I can to make sure she gets whatever she needs to help her through."

He sits there letting my words sink in and then nods his head in acknowledgement.

"I didn't think you'd do anything less than that but I had to make sure." He stands up and turns towards me. "I'm going to bed. Meeting in the morning with the guys. Let's pass this to them and see if they can get something we couldn't."

He goes upstairs and I lean back on the couch. I'm glad he's getting his head out of his ass when it comes to Sara. I just hope we find Len in time before Sara hides deeper into herself.

With that thought, I decide it's time to go to bed. As I stand up, I reach into my pocket and pull out her ring. I stare at it and the thoughts of seeing her smiling as I put it on her finger runs through my head. I take a deep breath and pray the boys will have better luck with this shit then we've had.

Sixteen

Len

Six months later...

I WAKE TO A SHARP pain going through my back. I glance over at the clock and see it's two in the morning. That means Steven's still here, which is a good thing since I'm pretty sure I'm in labor. Panic seizes me because I'm scared that he isn't going to follow through with our deal. Maybe I can talk him into taking me with him and dropping the baby off. I doubt it since I haven't been out of this basement in nine months. Another sharp pain goes through me, and I feel like someone is sticking a knife in my back.

I turn back at the clock again and see that I'm having contractions about nine minutes apart. I decide I have time to take a shower before I have to call Steven through the intercom. I get out of bed and head over to the shower.

Turning on the water, I think back to one of the memories that helps me get through the times when I need to remember the good in life . . .

We're walking into the house from leaving my parents' house when I'm suddenly pushed up against the wall. I gaze up into Dante's eyes and smile at the lust that's shinning bright in them.

"I want you badly, Len." He bends his head down and nuzzles my neck.

"Well, I think we need to talk first, Mr. I'm moving in, marrying you, and having babies."

He snaps his head back and looks down at me with confusion written on his face.

"You said you wanted that too."

"I know I did, but you didn't actually talk to me about it. You just stated what was going to happen after I said I did want the same. What if I wanted to wait for a few months?" I question and then slip out from under his arms.

"I told you I didn't want to wait any longer, Len. We've known each for years, it isn't like we're rushing into things. What are your worries? Let's get to the bottom of this, and then I'm taking you upstairs." He wiggles his eyebrows.

I'm trying to hold a straight face, but I know I'm going to break. While I was at the spa I talked more with OPG about how fast everything was going. She explained that sometimes men who are in the alpha sense just don't understand that a woman needs to have an opinion in the matter too. She explained that if I made it seem like I was upset then we could discuss it, and if I played it just right I could make it seem like it was his idea when it was truly mine.

I swear the woman's a genius even if she can be mean to people who aren't family.

"I just don't want people to think that we're rushing things. What if we just moved in for now? After a few months we could start on that wedding and move to babies." *I peek at him from under my lashes.*

He's standing there with his arms crossed shaking his head no with a smirk on his face. Shit, I have a feeling he isn't buying this, and it makes me want to stomp my feet like a teenager.

"There's a slight problem with your logic there. Did you forget that we didn't use protection last night? That you could be pregnant right now?"

I think quickly calculating if I'm currently ovulating, and with a moan I realize that he's right. Well, shit, maybe I can just have him hold off on the wedding for now.

"Okay, you've got a point. What if we at least just move in for now and wait for the rest. Use protection from now on until we know for sure I'm pregnant or not." *I smile big at him hoping that what I suggested worked this time.*

"I don't think that's going to work either, Len. Do you want to get married before or after your belly is swollen with my baby? It doesn't matter to me either way, I'm just trying to figure out what you're going to do when you realize that I did plant my baby in you last night." *He's now smirking full on with pride that he might've accomplished that fact.*

This sexy asshole isn't going to change his mind. Maybe I can seduce him. I grin full on at him, and he narrows his eyes.

"What are you thinking now, mio tutto?"

"Oh, nothing much. I was just thinking that it's time to go and take a steaming hot shower since I still have the oils all over me from my massage earlier that Bradley gave me."

He narrows his eyes more and uncrosses his arms while I see a flicker of jealousy run across his features.

"Len, you're pushing it. I know you didn't allow another man to touch what's mine. If so, then I'm going to have to take you up those stairs and reclaim that sexy body of yours to remind you that you belong to me." He starts taking a step towards me causing me to hold my hand out stopping him.

"Don't take another step, mister. If you want to show me who I belong to, then you're going to have to agree to my terms of holding off on marriage and babies."

"I told you that you may already have my baby in you. Now, you want to wait on marriage fine, but you will wear my ring while you plan the wedding. Deal?"

I start to think about that and consider that it wasn't that bad of an idea. Then, I can actually wait and plan the wedding. I could also see my ob-gyn about pills.

I'm snapped out of my thoughts when I go flying over his shoulder, and he's running up the stairs. He slaps my ass and then rubs it as he's rushing towards the bedroom.

"You're taking too long to think. Let's get in the shower and finish this discussion. I'm thinking with me on my knees between your thighs you will finally see reason and that it's a good thing for us to go forward with not only moving in, but marriage, and babies." He stops and places me on the counter. "Now, let's get you undressed and in the shower. I need desert and you need to get that oil off your body."

I giggle and jump down to start undressing while he starts running the shower. I step into the shower and right *when I got to start washing my hair I hear him murmur, "You really didn't have a guy massage you right? You were just shitting with me."*

"Nope, his name was Bradley, and his hands were magic," I moan out remembering the feel of his hands rubbing the tension away.

"That's it!" he growls out and pulls me to him taking me in a deep kiss.

I giggle into his mouth, and for a second I think that I need to tell him that Bradley is a gay married man. Then, as he deepens the kiss and rubs his hands down my back, I decide that it can wait until after this round...

I snap back when a sharp pain hits, and I feel a rush of water go down my legs. I glance down and see a little bit of blood at the bottom of the tub, and I know my water broke. Well, at least it happened in the shower. I finish washing up really fast. I dry off and get a long gown on and a pair of panties with a pad in it to catch the extra water that's still dripping out. I take a moment between contractions to fill the tub with very warm water so I can use it during my labor. After turning on some music, I decide to let Steven know it is time.

"Steven, I'm in labor," I say into the intercom.

"Okay, lovely, I'm on my way down. Get into bed," he tells me.

Crawling into the bed, I begin to pray that God will be with me and my baby. I pray that

Even though I'm so exhausted, I can't stop the smile on my

face as I gaze down at my son as he nurses. He looks just like Dante did when he was a baby. He has blue eyes, and I pray he keeps them. I glance up and see Steven cleaning everything up. I was in labor for a total of sixteen hours and didn't have any drugs. I didn't want to chance him doing something to him while I was still groggy. Steven's been quiet since I delivered, and I'm scared to break the silence. But I know I need to try and talk him into letting keep my child.

"Steven, are you okay?" I ask in a whisper.

"Yeah, Linda, I'm okay. I'm just thinking of everything that needs to happen now. I'm going to wait three days until it's stronger then take it to the hospital with me. I need to go buy a few things for it. Why don't you tell me what you think you need?" he says as he pulls out a piece of paper and a pen from a bag on the dining table.

"You picked up everything that was needed over the past few months. I don't think there is anything left to get. Did you get a car seat?" I ask him quietly while still looking at my son.

"Yeah, I'll be back," he says and walks off.

I glance back down; I know I need to name him. I think long and hard about a name. I want to carry on my pops tradition, but want to honor Dante as well. I put him on my shoulder to burp him and go through the countless names that I know. I look over at the table and spot Steven's bag. He forgot his medical bag?

I stand up slowly and feel discomfort from child birth, but I refuse to let it stop me from seeing what's in that bag. I place my son on my shoulder, move to the dresser, grab a few blankets, and walk to the table. I block the camera and make it look like I'm changing the baby. I reach over and open the bag. I spot needles and vials of medicine. I grab them, stash them in a blanket, and place the pilfered items between my chest and my son.

I head to the trash and throw the diaper away, acting like nothing's wrong. I head to the bed and put the baby down with my back to the camera again. I slide the blanket up my shirt and make sure the baby has pillows all the way around him so he won't fall off.

I head to the bathroom and turn on the water. I'm so grateful that the camera isn't on this area. I quickly put the blanket of stuff in the tub and get undressed. I step in the shower and close the curtain, but leaving a small crack so I can watch the baby as I take a shower.

I unwrap my stuff and see that the medicine is Dilaudid. This is a very strong pain medication and I know this is will be our ticket out of here. I get the syringe and pull out five units which is a lot, but I don't care; I'm getting my baby and me out of here. After I finish with my shower, I check on the baby again and see that he's sound asleep.

I take a few moments and pray to God that I can get us out of here without any hitches. I just need to be able to get through this. I'm startled out of my thoughts when I hear noises coming from upstairs.

This is it. This is my chance to save my baby and me. I walk over to the TV and angle myself as I get the needle out of my pocket. I'm close to the door, but it looks like I'm changing the channel. I hear footsteps coming down the steps and my heart rate begins to beat faster. The door knob starts moving, and all I can hear is my heartbeat in my ears. The door opens and Steven starts to step in the room. As quick as I can, I plunge the needle into his neck and press the plunger.

"What the fuck!" he roars.

I jump out of the way and watch him as he grabs at his neck. He looks over at me, and I can see the medicine's starting to work because his eyes are starting to dilate and his movements are getting slower. I made sure I stuck it in his artery so it would go through his system faster. He starts to walk towards me but stops and grabs his head.

"What did you do? You stupid girl! I'll punish you for this!" he roars and stumbles towards me. "Just wait . . . until . . ."

He drops to the ground, and I watch as he slowly relaxes. I continue to stare at him, dumbfounded that the plan worked. I need to get away and make sure my son and I are safe.

It's with that thought that I rush to start to pack things we're going to need. After I get everything I can think of, I rush to my baby. I have to get us out of here.

Seventeen

DANTE

I WAKE UP IN A cold sweat and look over at the alarm to see it's five in the morning. A feeling of dread rushes through me and normally, that means something is wrong. I look around and try to figure out what had awakened me. I see that everything is still the way it was when I went to bed so I decide to go downstairs and see if something is up there. After checking out everything, including the alarm system, I decide to take a shower to see if it will get this to go away.

I stand in the shower and still have the feeling of unease going through my body. I think about what's going on today and nothing standing out that would cause this weird tension in me. I just can't shake that something's off, and it bothers me. I normally follow my gut because it has yet to steer me wrong. It's one of the things that saved my buddies and me when we were overseas. Fuck it. I need to get some coffee and, when Lucky wakes up, I'll talk to him about this and see if we can figure it out.

I hurry through my morning routine and go down to the kitchen to make some coffee. I quickly decide to brew a whole pot since Lucky should be waking up any minute now. I decide to make us breakfast too. We have a meeting today with KCPD and some of the people from the hospital to see if we have any more leads on Len.

I feel like I've been hit in the chest with a sledge hammer at the swamp of emotions running through my system at the thought of my Len. I reach down into my pocket again and rub the metal in between my fingers. I'm finding I do this often, and it has become the one thing that gets me through my emotions of missing her.

It has been nine months since she went missing, and we still have no clue where she is. Nobody's heard or seen her since the party, and that scares the shit out of all of us. By now, there should have been some sort of sighting or some sort of contact.

Many think that it's too late and she's dead, but I can't even think that because I know I would be dead too. She's the reason my heart beats and my lungs draw in air. I know deep down that I'd know if she were dead. I'm more worried about her state of mind when we find her. I'll get her whatever she needs to make sure she's okay.

"Hey, what are you doing up before me?" Lucky asks, making me snap out of my thoughts.

"Woke up in a cold sweat," I tell him as I look over to him. "Tension, unease, and I'm not liking it. Need to talk through it with you."

"Shit, man, I hate your fucking gut feelings. Let's figure this shit out. We're meeting with KCPD and the hospital people, which are the only big things going on. Do you think that's it?" He gets a cup of coffee and snatches a piece of bacon from the plate next to the stove.

"I thought of that and I don't think that's it. Anything going on at the office that might be triggering it? Any cases that I don't know about yet?" I ask him, grabbing the eggs.

"Not that I'm aware of. I checked in with the guys and everything's on track. Missing Persons case is wrapping up nicely and SWAT is still wanting our help with the drug bust, but that's it. At least that's what Thing One and Thing Two are telling us. Should we check their work this morning to make sure? It's their first case without support." He starts setting up the table.

"No, let's give them the chance to prove they can do this without us. I trust that they will come to us if they need help. I'm glad the other Missing Persons cases are coming along. Shit, man, I don't know why I'm feeling this way. Maybe I'm just losing it," I tell him as I plate the omelets.

I start eating and do my mental check list, because I know it's the only way I'm going to figure out what the fuck's going on. I think of this gut check shit is a warning. I go through and think of all the places or things that are going to happen today. When nothing sets off the tension, I then go through the rest of the week's agenda. Again nothing.

What'll happen is that when I get to the situation or person that's causing this, I'll get an overwhelming rush of emotions all at once. It's almost enough to make me throw up because it's so intense to feel. If I can't figure it out I switch to names of people that I care deeply about. The scary thing is, it has never been wrong before, which is why I hate it when I get these fucking warnings.

When going through the day's events didn't trigger

anything, I decide to go through names. I hate it when I have to go through names because knowing who it is needing a warning makes the emotions even higher for me. I start with my family and don't sense anything which makes me ease up a bit. I go through my Seal brothers, and again nothing triggers it. I start to think of Lucky's family, and the tension's slowly starting to come with each name that passes through my mind. Then it happens, the name that has my gut clenching and dread washing over me, and it makes me want to roar.

"Fuck! It's Len!" I scream, jumping up from my chair.

"What the fuck do you mean, it's Len?" Lucky demands looking up from his plate of food.

"The feeling, it's Len. Damn it, Lucky, something's off with Len. We need to get to the office!" I tell him and then walk off to get my shit together.

I know Lucky's contacting the boys, which is good, because, right now, my only thought is getting to the office, getting the files, and scouring everything to see if we can find her.

"Ghost, there's nothing in these files. We've been going through them for months now. I hate that you have this feeling, but I'm not sure what else we can do here. KCPD will be here any minute now and hopefully they'll have something new," Eagle tells me while he goes through the papers again.

"I hate to admit it, but he's right. Let's get ready for our meeting with the detectives. I'm going to have Sara make some coffee and grab something to eat," Lucky tells us, gets up and walks out the door.

I lean back in my chair and stare out the window and try to calm down. We've been looking through everything for hours now and still can't find anything, which makes these emotions come stronger at me. It isn't going to go away until I figure it out or whatever it is happens, and knowing it has to do with Len just makes it worse.

"The detectives are here," Doc says, poking is head in the door.

I glance around and see there's coffee, water, and food in the center of the table. I wonder how long I've been out of it. I'm surprised the guys didn't say something to me to get me out of my head. I mean, it can't be helped because she's everything to me. I can't function in life without her, she consumes my thoughts. Even if she isn't here.

"Okay, since we're all here, let's get to work. Detective, you said you had some new information for us," Lucky he takes a seat next to me.

His words make me snap my head in the direction of the detectives.

"Yes, we're waiting for some test results to come back, but we have some news. A call was put into the tips line saying there was a dead body in a house in North Kansas City. A unit was sent out and found the front door open and, upon search of the home, we didn't find a body. However, we did find signs of a struggle and some odd things as well," Detective Walters tells us.

He opens his brief case and pulls out a file.

"And this pertains to Len how, Detective?" Lucky questions.

"We're getting to that. We found something odd in the basement of the house. Every piece of furniture was bolted down. That threw up tons of flags. When we checked inside the dresser we found clothes that belonged to a woman and a baby," Detective Edmonds explains as his partner hands over the file.

"A baby?" My heart starts to pound harder in my chest.

"Yes, a baby, and by the looks of the clothes, I'd guess the baby's male," Detective Walters says, laying out pictures of what I assume is the house.

"Baby?" My voice comes out in a whisper.

"We also found a placenta buried in the backyard and, from the looks of it, the baby had to have been born recently. The health of the baby's still unknown, however," Detective Edmonds says looking at his phone.

I sit there dumbfounded at the news. I understand why they are telling us this. There was a possibility that the woman was Len. And, that the child more than likely came from her.

If she had a baby that meant it was mine, right? I guess it could be his, if he'd violated her and if she had the baby early. That thought makes me sick to my stomach. But I don't think the baby's his. Honestly, the way I look at things, even if I'm not the father by blood, it won't matter one bit. Any baby that came from Len is my child, and that's all that matters to me. But I have a gut feeling he's mine which makes me wonder if she and the baby are okay. I take a second to let it sink in that I was a father.

"I want to donate a sample of my DNA," I tell them.

"And why would you want to do that, Dante?"

"If Len's the woman that you're assuming was there,

then there's a possibility that I'm the father."

I gather up the paperwork and photos off the table.

"That's what we're assuming, that it was Ms. Shields in the home in question. However, until the test confirms it, we're not one hundred percent sure," Detective Edmonds states.

"What makes you think it was Len at the house, Detectives? It could be anyone really," Eagle says.

"Well, that's the other thing we need to inform you of. We already informed your parents Neil of this because we have to do a news conference. The house we were called to was the home of Dr. Steven Adams. Currently, there's an alert out on both Ms. Shields and Dr. Adams. We're still combing through the home, but we have reason to believe that Dr. Adams is the kidnapper. We also believe that it was Ms. Shields who phoned in the tip. If you have a recording of her voice it would help a lot. The odd thing is, the caller thought he was dead so we're unsure of what condition Dr. Adams is currently in." Detective Walters stands up and watches my expression, which right now is in shock of the news he just dropped on us.

"Fuck," Sin mumbles out.

Fuck is right because both he and I cleared him of anything when we interviewed him months ago.

"Okay, Dante, we'll go with you for the testing. We just wanted to give you that information and also, if you hear from Ms. Shields, please contact us," Detective Edmonds tells us.

He stands and helps Detective Walters gather up everything else.

"Do you think he still has her?" Lucky asks.

I hand him over the papers and pictures so he can view them as well.

"Judging from, the phone call, I don't believe he does. However, we can't say that with one hundred percent certainty. That call could have come from anyone. Which is why I'm asking for a recording of her voice."

"I have a saved voicemail from her I can have sent over to you," I state.

"That would be helpful. Again, if you hear from her, contact us."

"Sounds good. Thanks, Detectives." Neil turns to face us. "Eagle. Doc. Sin. Stay with me and let's get to looking into what they just gave us. Ghost, go get your DNA done and get back here so we can find my sister and bring her and my nephew home safely where they belong." Then he's walking out the door.

The thought that Len's out there with a child worries me. I have this overwhelming need to go and search under every rock to find them. I just need to see them. I'm ready to bring my family home and *never* again let them out of my sights.

Eighteen

Len

IT HAS BEEN SIX WEEKS since that horrible night. Looking down at my son, I take a deep breath, knowing that for now, we are safe. I drove down to Clinton, MO and rented a small cabin that I was able to pay three months of rent in cash. There's a total of three cabins but they're spaced pretty far apart. I would guess there are about five acres in between each cabin. The old woman who owns the cabins, lives on the same land.

The only line of communication she has is a land line for her business. Reception here at the lake is really bad so it makes sense that she would have just a telephone. She didn't ask any questions and was really sweet. I used the name that Steven had given me before we got married because it is easier to hide.

I have been keeping updated with what's been happening through the local newspaper. I was planning on being gone for just a week and then returning home.

However, I saw that Steven and I are considered missing and that made me realize that I didn't kill him. My mind flashed to the picture that was with the flowers that I received before I was kidnapped, and I knew I couldn't go back home just yet. I needed to make sure the family was safe from harm. My fear of Steven killing one of them or my son, had me shaking and deciding that I had to stay put. It might not seem rational but it's all I can think about.

I've been sending messages to my OPG letting her know that I was safe. I call her cell phone weekly from a blocked number in town. I let it ring two times before hanging up, and then call back letting it ring three more times before hanging up for good. It's something that we've done over the years when we were hiding in a room and didn't want others bothering us. I'm hoping she realizes it's my way of telling her I'm okay.

I was able to get a call in today because I went into town and met with a doctor to get my six-week check. He also looked over my son and gave us the all clear. I'm grateful for it being a small town and the fact of confidentially. I gave a false name and paid in cash so they really didn't question anything.

I glance around the cabin and see that it's very simple. It's one huge room, which isn't a big deal since it's just us two. The living room is in the front of the cabin and has a fireplace, which would be perfect for the cold nights. There's a huge front window that all you can see is trees and the driveway. On the left side of the cabin is the studio bedroom that has a queen size bed, basinet, dresser, and nightstand. Next to the dresser is a bathroom that's just a shower, toilet, and sink.

In the back of the cabin is the dining room and the kitchen which is small but perfect. It has a huge sliding door that opens to a back porch which you can sit on and look out at Lake Pomme De Terre. There's also a barn style garage next to the cabin where I've hidden Steven's car from prying eyes.

The landlord stated she has someone who delivers food to her, and I'm more than welcome to get her a list of what I need and the money so I wouldn't have to take the baby out if I didn't want to.

I look down again and see that my baby boy has stopped eating and has fallen asleep. I gently cover my breast and put him on my shoulder to burp. As I pat his back, I think about what I found that night as I was packing suitcases to get out of that house . . .

I quickly rush around, holding my son while trying to fill the suitcases as fast as I can. I figure out quickly that I can hide out at the lake that I grew up at. The last time OPG and I came to the lake, we passed some cabins and we said the next time we came, we would rent them. It's perfect for hiding and there isn't much reception there either. I need to pack as much as I can, because I know going into town is going to be a rare thing for me to do once I find somewhere to hide.

I need to find his keys to his vehicle, so I start searching the house and I walk into what I'm assuming is the master bedroom and look over at the dresser. I notice on my quick walk through the house that everything looks perfect. Like the whole house was a museum, which leads me to believe that Steven might have OCD, as well as some other mental disorder.

I grab the keys and my foot bangs against something. I glance down and see a bag. I opened it to find it full of money, as well as passports for Steven and myself. I'm not sure how he got them but they look very real. He had to of paid someone a lot of money to forge them. I do a quick count and it's about ten grand in cash. I decide I have no choice but to take the money. I don't even want to think of what he had planned. All I know is I need to get out of here.

I get back to the basement and decide that I need to see if I can get my son to latch for breastfeeding. He is only a few hours old but I know we have a two-hour drive ahead of us. As he feeds I can only stare in amazement at how beautiful he is and I decide right there what his name is going to be. Smiling slightly to him as he finishes eating, I then speak his name to him for the first time.

"Marcus Anthony De Luca, I love you so much. I'll do everything I can to keep you safe and sound," I whisper while I burp him. It's time to get out of here.

The knocking on the door brings me back to the present. I look over and see Ms. Cindy at the window, waving at me. Slowly standing up so I don't wake up Marcus, I walk over to the door and open it up.

"Hi Ms. Cindy, what can I do for you?" I whisper softly to her.

"I came to see if you had that list for the grocery store. The young man who shops for me should be here in a few hours. How are you settling in?" she says quietly smiling at Marcus.

"We're settling in nicely, thank you for asking. I'm sorry

I haven't had time to make a list. Do you have a moment to come in?" I open the door wider, inviting her inside.

"Of course. Give me little Marcus here so you can get things together," she tells me and holds her hands out for Marcus.

I smile as I hand him over carefully, and I feel a sadness wash over me. I watch them both, and all I can image is OPG holding him in her arms. I quickly pull myself together and rush through a list of what I'll need for the week. I pull out some cash from my purse and then hand them over to her. I gratefully take him from her and the feeling of sadness comes again at thinking about my mom and Dante's mom missing out on this as well.

"Thank you, Ms. Cindy. Please tell your errand boy to keep the change," I quietly tell her.

"No worries, Ms. Adams. I'll be back with your stuff soon." She starts to walk out the door. She stops and looks over her shoulder. "If you ever want to talk, I'm here to listen." I see the concern in not only in her eyes but also etched on her face.

"Thank you," I murmur as she steps out the door. I wonder if she knows something, then I remember she doesn't have a TV. I'm sure she would've said something by now if she knew anything.

It's with that thought that I decide to take a nap with Marcus until she comes back with the groceries.

DANTE

I'm going over tons of files and searching everything trying to find Len and my son. The results from the DNA testing not only confirmed that Len was at Adam's house but that the child was in fact hers. Also, it confirmed that I'm the father. They were able to pull DNA from the umbilical cord to test this. From what we know, both are alive, however nobody knows where they have gone to. And Adams is still missing. We found a passport in Adam's bedroom along with some papers in the closet that suggest Len's new name is Linda Adams.

After an investigation on the new name for her, we found that she married Adams. We're currently searching for the person who signed the license because we have reason to believe that this is a forged document. There's a chance it isn't since it's very easy to get ordained to perform marriage ceremonies these days, especially in Kansas, which is where their license was from.

We had to put out flyers, did a press conference, and even had something written up in the Kansas City Star stating they are missing. We haven't mentioned anything about the baby yet. So far the tips that have been called in haven't turned up anything. It's driving me crazy that they both are out there, and we don't know if they're okay. I don't know how people can deal with their loved ones missing for years. I need my family!

"We're going to the lake to get away from here. OPG is wanting both families to go and relax. She's worried that we aren't thinking clearly when it comes to finding Len. Before you object, I think she's right. I loved going to the lake when we were little. It might do some good to get some fresh air and look at the files again and see what we can come up with," Lucky expresses with a sigh.

I know he's right, and it would do us some good to look at the files with a fresh mind. Maybe getting some good clean fresh air will be what we need. Maybe something will come to light and we can catch a break.

"Are the boys coming too? I think it would be good for them to get away."

"Yeah, you might be right and it's only two hours away so if anything happens, we can rush back here. We can tell Sara to just forward the system and work from home and call us if it's an emergency. We'll have to let KCPD know too so they know where to contact us." He pulls out his phone to text the boys and let them know the plan.

"All right, that works. When are we leaving?" I ask.

"Friday, around nine in the morning is the plan. Pops wants to leave Thursday night though. So, I would say make sure you're ready to head out then," he explains then stands up, and turns to leave.

"How late are we talking on Thursday?" I ask him right before he walks out of my office.

"Who knows. You know how Pops is. More than likely it will be around eight at night. So be ready," he yells back.

I have a weird feeling something is going to happen this weekend. I didn't tell Lucky this when he said we were going to go to the lake. I don't like getting these feelings, especially since the last one. I just hope that this time it's a good one, because I don't know if I can handle something else happening.

Nineteen

Len

AFTER OUR FRIDAY AFTERNOON NAP, I decide that I want to take Marcus on a walk by the lake. Right when I'm getting him dressed for the outside, there's a knock at the door. I peek out towards the window and see Ms. Cindy standing there, waving. I wave her in.

"Well, what are you two up to?" She walks in and shuts the door.

"I'm going to take Marcus for a walk by the lake. He needs to see the amazing beauty that is there. I have always loved this lake and walking by the water has always calmed me when my OPG and I came down here on the weekends," I absently tell her thinking back to those days.

"Your OPG?" Ms. Cindy asks and takes a seat at the dining room table. Her question snaps me out of my thoughts.

"Yes, my grandma. I call her OPG, it's a nickname I gave her as a kid. Sorry, I just miss her," I explain and finish getting Marcus ready for our walk. "Would you like to join us?"

"Oh, you sweet girl, that is kind of you to ask, but I think I'm going to go back home. I just wanted you to know that I have rented the cabin on the other side of me to a large family. They seemed very nice last night when they checked in. They're staying for a couple of weeks, so I wanted to give you a heads up in case you see any strange people walking around you'll know what's going on. I explained that they should stay on their side, so it shouldn't be a problem," she tells me and gets up to head out.

"Thanks, Ms. Cindy. Marcus and I will stop by later if you still feel up to having dinner with us?" I ask because she has dark circles under her eyes and it makes me wonder if she's sleeping alright. "Why don't I come by early and make dinner? You can get in some cuddle time with Marcus."

"That would be wonderful, sweet girl. Why don't you come around four?" She gives me a hug and kisses Marcus on his cheek. "See you both soon."

I lock the front door, pick up Marcus, and head out onto the back deck. The sun is shining brightly and there is a gentle breeze coming from the lake. It makes me want to run down to the water and splash my feet in the water like I use to when I was little. I haven't been past the back porch yet because I didn't want to take Marcus out that far. So I'm eager to look around the area. It's close to where we would normally stay when we would come down.

Thinking about my OPG again brings memories of the times we were here together. I know she would've loved to be here with us right now and see how amazing the view is. I look off the porch and down to the shoreline. The waves are very gently lapping up on the shore. Looking further out I see fish jumping out of the water. OPG would have loved to sit down on her chair and cast her line. Shaking my head, I start to head down the stairs toward the water.

After about thirty minutes into our stroll on the shore, I hear a boat off in the distance. I don't want the noise to wake Marcus, so I decide it's time to go back to the house. I glance up and can see the boat is going towards the cliffs across the way. I know they're going cliff diving and it makes me shiver at the memory that floods me. I used to love doing that until Pa screamed at me not to jump. He grabbed his shotgun and fired into the water. I climbed down and glanced at where he shot and saw a family of cottonmouths swimming around. Yeah, that stopped my jumping days.

I shake off the memory while I walk up to the house and lay Marcus down in his basinet. I grab a diet coke out of the fridge and stand by the sliding door. I'm watching the group that is cliff divers. I wonder who they are and if I know them. They're too far for me to see them or to recognize the boat. It's possible I know them from before but I'm really not sure. I decide I don't have time to figure it out, because I want to take a shower before Marcus wakes up.

I head to the bathroom and try to place if I know them. I'm hoping I don't so I'm not recognized and can continue hiding out until Steven is found.

DANTE

We ended up pulling into Clinton around eight thirty last night. Pops wanted to get there early enough so we could meet the woman who we rented the cabin from.

The one we have is big enough for all of us. She has another one, but it's small and is rented. I wish it wasn't because I would have rented it so I could get some quiet time.

Currently, we're loading into the boat Pops owns, because OPG says we need to at least enjoy one day without worries of anything. I protested, but, in the end, she won, because, honestly, nobody can win against that woman. So, we're loading into the boat to go cliff diving everyone thinks it's a great stress reliever.

"Okay, there are a set of cliffs over there that we'll go to. Mom can sit on the shoreline and still see us while she fishes. Before anyone gets out of the boats, I'll throw some rocks around to make sure there are no cottonmouths around," Pops explains before he starts the boat.

"I'll never forget that day, Pops. Shit, if Len were here, she wouldn't be cliff jumping. She hasn't since that day . . ." Lucky starts telling us about why Len won't dive anymore.

"Shit, I'm not sure I'm cliff diving. I hate snakes," Eagle tells us with a straight face.

"No, you'll get up there and jump at least once or you're going to have OPG on your ass." Lucky cracks up laughing, "And trust me she'll know if you did it or not."

"Fuck me, your grandma's freaking scary," Eagle states, which causes us to bust out laughing at the thought of this big ass ex-Navy Seal being scared of a tiny woman.

We watch as Pops and Papa throw rocks into the water near the cliffs. Something on my right catches my eye, and I glance over. I see a woman walking away from the shore. Something about her seems familiar, but I know I have to be losing my mind because I have never been to this lake before. I squint trying to see if I can make out anything other than she's wearing a yellow sundress and has blonde hair.

I shake my head and realize everyone's getting out of the boat. I stand up, take off my shirt, and dive into the water. As I swim to the shore, I think about the woman I saw a second ago and wonder if I will run into her during our stay here.

Len

I watch Ms. Cindy rock Marcus in her rocking chair while I clean up after dinner. I'm really glad I came over to eat with her, because it gives me a sense of how my OPG would be with him. Another pang of hurt rushes through me at the thought of not seeing her for a while.

Don't get me wrong, I miss my whole family so much, but I know she's getting up there in age, and I'm scared that I won't see her again.

I look back over at Ms. Cindy and wonder if she knows who I am. As if sensing I'm watching her, she raises her head and grins at me.

"I can hear your brain working overtime over there, Linda. What has you thinking so hard?" she murmurs.

"I don't know how to ask what I want to know. It's complicated," I say with a wobble in my voice and tears threaten to come to the surface.

"I'll tell you that I know, your name isn't Linda Adams. I've known who you really are from the moment I opened my door. I don't know the situation, but I understand that you need some time to gather yourself, and this little man here before you can face what you need to. I'm willing to give you that time. I know your OPG would expect that of me," she explains with a sly grin on her face.

"My OPG?" I gasp.

"Yes, May's a friend of mine. I met her a long time ago here at the lake shortly after your Pa married her. I remember when your pops, mom, Neil, and you would come with her and your Pa each weekend during the summer. We lost contact with each other about five years ago. However, she didn't know that, a few years ago after my Carl died, I bought these cabins and fixed them up for rentals," she explains while softly rubbing Marcus on his head.

"I don't remember you and I don't know what to say. I'm not ready to talk about what happened, but you're right, I need time to get myself together before I have to face the situation that's waiting for me," I choke out and sit down on the couch.

"Len, why don't you go take a walk and clear your head a bit? I have Marcus and we'll be fine. I think you need to think about what needs to be done," she gently suggests.

"I think that might be good. Thanks, Ms. Cindy." I give her a brief hug, and kiss Marcus on the head. "I won't be long."

"Don't rush. I'm enjoying my time with this little man. I didn't have children of my own so this is the closest thing to a grandchild I'll ever have," she tells me with a longing in her voice while looking longingly at my son.

"I would be honored if you would be a grandma to him, too. He loves you, and I can tell you love him," I say with tears in my eyes.

"I would love that. Thank you, Len," she whispers with

tears falling from her eyes.

I walk out the back door and down to the woods. I take in a deep breath and think about what I'm going to have to face soon. I know the longer I wait to return home the worse things can get. I called the police tip line and told them about Steven being dead. By now, they would have to have fingerprints and DNA that I was there, but I took the papers that were on his dresser so they might think I was there of my own freewill.

After some deep thought, I decide to stay one more week before I head home and face what is waiting for us. I think I should probably call Neil and have him meet us first before going to the police. I know they'll have to question me, but I'm scared that they'll think I went willingly. There were a lot of things in the house that might suggest I was never kidnapped.

I glance up from my steps and see an oak tree that has a carving in it. I take a few steps closer, and my breath catches in my throat. My hand shakes as I reach out and my finger traces the letters that are etched into the bark.

Dante + Len.

I'm flooded with memories of being sixteen and holding a knife marking the tree with what my heart hoped would happen. I carved this shortly after they left for boot camp on my trip to the lake with OPG before I started college.

I hear a chuckle that I know very well and snap my head towards the sound. I'm close to the shoreline, but still hidden in the trees. I look at the back of what looks like to be an older woman sitting in a chair with a fishing line in the lake. I stare in shock because I know for a fact that the woman is my OPG.

I watch her as she chuckles yet again, and I gaze out towards the water. I see the cliffs and the group from earlier still over there doing stunts off of them. A flash of red off to the side of them catches my eye and I glance over seeing a boat. I gasp out loud recognizing it's our family boat. It's at that moment that I realize the family that's in the other cabin, is mine.

"Len?"

I turn back and see OPG standing up with a look of amazement and wonder on her face. Tears are starting to stream down her face as her hand comes to cover her mouth.

"OPG?" My eyes start to well up with tears.

"Why didn't you come home by now? We've missed you so much. We've been so worried."

"I needed some time to process everything that happened. I also thought I killed Steven. So, when the paper came out and said we both were missing I knew he was still out there and I couldn't risk the family. I couldn't risk my son," I choked out.

"We know about my great-grandson. Len, I know you don't want to continue to run from this. Your family will support you through everything. There's no way we'd let anything else happen to you," she tells me with conviction in her voice.

"I came out for a walk and decided that next week I'll get ahold of Neil."

"Good! Now, I'll be by tonight to see you and my grandbaby. I'll knock twice on the door then pause and knock again three times. I'll just tell everyone that I'm going night fishing, and we both know they'll believe that. You probably should be getting back to the cabin because it looks like the boys are done. I love you, tons and bunches, Len."

"I love you, tons and bunches too, OPG." I smile at her and turn to hurry back to Ms. Cindy's house so I can get back to the cabin for my visit with my OPG.

Twenty

DANTE

AS I GAZE INTO THE fire, I can't help but get lost in thought. After cliff diving, we came back and grilled burgers for dinner. OPG finally returned from fishing right before we were finished setting up the table for dinner. She explained that nothing was biting, so she was going to do some night fishing once the sun went down and it was dark. I questioned it in my mind, but everyone seemed to be okay with it.

After dinner, Papa went to get the ice chest while Pops built a fire. The Moms gathered the stuff for s'mores and all us boys collected chairs and pulled them around the fire. Looking around, I start thinking about how amazing it would be to have Len and our son here with us. Everyone's smiling, but you can feel the loss of not having them with us.

"Hey, you okay? You look lost in thought." Eagle sits down next to me and hands me a beer. I didn't even notice the one I had was empty.

"Thanks, and yeah, I'm okay, just thinking about Len

and my son," I sigh and take a pull from my beer.

"I know, brother, we all are thinking about them. I just wish we could figure out where she would of ran to for safety. I bet it won't be much longer before she's right here with us." Confidence is strong in his voice.

"I have no clue where she would go. I thought by now she would've let us know where she was. All we know is that she has been calling OPG weekly. I wonder if I should go and talk to her by myself," I murmur out.

"I don't think any of us thought of that, because Pops has been adamant of keeping her out of it. He says she's really sad and depressed about Len so he didn't want us bringing it up. With her illness, they've been more careful about what she's told. Why don't you go down to where the crazy lady is and talk to her? I'll cover you." He moves to Lucky's side and strikes up a conversation.

I stand up and walk towards the house to go to the bathroom. After I finish up, I decide to go out the front door so nobody will see me walk down towards the shoreline where OPG is fishing. I'm really hoping she gives me something that we haven't thought about yet that will help me find Len.

I arrive at the area where she's supposed to be, but notice that her stuff is there, but she isn't. I wonder if she's in the woods and decide to call out softly so as not to scare her.

"OPG? You there?" I whisper loudly. I stop and listen to see if I can hear her. "OPG? It's Dante."

Nothing.

That's odd.

Scanning the area, her pole lies dormant; like it was never thrown into the water. The lantern's missing and so is the small cooler she had with her snacks and water. I wonder if she went up to the owner's cabin. I don't want to bother her visiting but, I need to make sure she's okay.

I walk towards Ms. Cindy's place, and as I get closer, I can see lights on and a couple of figures in the cabin. I knock gently on the door and step back into the light.

"Oh, hi sweetie, what can I do for you?" asks the lady who answers the door.

"I was just looking for Ms. May and wanted to make sure she was okay. Have you seen her?" I ask with a small smile but it drops when I see panic flash across her face.

"No, she isn't here. I know she likes to walk in the woods at night looking for mushrooms. She usually does that if she catches fish. Have you checked the woods?"

"I haven't checked the woods. Thank you for letting me know. I'll go and tell her son she's mushroom hunting so he won't freak out. Thanks again." I grin trying to throw off that I caught the panic that she tried to hide.

"No problem. Let me know if you can't find her, and I'll help look," she calls out and then shuts the door.

I see her watching me through the window, so I keep walking until I'm deep enough in the woods to turn and watch the house. I'm grateful that I didn't bring anything with me to light my way and that I'm also wearing dark clothes. After about five minutes of waiting, she peeks out of the door and looks around. She grabs her jacket, walks out of the door, and towards the cabin on the other side.

I quietly follow, hoping to figure out what's happening. As I get closer to the other cabin, I get a churning in my gut, signaling that something's about to happen. I stop right before the light shines into the woods. I watch her knock on the patio door. A woman walks up to the glass door, and I realize it's the same woman from the shore earlier, however, I still can't really make out her face because she's standing in the shadows.

I can't help but think that I know this person. I strain even more trying to make out who she is. I see the owner take a small step back, and then I see OPG take a step out from behind the other woman and onto the porch. It looks like she has a bundle of something in her hands. Why is she here? I don't understand what she's doing and how she knows this person.

I hear a cry and see OPG look down at the bundle and rock it like it's a baby. At that moment, the woman in the house steps out and looks down at the bundle, and its right then that I see who it is. Before I realize what I'm doing, I'm off at a dead run towards the house.

"Len!" I yell, and her head snaps up, and she looks right at me.

My heart is pounding while I rush to get to her. I reach out to her, and I see fear in her eyes but I don't let that deter me as I pick her up and hold her tightly to me. My head goes directly into her neck, and I take a deep breath, trying to soak in as much of her as I can. My emotions get the best of me, and I feel the wetness sliding down my cheeks. I have a feeling of home and content with her in my arms finally. I never want to go without this feeling again.

I'll do whatever it takes to make sure Len and my son are safe. No matter what the cost.

Len

One hour before...

I'm hurrying around the house trying to pick up and get everything ready for OPG's visit. I just finished feeding, bathing, and dressing Marcus so he'll be in a good mood for her visit. I'm so nervous. I feel tears welling up at the thought that I get to finally spend time with my OPG.

I hear someone walking up to my patio door. I glance over and watch as she comes into view. I head over and open the door before she could knock. I grab her and start sobbing as she hugs me tightly and rubs my back murmuring how much she loves me and that it's going to be okay.

"I can't believe you're here! I have missed you so much and thought of you daily. Honestly, Dante and you are what got me through the kidnapping." I start breaking down again.

"I know, Len, it's going to be okay now, so calm down. Let's get inside, so nobody will see us," she quietly tells me while rubbing my back.

After we get inside, I go to the sink and splash some cool water on my face. I take a few deep breaths and turn towards the living area. I stop at what I'm witnessing in front of me. OPG is sitting on the bed beside Marcus with tears running down her face. She's stroking his head and has a look of pure love on her face as she takes in my sleeping son. I get choked up again, because I have dreamt of this day since I found out I was pregnant with him. It also has me thinking of what Dante will be like. It almost makes me want to run to the other cabin and drag him here, but I know I need a little more time.

"He's perfect, Len. I love him so much. What did you

name him?" she asks me.

"Marcus Anthony De Luca," I quietly tell her.

She stands, picks him up and walks over to the rocking chair in the corner. She rocks him and sings the same lullaby that she used to sing to me when I would sleep with her or when she would just hold me. I cross the room and sit on the couch and silently cry as I watch them together. I missed her, and my family, but this makes it so much worse.

"He looks just like his daddy. What color are his eyes?" she asks after about twenty minutes of just rocking and staring at him. He hasn't woken up yet.

"Right now, they're blue, and I'm hoping they stay that way since that's the only thing he seems to have inherited from me so far." I glance at him and know that if people went just by looks they would swear I wasn't his mom.

"I'm not going to ask you what happened just yet. We'll have time to get into that later. I want to know how you're doing, Len. I missed you, but I knew you would be okay because you're a very strong woman," she unsteadily tells me. I know my kidnapping was hard on everyone, but I really am scared to tell her everything.

"I'm having nightmares about what I had to do to get us out of there. I know I'm going to need help when I get back home. I'm also scared that Dante isn't going to want to be with me anymore. Who wants someone who's damaged?" I choke out.

"Len, you need to stop living your life as if you have baggage and start living it as the survivor you are. I don't know the trouble you had to endure, but I know that you are stronger than this. Also, Dante not wanting you . . . Len, you have no idea how torn up he's been. Len, he was going to ask you to marry him that night. Neil and Dante have been sleeping at your house since the night you went missing. They have studied files and poured over every tip that has come in trying to find you. If that doesn't tell you how much you're wanted, sweetie, I don't know what will." Her voice is firm and stern when she speaks to me.

They slept in my house? I don't know how to take that.

The knock on the door shakes my thought process, and I stand up. I go to the back door. I push it open and see Ms. Cindy standing there with a troubled expression on her face. I look behind her, but don't see anyone there.

"What's wrong?" I ask her, fear evident in my voice.

"I had a visitor looking for May. I figured she was here since she wasn't at her fishing spot, or at my house. I told them she was hunting for mushrooms. It was one of the gentlemen that came with your pops and brother the other night to check in. I don't know his name." She peeks over my shoulder.

I turn and OPG walks towards us with Marcus bundled up against the night chill. She goes outside and stands in front of Ms. Cindy. They're talking so quietly that I can't make out what they're saying. I strain to hear what they are saying, but only catch a word here and there.

Marcus lets out a cry, and I step outside towards him. I glance down and he seems to be okay. OPG starts to bounce him, and I wonder if he's hungry. Just as I was about to take him from her, I hear something coming from the edge of the yard, where it meets the wooded area and realize it's a voice I wasn't ready to hear. Fear consumes me and I snap my head at the sound of my name.

"Len!" Dante roars as he runs towards me, and I know

immediately that he was the visitor that Ms. Cindy was talking about. Before I can do anything else, he lifts me up by my thighs, wrapping my legs around his waist, so he can hold me tightly in his arms. I hear him take a deep breath. There's wetness seeping into my shirt, and I realize that he's crying. I've never witnessed Dante breaking down before, and it overwhelms me to the point that I need to get as close as I can to him.

I wrap my arms around him, shoving my face into his neck and cling to him. I sob while taking a deep breath of his scent that I have missed so much. The fear I felt a moment ago at his presence slowly fades away, and the feeling of being completely safe replaces it. I have always felt this way in his arms and know, without a shadow of a doubt, that I never want to leave them again. I haven't felt this since the night I was taken and I was scared I wouldn't ever experience it again.

"Len, I never gave up hope of seeing you again. Why didn't you call me when you got out? Why did you hide from me?" he cries into my neck.

"I c . . . couldn't. I had t . . . to keep everyone s . . . safe," I sputtered out between sobs.

"I'll keep you both safe. Never doubt that again," he growls and then looks up.

"God, *mio tutto*, I have missed you so much. I love you and never want you or our son out of my sight again. But before we get into all that tell me about my boy," he whispers and turns towards Marcus, who is still in OPG's arms.

"OPG, bring my son to me, please. I'd like to meet him," he asks while sitting me down.

"I'm going to leave the three of you to work through

things. If you need me, I'll be staying with Cindy tonight. I'll let everyone know that I saw you walking and that you will be back later." She gently lays Marcus in Dante's arms.

"Talk to him, Len. Tell him everything," she murmurs in my ear, kisses my head and walks away.

I turn back and watch Dante with our son. My heart aches as I see my strong alpha man break down once again at seeing him for the first time. He slowly turns and makes his way into the living room, taking a seat on the couch. He glances up and smiles at me.

"Come sit with us, Mamma."

I take a deep breath trying to control the emotions that are trying to consume me. I slowly make my way to his side and sit down next to them.

"Daddy, meet your son, Marcus Anthony De Luca," I whisper to him.

He snaps his head up and a slow grin crosses his face. He glances down again and in a voice so gentle that I almost don't hear it, whispers, "I love you so much, Marcus. Your mamma and you are my world. I'll stop at nothing to make sure you're both protected from this moment on." He glances at me, tears in his eyes. "Tell me about my son."

And right then, I fell even deeper in love with Dante.

Twenty-One

DANTE

I WATCH AS LEN BREASTFEEDS Marcus and think what beautiful sight they make; I still can't believe that she's right here in front of me. It amazes me how much my son looks just like I did as a baby, but with Len's eye color. I pray that he keeps the blue.

I think back on the phone call and the emotions I felt when I discovered the results of the paternity test. Regardless of those results, I knew I loved him the instant I discovered Len gave birth to him. She was mine, and so was he.

Staring out the window, thinking of where my family could be, is torture. We know that Len was there and that it was under a different name. I try to think about what happened and how she managed to get out. I also pray that she isn't still being held by him. The longer they're both missing, the more I'm worried that he has them still.

The phone ringing pulls me out of my thoughts.

"De Luca."

"Mr. De Luca, this is Detective Walters. I'm calling about the results from the DNA test. Do you have a moment?"

"Absolutely. Do you need me to come in or do you want to meet here?" I ask him, hoping he'd be okay with doing it over the phone.

"It's up to you. However, I can give you the results over the phone and have the papers faxed over, if that's alright?"

"Yes, that's perfectly okay." I take a deep breath and wait anxiously for him to start speaking again.

"It's a ninety-nine point nine percent chance that you are the father of the child that's in question," he reads off the results.

"Thank God! Can you rush those papers over as fast as you can? Also, where does that leave everything once Len and my son are found?" I breathe out a sigh of relief knowing I'm indeed the father to Len's baby. It wouldn't have mattered if I wasn't because any baby from her I would consider mine. However, if I wasn't the father, then the realization that his other family could demand to be part of the baby's life hit me. A problem I wasn't sure how Len would deal with.

"Well, after we question her then she's free to go. Depending on what happened, she might need some counseling."

"Thanks for the update and for the information."

"No problem."

I lean back, close my eyes, and think about the news I just received. A sense of love so strong blooms from me that, at first, I don't understand it. I've yet to meet my son, but my love for him is there. I never thought I could love anyone as much as I love Len, but I was wrong. The love I have for him is indescribable. It's a different kind of love, and it overwhelms me.

In that moment, I understood the worry and fear that my parents felt when I couldn't contact them on missions. The thought that I might never get to hold him or show him the love I feel haunts me. It's then that I vow to be the best father I can be. I'll protect him and his mom from everything that I humanly can.

There'll never be a day after they are finally in my arms that they don't know the love I have for them. It's with that thought that I turn back to my desk and start digging into the files.

I hear a burp and a giggle which makes me turn and look over at the bed. Len gently places Marcus down in his basinet. I was so lost in thought I didn't realize she was done feeding him and was putting him down for the night. I take a deep breath, knowing it's time for the talk I'm dreading.

"Len, *mio tutto*, I need to know everything. Are you ready to talk?" I carefully ask her.

"No, I'm not ready," she whispers and walks into the bathroom, closing the door.

I sit back and give her a few minutes to pull herself together. After a few moments, she walks back out and I see the circles under her eyes. It causes a slice of pain in my heart knowing she's tired and has been taking care of Marcus on her own.

"We need to talk, but we can do that in the morning.

Just know that I'll always keep you safe from now on, and he isn't going to take you again. Let's get dressed and get to bed. We need some sleep before Marcus wakes up." The firmness in my voice leaves no room for argument.

Just as we walk back into the room, Marcus starts stirring and whimpering. I look over at Len as she walks over to the basinet and picks him up.

"Welcome to fatherhood, Daddy. I think your son needs changing." Smirking at me, she hands me my son and walks over to where the diapers are.

"Well, there's no time like the present to learn. However, grade me on a curve, will you? I've never done this shit before," I say out loud to both of them and start to undress him. The smell of his dirty diaper hits me, and I realize it's going to be a hell of a long night.

Len

I slowly awake to the sound of a small whimper and soft whispers. Smiling slightly, I peek open one eye and see Dante on the couch changing our son. I swoon a little at the sight of him taking care of him. I strain my ears trying to catch what he's saying, and what I hear, makes tears come to my eyes.

"Little man, I have so much to teach you. I still can't believe I'm your daddy. I love you so much, and I'm sorry I wasn't there while you were in your mamma or for your birth. However, I promise to be here from this day forward. Your mamma is the best woman there is, and we'll have to team up to make sure nobody hurts her again. Women are meant to be treasured at all times." He smiles at our son when he makes a gurgling sound. I know at any minute Marcus is going to want to feed, but I don't want to interrupt their male bonding time.

"It's almost football season which means it's time to teach you which team is the best. We both know it's the Seahawks, but I know if your mamma and her family have any say, they will tell you it's the Chiefs. Don't listen to that nonsense. You will see that blue and green is the way to go." Dante chuckles.

"Red and gold, baby boy. Don't listen to your father, he really is delusional. Everyone knows the Chiefs have the loudest and the best fans in the world. Nobody wants to say they are sea chicken fans," I speak up, defending my team and setting Dante straight. At the sound of my voice, Marcus starts crying out which causes my breast to tighten up.

"Oh, I see how it is, son. Mamma wakes up, and now I'm no longer needed. I don't blame you though, I would want her too." Dante smiles at me and brings our son over. "We need to get you two to the doctor to get you checked out."

"I already saw the doctor. I went yesterday, and we both are fine. If you want to see the paperwork I hid it in the kitchen drawer," I tell him.

"We'll make sure to bring it with us when we go home. I still would like it if you could be seen by your doctor there. I'm going to go over to Ms. Cindy's cabin and ask them to watch Marcus for us this morning. I'm also going to go and talk to Lucky and get him to come over. Len, we need to talk about everything," he quietly tells me as he sits down and rubs my back.

"Okay," I whisper, because what else am I going to say? I don't want to do this, but I know it's going to have to happen.

"I'll be back soon, and we'll get this fixed. I love you, Len. One more time." He kisses my head and bends down to kiss Marcus before he walks out the door.

Staring down at my son, I realize that we have a long road ahead of us. I just hope that everything turns out for the better.

Just as I'm finishing up my cleaning, I hear a tap on the door and it opens. I look over as I watch OPG and Ms. Cindy walk in.

"Hey, Len, Dante came over and asked us to get Marcus. I'm proud of you for wanting to get this over with and taken care of. You need to come home and back to your life. Running won't help," OPG firmly tells me after she gives me a huge hug while Ms. Cindy is packing a bag for Marcus.

"I know. I'm just scared of how they are going to react to this. I'm scared that he's still out there, and once they know everything I'm even more afraid that they'll find him and kill him. I don't want them in prison." I start breaking down at the thought of them in jail.

"Len, you can't control what the future holds. Are they going to be upset with what happened to you? Yes. Are they going to protect you and Marcus? You know they'll do anything to make sure you're both safe. Are they going to kill him? You have no control over their actions. You do control your actions and keeping anything from them that will keep you safe is wrong," she whispers in my ear while patting my back. "Now, get your face dried up and get your ass in gear for them to come see you. I have a feeling Neil's going to go nuts when he sees his sister."

"Okay, let me kiss Marcus goodbye. He just ate thirty minutes ago, so he should be alright."

After making sure they had everything they needed for him, I give him a kiss and hug them both, thanking them for watching him for me. I watch as they walk over towards the other cabin. I go into the bathroom to wash my face and decide that I need to grab a cup of coffee so I can sit on the back deck while Dante goes to get Neil.

Twenty-Two

DANTE

AFTER I TALKED WITH MS. Cindy and OPG, I went back to the cabin to find it empty. I found a note on the counter telling me they went to breakfast in town. I decide to jump in the shower really quick before they return. I'm trying to figure out how to get Lucky away without the others wanting to join us. I'm also trying to think of what I'm going to tell the others as to why I didn't come back last night.

I'm brought out of my musing when I hear car doors. I rush through getting dressed and head down the stairs.

"Where the hell you been, Ghost?" Eagle barks out.

"I ended up walking through the woods and then fell asleep," I say vaguely. "Where's Lucky?"

"Outside with Pops talking about what we're doing today. I think we're going to be meeting up on the deck with files to go over things since Ms. May isn't here to talk us into something else," Doc announces as he walks into the house.

I nod at him and then walk out the front door. I see

Lucky and Pops in a deep conversation which stops when they spot me.

"Where were you last night?" Lucky asks me, cocking his head. "OPG came and said she saw you walking around and that she was going to stay with Ms. Cindy. We figured you would be back, but when we checked the bed it was never slept in."

"Had a lot of thinking to do. Want to go for a walk and figure out what we're going to do next? We need to work out a plan."

"Okay . . ." he murmurs and looks at me trying to figure out what's up. He knows me and knows that I'm hinting something's going on that requires just the two of us.

We turn and head towards the woods. Once we're a good distance away from the cabin, and I make sure we weren't followed because the guys will follow if they know something's up. I find a log on the ground and plop down. Lucky sits down on a stump in front of me and leans towards me, waiting for me to speak.

"I need you to keep your head on, brother, and hear me out before you take off on a run or demand answers." I look him dead in the eye.

"What the fuck did you find out from OPG? Eagle told me you went to talk to her."

"She didn't tell me anything. I kind of fell into this information from following Ms. Cindy."

"What do you mean you fell into this information, and why the fuck were you following Ms. Cindy?" He cocks his head with a confused look on his face.

"Just promise me that you'll wait until I tell everything before you freak the fuck out." At his nod, I continue and explain about me following Ms. Cindy.

"So, OPG was with someone in the other cabin? Who the fuck was she with?" he asks me. Ever since OPG got sick, we all have become really protective of her.

"When I saw who it was, I ran up to the cabin and ended up staying there all night until this morning," I whisper out because my emotions are getting the best of me that I found my woman and child.

"Would you just fucking tell me already," he growls out getting impatient with me.

"Len and my boy," I choke out, and a tear falls from my eye.

I watch him as he takes in what I just said. I see the emotions go through him at knowing his sister and nephew are, not only safe, but so very close. Once it fully sinks in, he turns to go towards the cabin. I jump up and grab him to stop him.

"Stop. We have to talk about this and work out a plan. You need to know she's scared. She knows he's still out there, and she's scared he's going to come for her. Right now, Marcus is with OPG and Ms. Cindy. Len knows I'm bringing you back, so you need to work through your emotions before we face her."

"She knows I'd fucking protect her! Her not coming to me pisses me the fuck off. What in the hell was she thinking?" He starts to pace in front of me, and I watch as something I said sinks in. His face changes from anger to disbelief.

"Wait . . . Marcus? My nephew's name is Marcus?" he whispers out my son's name.

"Marcus Anthony De Luca. She explained she wanted to

keep the tradition that your family has with the Chief players. Marcus Allen for the first name and Anthony after both dads. Lucky, he looks just like me, but with Len's eyes. He's perfect."

The pain of missing his birth and the first six weeks of his life hits me hard and makes me drop to my knees. I can count on one hand how many times I've broken down like this, and the last time it happened was the day she was taken.

I should be angry that Len kept him from me all this time, but I can't bring myself to direct that at her. I agree she should've known we'd do anything to protect her, however, that asshole did get her on our watch.

I feel Lucky drop down beside me, and I wonder what he's thinking seeing his friend like this. I feel his arms wrap around my shoulders, and he hugs me while I try to pull myself together.

He drops down beside me and grabs me in a hug.

"Okay, brother, let's get our shit together. I need to see my sister and nephew," he demands, but looking at him, I see he has tears running down his face too.

After a few moments, we pull ourselves together and start towards the other cabin. We approach the backyard, and I see she's sitting there, looking off towards the water. The way the light is shining on her makes her look like an angel. I smile so big, because I'm so happy that I have found my family.

I step on a twig which breaks and alerts her that we're here. She snaps her head toward us, and I see her stiffen. She puts down her mug and slowly starts to walk towards us. Once she gets down the few steps, she begins running towards us. Lucky rushes towards her and opens his arms just in time to catch her when she jumps at him. He holds her tightly to him as he whispers to her and rubs her back.

Seeing this just makes me want to kill the fucker that took her. I shouldn't have to witness a brother and sister seeing each other for the first time after a kidnapping. I shouldn't have to witness the emotion that's pouring from them from the knowledge that she's alive. It pisses me off so bad and makes me want to find him to take out the rage that's coursing through me.

Off to the side, I quietly deal with the anger. I don't want to break their reunion up, but I know we need to get inside before someone sees us. I also know that we need to get the story from her. I don't want to hear what happened, but we need to know as much as we can to protect Len and Marcus. There is no way in hell I'll let that fucker near them again. Even if it means I take his life with my bare hands.

Len

Ten minutes earlier...

I'm watching the waves come up on the shore, and I think about what's about to happen. I'm not looking forward to telling them about my months in captivity. I know my brother and know he will want to go and kill the bastard. Even though he didn't rape me, nor did he physically hurt me, he still did a lot of mental abuse. I know I'm going to have to go through some sort of counseling when I get home.

I'm brought back to the present at the sound of a twig breaking, which makes my head snap towards the sound. My breath catches in my throat at the sight of Dante and Neil. I slowly stand, set my mug down, and start heading towards them. The moment my feet hit the grass, I take off at a sprint towards Neil and see him rushing towards me.

The emotions etched on his face are pure joy, mixed with disbelief. Right before I get to him, he opens his arms, and I jump into them. The moment his arms come around me and hold me tight, I start sobbing into his neck. I can't believe my brother is here and holding me. I often dreamt of this moment, but was too scared to really hope, just in case I didn't get to see him.

"Squirt." Hearing my nickname from my brother makes me cry even harder.

"I was so worried and scared. I didn't think I would ever hold you like this again. I never thought I would get another day to tell you how much I love you. I missed you so much!" Neil chokes out while holding me. I feel his tears soaking my shoulder as he continues to tell me how much I mean to him.

I can't talk. My emotions are crazy. It also doesn't help that my hormone levels are still unbalanced after my pregnancy. At that thought, it reminds me that he knows he's an uncle.

"You're an uncle."

"I know," he sobs out in my neck, squeezing me even tighter.

"Hey, you two, let's get inside. We don't want to chance everyone seeing us just yet." Dante steps up and starts to reach for me like he's going to take me from Neil.

"No, you got all night with her. Fuck off, Ghost, I just got my sister. I'm not ready to let her go just yet," he growls out and walks off with me still in his arms.

"Fuck me. You're not going to leave our house anytime soon when we get back, are you," he states rather than questions.

"Nope."

I giggle at my brother's response. It's a good thing we have a big house, because I have a feeling a lot of people aren't going to want to leave.

I'm placed on the couch and Dante plops next to me. Faster than I can realize, I'm picked up and in his lap, which makes my brother crack up with laughter as he takes a step back. I just shake my head and lay it on his shoulder.

"Now, let's get to the bottom of something Len. Why in the fuck did you not contact us when you got out? Do you know how much worry you not only put on our parents, but the rest of us? What part of security and Seals do you not understand?" Neil screams the last question at me.

I knew this was coming. I'm not proud of myself for staying away for so long. I know I worried everyone, but they need to understand that I thought I was doing them a favor by hiding so Steven wouldn't hurt them.

"Neil, at first I needed time to process everything. I was only going to stay away a week, but I saw he was still alive. I kept flashing back to what I saw in the picture, the one he sent to my house. I thought if I stayed away he wouldn't harm you guys . . ." is all I'm able to get out before Neil starts yelling again.

"You were worried about us being harmed? Do you not remember what our jobs were in the Navy? Len, that's the most fucked up thing I've ever heard you say!"

Dante holds me tighter to his chest, and I worry for a brief moment he's going to start yelling at me too. I squirm and finally get loose of his hold. Jumping up quickly, I rush over to Neil and get right into his space.

"Look, I know it was stupid, okay! But I didn't know what else to do, Neil! I couldn't let him harm my family. If it meant staying away until he was caught, then I would have done that. You don't have to yell at me, I already feel bad enough, and I will have to deal with keeping, not only my family from my son for six weeks, but his father from him as well! So, please j . . . just stop." I can't hold back the sob that comes through at the end of my rant.

Neil's arms come around me, and he holds me to him.

"Don't do that shit again, Squirt. You're everything to me and the family. We were without you for over nine months. The thoughts . . ." he takes a deep breath and continues. "Protection and security is our job. Let us do our job now to make sure Adams is caught."

I nod and finally let him go. I go back to Dante and crawl into his lap.

"Why didn't you yell at me?" I ask him.

"Oh, trust me, it was coming. Right now, I'm just glad you're safe. Since Neil just took care of it. I don't think I need to say anything more." He turns his head towards Neil. "Don't yell at her like that again. I understand your emotions were running high, but I don't appreciate the way you were talking to her. Brother or not, I will knock you on your ass if you do it again."

Neil rolls his eyes and goes to the fridge in the kitchen.

"Okay, Squirt, let's have it. We need to know everything you can tell us. I know you don't want to talk about it, but we need to know it all. This will help us in finding him so we can keep Marcus and you safe," Neil states as he walks in with three bottles of water, a notepad, and a pen. He hands Dante and me a bottle of water, then sits on the chair across from us.

Taking a deep breath, I tell them everything. I start with the night of the party and then describe the house. When I tell them about how he drugged me, I feel Dante tense under me. I knew this was going to be hard, on them and on me.

"Tell us about the wedding," Neil murmurs, which makes Dante growl.

"The reason I agreed to marry him was because I knew I was pregnant. He wanted to give me an abortion, but I made a deal with him that I would marry him if he let me keep the baby. He agreed, only if after the baby was born, I'd allow him to take Marcus to the hospital with him. He was supposed to tell them that he found the baby somewhere and brought him in to be checked out." I take a deep breath and close my eyes at the emotions on Dante's face.

"The next day, there was a man I'd never seen before with papers that had my fake name on them. He didn't perform anything really, just said you both ready and waited for our answers. He then had us sign the papers and gave them to Steven, which he was supposed to file with the city. I don't remember much about the guy, but if I see his picture, I can identify him," I explain in a whisper.

"He did file, but never told anyone that he was married until the day, I'm assuming, you went into labor. He called the hospital that day and said that his wife was very sick so he couldn't come into work," Dante tells me.

Silence descends over us as I take in his words. I honestly thought he would mention getting married to someone before then, but I guess it would have brought up too many questions.

"You know; the marriage isn't legal. You're not his wife, Len. Since it wasn't in your real name, it isn't legal," Dante whispers into my ear.

I nod, but it still felt real.

"Did you notice any habits that he had?" Neil murmurs as he writes things down on the pad.

"Honestly, when we were in the room together, we were eating or watching TV. There was really not a lot of talking that happened. I did notice the more I rubbed my belly as I got bigger, the madder he would get. Oh, I found a bag with money and two passports." I get up, grab the bag, and hand it to Neil.

"This might help. Was there anything else in the bag?" he asks as he opens it.

"I don't know because I didn't look through it really. Oh, and his car is in the shed in the back." I grab the keys out of the drawer in the kitchen and hand them over, too.

"Okay, we'll check it out in a bit. Tell us everything else," Dante gently says as he grabs my wrist and pulls me into his lap. Taking a deep breath, I start from the wedding and go from there.

After telling them everything, I'm exhausted and emotionally drained. I had to stop several times to gather my thoughts and explain the situation.

I glance up and see it has been about three hours since we started. My breasts are heavy with milk so I know Marcus should be returning soon. I turn towards Dante and Neil who are sitting at the table and looking over the notes they'd taken.

Just as I'm getting ready to let them know I'm going to

Ms. Cindy's, there's a knock on the door. I peek out the window and see OPG there holding Marcus. I wave them in.

"He's fussy. I'm assuming it's feeding time."

"My breasts hurt so I know it's time," I tell her as I reach my arms out for Marcus.

I sit on the bed, scooting up to the headboard so I can lean back. After getting Marcus settled into position, I start to raise my shirt, and I'm startled at the sound of a grunt and footsteps. I turn towards the sound and see Neil heading to the back porch.

"I can't sit here and watch you pull your breast out, Squirt," he grumbles out. "No man should see his sister's breast. Feeding a child or not."

"Sorry. I'm just used to it being me. I'll cover myself. You don't have to leave." I giggle and grab a blanket to cover up.

He turns around, sees I'm covered, and ends up going back over to Dante who is laughing hard at the situation. OPG's trying hard to hold in her chuckles but she's failing.

"Be happy it's me and not our friends, fucker!" he grumbles again, but at Dante.

This stops Dante in his tracks. He turns and gives me a glare. I start snickering because I know what he's going to say before he even opens his mouth.

"I know, I know. These are your breasts, and if I'm going to feed Marcus I need to make sure I'm covered. Got the glare loud and clear, caveman." I roll my eyes at him.

"Damn fucking right! You won't be sharing that view with fucking nobody. I don't care how natural it's supposed to be. I won't have those perverted asses seeing my woman's tits," he growls.

"Shut the fuck up, Ghost! Or I'm going to fuck your shit up!" Neil yells out which causes OPG and me to laugh even harder.

Dante and Neil turn back to what they were doing, and I gaze down at Marcus. I say a quick little prayer that Dante and Neil can find Steven so we can be safe again.

I finish up Marcus's feeding, cover up, and burp him. It's then that I notice it's quiet. I turn towards the boys, and I see Neil in tears staring at me. I get choked up at seeing tears in my brother's eyes.

"I didn't think I'd ever get to see this, Squirt. You're going to be an amazing mother," he whispers. "Can Uncle Neil meet his little man?"

I walk over and hand Marcus to him.

"Marcus, this is your uncle," I choke out.

I stand there and watch my brother bond with his nephew. I feel Dante behind me, and he wraps his arms around me from behind, placing his chin on top of my head. We stand there and watch my brother as he stars at Marcus. His face shows the excitement of finally being an uncle, and the love that he feels for him, shines from his smile. Before the guilt of not going to them right after I escaped can consume me again, I hear my brother speak at Marcus.

"Your grandparents are going to flip when they meet you. Speaking of which, I think we need to let everyone know you're here. We're staying for another week at least. Letting everyone know you're here will be good so they can help keep an eye out. We don't know if Adams knows your both here," Neil states, not taking his eyes off our son.

"I agree. Did you ever tell him about the lake, Len?" OPG pipes up from behind us.

"No, I never spoke about you guys when I was there. I kept that part just in my head. I used to have dreams of us here to help keep me going during the day. I'm sure I didn't . . . Fuck!" I scream out and spin around to look up at Dante.

"What?"

"I might've mentioned it in school. Actually, I know for a fact I did because I was telling everyone about the family trip we were planning the year before I started my residency. If he remembers that . . . God, Dante what if he remembers?"

Dread courses through my body at the thought that he might be able to find us after all.

"Listen to me, Len, nobody will take Marcus or you from me again. Do you understand? I'll fucking kill anyone who tries. You're not going anywhere, so get that fucking thought out of your head. You're not to be left alone until he's found. Let's get a bag together and head to the other cabin," Dante says, holding me close.

I nod against his chest and try to relax. Just when I'm almost calm, it dawns on me that I'm about to see the rest of my family again. I hope they give me time before they'll want to know what happened to me, because I don't know if I can retell that story again.

Twenty-Three

DANTE

I SUGGESTED OPG AND NEIL take Marcus and head over to Ms. Cindy's until we get everything together. We're just about finished packing when Len states she's going to get a shower in now because it isn't often that she can take a shower without having to hurry because of Marcus.

The water turns on, and I immediately go hard at the thought of her in the shower. I can't stop myself from thinking of all the things I want to do to her. The image of her washing her body has me snapping and making the choice to go and join her in.

I stalk towards the bathroom door, pulling off my clothes as I go. Opening the door, her silhouette greets me through the curtain. I notice it isn't a big shower, but it'll do. I can't wait to get her back home and in our shower.

I make noise so she isn't startled, push back the curtain, and she jerks around to face me. I give her a cocky smirk and let my eyes trail down her body as I grab my cock.

"Dante, what are you doing?" Her breasts heave as she asks, which makes me focus on them. Her nipples tighten, and I grin knowing that I'm affecting her.

"I need you, Len. It has been over nine months since I had you. Now step back, *mio tutto*, we're getting ready to get reacquainted with each other," I growl as I step into the shower, jerking my cock.

I crowd up against her still stroking myself. With my other hand, I reach up, grab her hair, and pull until her face if looking up at me. I stare into her eyes, gauging her reaction. Her eyes are dilated and her breathing is starting to pick up even more. I don't see any fear or panic coming from her. I take a moment to figure out what step I'm going to take now.

"Fuck, Len, I want you badly, but I also need to taste you. Be a good girl and lean against the wall for me. Put your hands on the bar above your head, and don't let go. You let go, and I won't let you come, you understand?" I demand and let go of my cock.

She slowly raises her hands above her head and grabs hold of the bar. I pull her hair to the side making her head tilt giving me a view of her amazing neck. I lean down and bite down hard enough to leave my mark on her which causes her to cry out in pleasure, but it is muffled. I glance up, her eyes are closed and she's biting her lips to help keep her noises in. I kiss my way up her neck to her ear.

"You don't have to be quiet, *mio tutto*. I want to hear you scream for me," I whisper in her ear and smile against it when I feel her shiver from my breath. I pull my head away from her neck and look down at her face. She opens her eyes and grins at me. Oh, this is going to be fun.

I slowly make my way down to her nipples, kissing and nipping as I go. I lick each nipple to ease the sting that I cause on her skin. I gently graze my teeth across the peeks and get a slightly sweet flavor on my tongue. She hisses, and I jerk back to look at her.

"They're sensitive. I'm still trying to get used to nursing." She blushes and looks away.

"Len, look at me. It's okay I'll be easier with your breast. I'll say I'm loving the fact that they're bigger." I smirk, lean down, and kiss the top of her breast. "Also, your milk's sweet so I now understand why Marcus is such a pig when it comes to feeding time."

She bursts out laughing at that comment. I start to kiss down between her breasts when she stops me.

"Dante, you don't have to do that. I really am all right with just making love," she tells me. Her voice has a tremble in it, and I realize it isn't from what I'm doing to her.

"What's wrong?" I'm starting to get concerned that something more happened then what she told us.

"Dante, calm down. I just don't look the same as I did before Marcus. I have stretch marks, and I have baby fat still from the pregnancy," she whispers the end to me and looks away.

I take a deep breath and frame her face with both hands forcing her head to turn towards me. She has her eyes closed, which pisses me off. "Open your eyes," I growl harshly at her which causes her to snap her eyes open.

"I want you to listen to me, Len, and listen well," I demand, looking directly into her eyes. She nods.

"I don't know why you think having stretch marks or as you called it *baby fat* is a bad thing. I don't find that shit bad at all. If anything, I find it even sexier because I know you got that from carrying my baby in your belly." I drop down to my knees and kiss her marks and look up into her eyes.

"When I see these marks, I see the love that created them. I feel admiration for you because of your strength and willingness to endure the pain, agony, and struggles that created life. I believe they are marks of honor that our son gave you. I love that you have them, and I cherish them," I tell her as I kiss each one I come to.

I gaze up into her eyes and see she isn't really believing what I'm saying. I take a moment to reword what I just said hoping it will get my point across.

"I look at these marks as love marks because you got them from giving our child life. Len, these are the most precious marks on your body to me because my son created them. I truly can't wait to see more form on your body due to the other babies you will give me in the future," I gently whisper against them.

I look back up into her eyes and see tears streaming down her face. She grabs my face, pulls me up to hers and leans her forehead against mine.

"I love you so much, Dante. One more time," she whispers against my lips.

"TI'mo, Len. Un'altra volta," I whisper back to her before I crash my lips against hers and deepen the kiss.

I forget all about tasting her, and the overwhelming need I have for her takes over as I pick her up and slam her against the wall. I reach down, test her wetness, and line my cock up against her pussy and surge into her in one hard thrust.

I groan in pleasure as she cries out against my lips at the

invasion of my cock entering her. She's tight as hell so I hold still while she adjusts to me.

"Fuck, Len, you feel fucking amazing," I murmur against her lips, trying to hold off from taking her hard.

I start to feel her relax a little which makes my cock jerk more. I pull out and slam into her again which makes her bite my neck to contain her cries of pleasure. That move alone makes me even harder and brings out my dominate nature.

"Grab the bar and hang on, *mio tutto*," I roughly tell her and wait until she obeys me. "Remember, you can't come until I tell you to."

She nods and grabs the bar. I grip her hips hard enough to leave my finger prints on them and pull almost all the way out. I thrust hard inside her and feel her jerk at the impact.

I feel her starting to tighten as I'm thrusting and it makes me pull out of her. She whimpers at the loss which causes me to smirk and put her legs down.

"I felt you getting close and I haven't tasted you yet, baby. You can't come until I taste your sweetness on my lips." I drop down and throw her legs over my shoulders.

I look at her lips and see they are swollen and pink from my thrust. My mouth waters as her smell reaches my nose. I can't hold back once that scent hits me. I latch on and eat her like she's my last meal. Her flavor of sweet and slightly musky hits me, and I can't contain the moan of pleasure that comes out of me.

I feel her on the edge, and I need her to come in my mouth. "Give it to me, Len. Let me taste your pleasure." I go back to her clit and suck hard.

She moans out as her orgasm hits her, and I continue to

circle her clit slowing down to draw out her release. I can't hold back anymore so I stand and plunge back into her. I slam my mouth on hers and start thrusting hard and fast.

I feel her starting to tighten again, and I know she's getting ready to have another one. I go faster and deeper into her, wanting to come with her.

"Give me another one, Len. I want to come with you."

I lean back so I can watch myself move in and out of her. I slide my hand between us and start rubbing her clit. I feel my balls tighten, and lighting shooting through my spine. Right when I don't think I can hold off, I feel her tighten against my cock, so much that I can barely move. I groan her name and thrust as deep as I can while I unload inside of her.

I reach up with one hand and undo her grip on the bar. She lets go and wraps her arms around my neck. We hold each other tightly as we come down from our high. Finally, after a few minutes we relax and let each other go.

Without any words, we wash each other and hurry out of the shower before the hot water's gone.

I look over at her and smile seeing the satisfied look on my woman's face.

"What's that smirk for?" she shyly asks.

"I like seeing my woman satisfied because of what I did to her." I smile even bigger when I see her stumble from drying herself off.

I snatch her towel away from her and pull her into my arms. I kiss her deeply and hold her close. After I feel her relax and start kissing me back, I slowly break up the kiss.

"Let's get dressed, go get our son, and head to the cabin," I murmur against her lips.

Len

I nod my head at his suggestion and pull at the towel he took from me. I start thinking about what just happened as I dry myself off, and realize that we didn't use a condom. This makes me stop everything and turn towards him.

"Dante, did you wear a condom? I'm not on protection."

He jerks his head towards me and takes a deep breath. That's when I know he didn't think about it either.

"I don't think it's wise to get pregnant right now with Steven still out there. Plus, Marcus is only six weeks old." My hand goes to my chest as I try to calm my breathing. Steven is still out there!

"Len, calm down. I agree with holding off until Steven isn't a worry anymore. However, it doesn't matter how old Marcus is when you get pregnant. I'll be with you every step of the way." He walks up to me and wraps his arms around me. "I missed everything with Marcus, so the thought of you getting pregnant again with my baby makes me extremely happy."

"Dante, I want time between kids. I have a career that I don't want to give up. I don't want them too far apart, but I don't want them one right after another," I murmur out against his chest.

I feel him tense up when I mention my career. I hope he isn't about to tell me I won't be working because that isn't happening. I've always dreamed of being a doctor, and I won't give up that dream for anyone. Even though I'm a

243

mother now, that doesn't mean I have to give up my career. I'll probably work less because the thought of being away from Marcus or any future children for long hours just doesn't sit well with me.

"*Mio tutto*, you're still going to work?"

"Yes. I'm not giving that up. Don't ask that of me." I gaze up into his eyes hoping he understands what I'm trying to tell him.

"I don't like that, but I don't want to argue. Can we discuss it more when this mess with Steven is cleared up?"

With a nod I stand up on my tip toes and give him a quick peck on the lips.

"Come on, we need to get going." I walk out of the bathroom and go to get ready to see my family again.

Twenty-Four

DANTE

WE HEAD OVER TO THE cabin, and I try to control the rage that has been going through me since Len told us the story. I have a feeling that fucker wasn't going to take Marcus to the hospital after he was born. Len doing what she did saved not only her life but the life of our son. For that, I'll always be indebted to her, and I vow to make sure she knows daily just how much I adore, love, and need her.

An anger like no other starts to consume me, yet again. I feel a jerk on my arm and turn to see OPG giving me a look telling me to get it together.

I know she's right, because Len is going to need all the help she can get to control the family when they see Marcus and her. I nod and take a deep breath.

We decided that Neil and OPG will go get everyone together in the backyard. Len, Marcus, and I will be off to the side of the house until we hear Neil whistle the signal to step forward. I will be holding our son to ensure he isn't trampled in the rush to get to Len.

Stopping just shy of being in sight, I pull Len to my side and kiss her forehead. I try to give her as much of my strength as I can.

"You know you don't have to do this, right? We can just bring one family member at a time to the cabin," I whisper into her ear and feel her shiver. I smile knowing I have that effect on her.

"No, the sooner the better. Then, we can get more alone time maybe. Just be ready to . . ." She stops and looks at me with tears in her eyes. I know she was going to use the word 'kidnap' her.

"Don't worry, *mio tutto*, I'll pull a caveman and just throw your sexy ass over my shoulder. They can't stop me." I smile and wink trying to lighten the mood.

"Thanks," she whispers so softly I barely hear it.

At that moment, we hear a whistle and know it's time. I give her a hard peck on the lips and a small smile. With my hand on her back and the other cradling our son close, we walk around to the back of the house. I glance up and see the shock on all their faces. We stop shy of where they are.

"Hi," she sobs at the sight of our family, which breaks the trance they are all in.

Mom and Momma Connie rush to her and wrap her up in their arms, one on each side. That seems to snap Pops and Papa out of their thoughts causing them to go to them.

I turn to the guys, and they're standing there, trying to figure out how the fuck we were able to find her. I smile and nod my head at OPG when they shift their eyes over at me. It's then they notice the bundle in my arms and a huge smile breaks across their faces.

"My angel and my little man are home!" Sin calls out at the top of his lungs and starts making strides towards me. "Give me my baby boy. I need to see if he looks like me."

"Step the fuck back, asshole! No touching my boy!" Doc hollers and knocks him out of his way as he tries to get over to me. "Tell him, sugar, that I'm the daddy."

"Both of you better knock your shit off! Stop saying you're the daddy, or I'm going to kick your ass. Everyone knows that she prefers me since I'm the nice one." Eagle winks over towards Len who's laughing at their antics.

"All three of you are going to get your asses knocked the fuck out if you keep saying you slept with my woman. Marcus is the best looking baby in the world, which means he must take after a De Luca," I say with a huge cheesy grin on my face.

This makes everyone burst out laughing. I glance around and notice the twins are missing. Just when I'm getting ready to ask where the they are, I hear a car door. I turn back to Len and give her a huge smile because I know they are going to flip their shit. Currently, she's being smothered by the boys, but she gazes at me and grins.

We hear the twins arguing over who was going to drive the boat after lunch, which makes Pops chuckle, because we know he won't let anyone touch his boat. I see the small twitch on Len's lips and tears starting to flow even more down her face. She turns towards their voice and waits for them to come into view. I know the moment they do because she falls to her knees and gives out a cry at seeing them in person. They've always been close.

They stop in their place and turn trying to find who made that sound. I watch their faces when they spot me with a bundle in my arms. Confusion is on their faces and they tilt their heads. I nod my head towards Len, and they follow the movement.

They stare for a second trying to figure out what they are seeing. Disbelief and then relief crosses both of their faces once they realize it's Len. They both rush towards her. Once they reach her, they lift her, and squish her between them. I can hear the cries from all three coming from their circle.

We all just sit and watch while they hold each other. This makes me wonder how her girls are going to react when they see her. I'm thinking that's going to be a hell of a reunion. I'm going to have to make sure we do it at the parents' houses, because then Marcus doesn't have to hear the squeals and cries coming from the girls.

Right at that moment, Marcus decides he isn't happy, so he lets out a cry. I gaze down at him and start bouncing and shushing him. I get a nasty smell from him, and I know it's time for a diaper change. I turn to head into the house when I'm blocked in by the Mom's and Dad's.

"Hand my grandson over and nobody gets hurt," Pops demands with his hands out.

"No! Grandma's first!" My mom steps in front of Pops.

I shake my head at the four of them arguing. Since they aren't paying attention to me anymore, I end up sneaking around them and heading into the house. I hurry up to my bedroom thinking I'm free and clear.

I try to shut the door and end up seeing that I was indeed followed. By five grown fucking adult men who have sappy smiles on their faces. I just shake my head again and walk over to the bed preparing to change him. I wonder which ones will stay once the smell hits the room.

"So, you going to tell us his name?" Eagle pops out while he takes a seat on the side of them bed.

"Marcus Anthony De Luca," I say with pride ringing through my words.

"Let me guess . . . Marcus is a famous Chief's player," Carlo states instead of asks.

"Yep! Then, Anthony is named after the Dads. He has Len's eyes, but the rest is all me!" I proudly proclaim as I start to change him.

"Fuck, that shit stinks. What they hell are you feeding him? Isn't he on breast milk or some shit like that?" Sin states and walks over to the window to open it.

"Yes, dumbass, he's on breast milk. Anyway, are the parent's still fighting?" I ask him as I finish cleaning him up.

"Sounds like it. Lucky and Len are just watching off on the side shaking their heads at them. I wonder how long it will take them to notice we left," he murmurs while he watches them from above which makes all of us chuckle because we can just imagine how it's going to be when they see we left the area.

After about twenty minutes of me fending off the boys who are demanding to hold their nephew, we hear footsteps on the stairs leading to the bedrooms.

"About time you four stopped fighting and came meet your grandson," I hassle them as they walk into the room I'm currently in.

"Whatever. Hand my grandson over. Also, would someone tell us his name for God sake?" Momma Connie holds out her hands.

Pops comes up next to her, wraps his arms around both of them and they take in their grandson. I turn towards Len who has tears streaming down her face. I open my arms and wave her over to me, which she gladly comes over.

"Why don't you tell them what you named him, *mio tutto*?" I whisper in her ear as I pull her down on to my lap.

"I decided to follow tradition, Pops, so I named him Marcus, after Marcus Allen. Anthony is his middle name after you and Dante's dad. De Luca is of course his last name," she explains.

"Thank you," her dad says, looking down at his grandson.

I hear a sniffle and spot my dad wiping away tears. I glance down at Len and smile. I give her a small peck on the lips and lean back on the headboard, taking her with me. We sit and watch as our family gets to know our newest family member.

Twenty-Five

Len

I AWAKE SLOWLY FROM MY nap. We were so emotionally drained after the morning's activities that we needed to rest. I find that I take naps more often than I did when I worked at the hospital. I know it's because my body is trying to adjust to being a mom and getting a balance on my hormones too.

Turning over, I notice Dante is still out of it. He didn't get much sleep last night between Marcus and my nightmares. I decide to let him get more rest. I just need to figure out how to get out of the bed since he has me locked tight in his arms and legs.

I glance over to the small basinet that Ms. Cindy had gotten for me and notice that it's empty. I start to panic, but then stop, because I'm sure that one of our family members probably snuck in and took Marcus out of the room.

Wiggling out of Dante's arms, I'm almost free when he tightens his arms and squeezes me into him. I feel his lips on my neck, and I'm instantly turned on.

"Where do you think you're going, *mio tutto*? I was having an amazing dream and, since I didn't get to finish it, you're going to have to take care of the problem I have going on," he groggily tells me while he rubs his hard cock against my ass.

"Dante, I need to go and see where Marcus is. Also, the house is full of people. We can't." I know it sounds so damn lame because I can't control the moans that are coming from my mouth.

"Marcus is with OPG. I heard her when she came in and snuck him out of his basinet about forty-five minutes ago. We can be quiet. Come on, Len, it's been a while since I felt your sweet pussy on my cock. I need it bad." He chuckles into my neck.

"Dante, it has only been about five hours since the last time we've had sex."

"Like I said, it's been a while. You know I'm in control in the bedroom so I don't know why you're arguing and not getting naked for me," he murmurs and bites my neck where it meets my shoulder.

Damn it, he knows my triggers. I decide not to argue with him after that because I'm in dire need of him since he has me all wound up.

I sit up and to take off my clothes. I know it's almost time to feed Marcus so we're going to have to make this fast. Just as fast as my clothes are gone, so are his, right before he pounces on me.

He ravages my mouth which makes me grab his hair at the nap of his neck. He's let it grow out a little while I was gone and I have fallen in love with it.

"Len, this is going to be quick." He reaches down to test how wet I am. "Fucking soaked."

He lines up his cock and slams into me. It makes me moan loudly which makes Dante cover my mouth with his hand.

"You have to be quiet. We don't want anyone to know what we're doing." He chuckles in my ear as he thrust hard into my body.

I wrap my legs around his waist and meet him thrust for thrust. It isn't long before I'm already feeling myself on the verge of falling over.

"That's right, you're almost there. I'm going to let you come and do you know why?" he whispers into my ear and I'm too far gone to answer him so he answers for me. "Because I own this body, *mio tutto*. It was made for me and me alone. I'll always give you what you need."

He thrusts in twice more, and I fall over the edge. Wave after wave of pleasure washes over my body. I'm vaguely aware of him growling his release in my ear as he empties into my body and then collapses on top of me. We hold each other as we come down from our releases.

"Condom," I mumble against his chest.

"I got some from Sin earlier, Len. We're covered."

A knock on the door makes me jump which makes Dante laugh in my ear.

"Hey, sex addicts, Marcus is starting to get fussy. I think he needs Len's spectacular breasts," Sin yells through the door.

This causes Dante to mumble out something I couldn't make out and causes me to giggle. He jumps up and opens the door butt naked.

"You better not be talking about my woman's tits. I'm going to fuck you up for those comments!"

"Dude, you are so easy to get going," Sin says, snickering out in laugher. "But seriously, you need to get your woman out here to feed your son. Lucky also wants to talk to us about what we're going to do. We went through the car while you were 'napping' so we need to talk."

I see Dante stiffen at that comment and then look behind him at me. He then nods at Sin and shuts the door.

"Come on, Len, let's go get our son taken care of."

I slowly get up and worry about what was found. I have a feeling this isn't going to be good.

DANTE

I watch Len as she feeds Marcus. Each and every time I see her feeding him makes me fall in love with her a little more.

"Let's go outside and chat about what we found in the car. We also need to figure out if we're going to call the detectives or if we're just going to wait until he's found," Eagle quietly murmurs to us.

We all head outside and sit around the table that's out on the deck.

"Eagle, Sin, and Doc looked into the car. They found papers under the spare tire hatch and something that threw up tons of red flags. Dante, you're not going to like this." Lucky pushes a bag my way along with a pair of gloves.

I notice he has gloves on so I grab the pair he hands me and put them on. I open the bag and look inside, and what I see makes me sick to my stomach. Right there on top is a picture of Len when she was about seventeen, naked laid out on what looks like a bed. I get the feeling that she didn't do this on her own because her eyes look glossy like she's drunk or high.

I reach in, pull out a few more images, and each one gets worse. There are some that are close ups of her body and some of her laying on a guy. I'm assuming it's Steven but can't be one hundred percent certain because his head isn't in the pictures and no tattoos are visible. There are some of her in her dorm, shower, walking across campus, in the hospital, and tons more of her in town with family and friends.

There are notes about how much he loves her and all about the night when they partied together. He explains how he knew she was the one for him since the moment he laid eyes on her. There are plans on how they were going to get married, have babies, and move to another country so they could help third world countries. There are also notes of how angry he is with her for being with me, and how he's going to punish her.

We find a detailed list of every man he thinks was after her, and how some of them disappeared. I catch my breath when I see all of our names on here.

"I guess you got to the list of names . . . we're dealing with a man who's not right. He's obsessed with her, and I have a feeling we're going to have to get the detectives involved. The question is, do we wait or call them now?" Lucky sits back.

"What list?" Carlo asks while he takes a seat. I glance up and see that Nicoli, Pops and Dad are with him.

"What you're about to see isn't something any of us want

to see of Len," Neil warns them.

I don't say a word as I toss gloves at all of them, and then push the contents towards them. I get lost in thought as the boys get them caught up with what's going on. I'm not sure what the fuck to do now. I know we need to let the detectives know what's going on, but I don't want to just yet. I want to wait and see if we can figure out his next move.

I snap out of it when I hear a roar and a chair crash to the ground. I turn towards the noise and see Pops glaring down at the picture in his hand. I have never seen him like this and I'm not only in shock, but also kind of freaking out.

"Pops, take a deep breath and calm down. I know the rage your feeling, but we can't alert the women right now. We need to figure out what we're going to do before we question Len about the pictures," Doc states in a calm voice which also shocks me, because I know he has deep issues when it comes to woman being taken advantage of.

"Calm down? That's my baby girl, and I couldn't protect her from the asshole when he kidnapped her. Now I'm finding out he also violated her!" he says through his clenched teeth.

"Trust me if anyone understands that feeling it's me. My high school girlfriend was raped by her grandpa our senior year, and I didn't have a clue. She ended up writing me a note telling me about it, and then she took her life. The bastard got off because her family made it look like she was crazy. I understand the feeling of not being able to be there for the one you love," Doc tells pops in an eerily calm voice.

We're all staring at him because he's never told us this. We knew he had issues from the past as well as issues from the mission that made all of us leave the Seals. We just never heard him open up about those issues.

Pops snaps his mouth shut and stares at him. He nods, picks up his chair, and sits back down.

"What I'm wanting to know is, what does he mean by disappear?" Nicoli murmurs while he reads the notes.

"Not sure what Adams meant. We need to do a search of the names and maybe we can put it together. We're going to have to talk to Len about the names of the guys she was friends with or dated and ask her if any just disappeared. The question is, what do we do with the information once we have it?" Dad pops up after shuffling through some of the images with anger and disgust written on his face.

"I think what we should do is first talk to Len. After we get names we can do an intense search on the secure laptops I brought, and then we can talk about everything," Sin offers, getting up to get his electronics he brought with him.

"Who's going to talk to Len?" Carlo asks and glances around the table.

"I suggest Lucky, Doc, and I do it," Nicoli answers, looking at me. I open my mouth, and he holds his hand up, stopping me. "Hear me out, I think she might be afraid to tell you names because of how you get all caveman on her. With Lucky and me, we're brothers who are protective, but not caveman. Doc can be there to help gage her body language and help us keep her calm."

I sit back and think about what he's saying. I know he's right but I don't like it. I need to be there to help her through this.

"I agree, and this will give you a chance to go and look over the car with Carlo. Just in case anything else was overlooked. It's good to get another set of eyes, because once the police get that car, we won't get the chance to see it again," Pops says looking over at me.

"Shit! Fine, but the moment you feel she needs me someone better come get me. Understand?" I growl at Lucky.

"Absolutely."

We all split up and I head towards the shed. I'm not liking the info we found out today. And by the way my gut's responding to everything, something's about to happen, and I know it isn't something good.

Twenty-Six

Len

I'M DUMBFOUNDED AT WHAT I just learned from the guys. Seeing the images of me like that just makes me want to run and take a shower. They make me feel so dirty.

I remember a morning where I woke up in a weird room and didn't know where I was. I felt horrible and couldn't remember a thing after eating dinner with a group of college friends, and then arriving to the party. Looking at those pictures, I realize I was at the fraternity house, where the party was hosted, and I was in someone's room. However, I don't recollect whose room or exactly when I went down stairs. All I remember is waking up and finding Sara knocked out on the couch.

When we talked about that night she told me that I drank a lot, and that I must have passed out. After that night, I didn't drink at parties anymore, which I really didn't mind overly much, because I was so wrapped up with school and residency. Now, seeing the pictures in front of me, I have a feeling that I was drugged. It makes me ill thinking that, not only could I have died due to drinking with the drugs in my system, but that I could have been violated even more than I was.

I glance back down at the note in my hand, and a sense of fear washes over me seeing the names on it. I don't know all of them, but I do know four of them and they are all dead. Three are male friends from college that went missing and one that ended up committing suicide from what the note stated.

"Len, are you sure that's all that you can think of?" Doc murmurs at me with a gentle voice. It's like he can sense I'm on the verge of losing my sanity knowing that they could also be victims, and it's all because of me.

"Yes," I whimper out.

"It isn't your fault. Adams is a very sick man. You can't take the blame for something that he did," he gently tells me while rubbing my back.

"I know that in my head, but my heart won't accept that answer. If they weren't friends of mine, they might still be here and not missing," I sob out and lean into his shoulder.

"I know, Len, but you can't take that on your shoulders because it will drag you down."

I just nod, because what else was I supposed to do or say? I don't know how to get this feeling away from me. Doc picks me up and places me on his lap. He continues to hold me while I sob on his shoulder. I finally start to calm down and relax from the crying fit I just had.

I hear whispers around me but can't seem to open my eyes to see who's talking. Strong arms lift me up, and I know immediately they are Dante's. I relax and drift off to sleep feeling safe in his embrace.

DANTE

I stretch in my seat and rub my hands across my face. I've been staring at this damn laptop for hours, searching for the names that Len gave us. I think back to what I saw when I walked into the house after searching the car and finding nothing that the boys missed.

Seeing her asleep in Docs arms with tear stains on her cheeks, broke my heart. I was pissed they didn't come and get me when she broke down. Eagle stopped me before I could go off and explained that it happened about thirty minutes before I got there. They were getting ready to grab me when she finally fell asleep.

I ended up picking her up from his lap, carrying her to the bedroom, and holding her before Mom and Momma Connie came in to take my place. I didn't want her waking up by herself after what happened.

Now, we've been pouring over everything we could find, but we're still running into dead ends. I'm beginning to think we're going to have to get the detectives involved.

"Fuck! We're going to have to call them," Lucky says as he leans back in his chair.

"I was just thinking that. Why don't you go and give them a call? Also, have you heard from Mace and Coleman? I'll let everyone know that we'll more than likely get a visit from them shortly."

"Yeah, they have their teams searching for Adams. So

far, nothing is popping up." He stands up and heads off to the edge of the tree-line.

I walk into the cabin and come to a stop at the sight before me. Len is in a rocking chair holding Marcus with a grin on her face. The love that shines from her takes my breath away.

"Anything come up?" At the sound of Dad's voice, Len pops her head up.

"I just came to tell you that we'll have to call the detectives. Nothing's coming up, and we need their help with this."

I walk over to Len and kneel down in front of her. I kiss Marcus on his head and then lean up and peck her lips.

"I love you, Len. One more time, *mio tutto*," I whisper against them.

"I love you, too. One more time."

I think about the ring that's in my bag upstairs. I kept it on me when she was gone because it was what helped drive me to keep going through the files. I decide that, after the detectives leave, I'll make sure I give it to her. I won't give her a choice if she's going to marry me. She gave up that option when I took her virginity. However, I do plan on making sure I take her to a spot I found in the woods when I ask her to marry me.

"They're on their way. They weren't too happy we didn't call them right after we found Len, but oh fucking well. They're also going to bring a tow to get the car." Lucky's voice breaks my thoughts up.

"Let's go for a walk along the shoreline while we wait for them," I murmur to Len.

Nodding, she goes to get Marcus ready to go outside. I

rush upstairs and dig in my bag for the ring. I can't wait anymore.

"What are you looking for?" Lucky says behind me.

"I'm going to put my ring on your sister's finger finally. Don't tell anyone, because we both know they'll follow us just to see the proposal," I grumble.

"About fucking time. I figured you would've done that right when you found her. That's actually why I followed you up here."

I grunt at his words as I grab the box and shove it into my pocket. I turn towards him, but end up doubled over in pain.

That son of a bitch just punched me in my gut.

"What the fuck was that for?" I groan out in agony.

"For getting my sister pregnant without a ring on her finger. I warned your ass that I was going to get a hit in. I didn't get a chance to do it before due to the fucked up shit that happened. Let's call it even now," he proudly tells me while cracking a huge grin.

"Fucking asshole," I groan and walk off before I punch his ass.

I meet Len in the backyard and see some of the guys are standing there. I shake my head because I have a feeling they are going to want to jump in on this walk, but that isn't happening.

"Ready to go for our family walk, *mio tutto*?" The boys snap their heads at me.

"We were just talking about going for a walk with you," Eagle says with a sly grin.

"Not happening." I wrap my arm around Len's shoulders and guide her towards the water.

We walk along the shoreline and are just content in the silence that's between us.

"Isn't it beautiful, Dante?" she says as we gaze over the water.

"So very beautiful that it takes my breath away." She turns towards me and realizes I'm not talking about the scenery. "Come. I want to show you something I found."

She nods and I guide her into the wooded area. I find the tree that I saw when I went for a walk earlier. I point to the tree that has our names carved into it and raise an eyebrow at her.

"Yeah, I was sixteen and you'd just left." She blushes, and it causes me to chuckle out at her.

"Give me your left hand."

She cocks her head, but holds out her left hand.

I reach into my pocket and pull out the box. I pull the engagement ring out and slip it onto her ring finger. I take a second and let the feeling of ownership run through my system. I lift her hand and kiss the ring on her finger.

"Len, marry me," I say and drop down to one knee.

She stares at me and just nods while I hold her hand. I jump up and take her in a deep kiss while making sure I don't crush Marcus who's sleeping in the carrier that's attached to my chest.

"We're getting married as soon as we can. I'll protect you from anything. I'll die for Marcus and you if that's what I have to do."

She has tears falling from her eyes as she stares into mine, and I can see the love in them. I also see fear, and I know she's worried. Let's hope the detectives can help find this asshole so we can move on with our lives.

"I love you so much, Dante. I don't know what I would do if something ever happened to you," she whispers.

"I love you, Len, and I'm not going anywhere if I can help it. One more time."

"One more time." She tilts her face up for a kiss.

I ravage her mouth in a deep kiss. I show her in that one kiss just how much she means to me and that nothing will keep us apart besides death.

A twig snapping pulls me out of the kiss. I glance over to see Sin off in the distance. He nods towards the house and walks away. I turn back at Len and grin.

"We need to head back, *mio tutto*," I whisper to her.

We walk back hand in hand towards the house. Once we get to the clearing the Moms are rushing towards us squealing. I look over at Lucky who has this huge grin on his face. Fucker couldn't keep a secret.

"Let's see the ring!" Momma Connie yells out after she had smothered Len in hugs and kisses.

"Isn't it perfect?" Len exclaims while holding out her hand.

"It is, and knowing he got it when he was overseas years ago makes it even perfect!" Mom tells her.

"What?" Len asks.

"I bought it overseas during one of our R and R times. I saw it and knew it was the ring I was going to put on your finger one day." I shrug my shoulders at her and her face goes from confusion to disbelief.

This causes a new set of tears to trickle down her face. I walk over, frame her face with my hands, and lean down to kiss her again.

"I told you, I knew four years ago that you were it for me, but I had to wait until it was the right time. Now, dry up your tears and go show everyone your ring. I'm going to go and lay Marcus down." I lay another kiss on her and walk away before the urge to take her upstairs with me gets too strong.

We have been going through the papers for hours now with the detectives. Len explained, yet again, what happened to her and what she knew which was harder this time since everyone was in the room to hear it. After her last breakdown, I made her go upstairs with the Moms and rest.

"I have a feeling that he might be back in Kansas City waiting for her to show up. I would think, since the pictures show that he knew where your parents lived, that he's probably watching the houses. I'm thinking that maybe we should set up a trap for him to fall into. We just have to be careful about it. We don't want it to look like a set up," Edmonds roughly grinds out, looking at the pictures again.

"What do you mean a set up? What are you thinking about?" Doc murmurs out, leaning back looking over at him.

"We're thinking of having Len be the bait, so to speak. This will draw him out and he won't know . . ." Walters starts to say.

"Fuck no!" I roar.

"I agree. You're not using Len for this. Hasn't she been through enough?" Carlo clenches his fist.

"You have to understand we're thinking that this may be the only option," Edmonds spits out.

"So, you want to put her in danger? And before you state you will be watching and protecting her, you can't guarantee that she'll be safe. We both know that shit can happen, and that isn't something I'm going to allow with my fiancé," I tell them though my clenched teeth.

"We could make sure she's as safe as we can make her. I think this is the only way to get him. The faster we do this the better it will be for her," Walters tries to tell us.

"No! I'm not going to allow her to do this. I just got her back, and I refuse to put her in danger. Think of something else." I jump up and slam my hands down on the table.

"Dante, you have to . . ." Walters says, but is interrupted by a voice I didn't expect to hear.

"I'll do it."

I spin and face Len who is flanked by Momma Connie and OPG. I shake my head and open my mouth to speak, but I'm cut off when she holds her hand out to stop me.

"Dante, I refuse to live in fear anymore. I have to help end this so we can move forward with our lives. I'm done looking over my shoulder. Don't tell me not to do this, because I'll go behind your back and do it, Dante. You want me to be safe then work with them and make sure I am," she spits out, then looks over at Edmonds and Walters. "The plan was to head home in a week. So, can we hold off and do it then? I want to enjoy my family a little more before the chaos starts."

"Yes, Ms. Shields, I think that's great and will give us time to plan everything, as well as go over all this evidence that we now have from the car," Walters says quickly before I can, yet again, demand her not to do this.

She nods then turns and goes back up the stairs. I'm way

too pissed to follow her, so I go for a walk. I storm outside and head into the woods. I can't believe she's willingly putting herself in danger. I can't allow this to happen, because it would destroy me if something happened to her again. I'm thinking about tying her to the bed to keep her from doing this, which really is sounding good for more than the reason of keeping her from going, but I know that wouldn't go over well.

I hear footsteps and turn to my right. OPG is standing there watching me with understanding on her face.

"You can't stop her, honey. We both know if you try she'll fight even harder. This is also her way of showing that she isn't afraid of him and that she'll defeat him. She needs to do this so she can move on," she quietly tells me.

I stare at her and take in her words. I know she's right, but I don't have to like it. I'm just not sure if I can handle the possibility of her being taken again. I just got her back, damn it.

"What you need to do right now is go and work out the best plan to keep her safe. After you get that worked out, get your ass upstairs and make sure Len knows you're on her side." She turns and walks away.

"OPG, can you let them know I'll be in shortly? I just need to think things through before I can go in there. Also, tell Len I love her and will be up shortly."

She turns back to me with a smirk and nods before walking away. I head deeper into the woods because I have a lot of thinking to do if I'm going to be okay with Len doing this set up.

Twenty-Seven

Len

MY HEAD POPS UP WHEN I hear someone coming up the stairs. I'm hoping it's Dante, but a second later the door opens and OPG steps into my room. She gives me a sad smile as my face falls.

"He went for a walk. No worries. He told me to tell you that he'll come back once he calms down."

I nod at her, then walk over to the window, and stare at the woods. I knew he would be pissed, but I didn't think he would want to be away from me. I just can't stand being in hiding anymore, and I'm ready to get back to life.

Marcus starts to fuss and I know it's time to feed him again. Walking over to the basinet, I pick him up and comfort him while I head over to the rocking chair. I glance back out the window as he eats and I wonder how long it will take Dante to get back to us.

"Stop worrying, Len, he'll come when he's ready. Your Pa used to do the same thing with me. I learned over time that it was better to let him go off to calm down some," she murmurs and pats my shoulder.

I just nod because I can't talk around the lump in my throat. I try not to think about how upset he is with me. I hear OPG quietly leave my room and I know that she's giving me time to process things.

By the time Marcus is done eating, I still haven't worked through how I feel about Dante leaving. I'm just hoping that he won't hate me for the choice I made. I see that the sun is starting to set, so I get Marcus ready for bed.

After a bath and another feeding, I place him in his basinet. Dante hasn't come back and that makes my mind start to wonder just how upset I might have made him.

I'm trying to decide if I want to go downstairs or just stay here. I know they have to work out the plan for the set up and I should be a part of it. I don't want them to see the disappointment on my face if he isn't down there.

I jump at the sound of the door opening and turn to see Sara, Julia, and Ashley standing there with narrowed eyes. My breath catches at seeing my best friends after being away from them for so long. I try to swallow but it's like my throat's closed and I can't pull my emotions together. Not being able to hold off any longer, I immediately leap off the bed and run to them with tears running down my face.

"I can't believe you didn't call us when you got away. What the hell, Len?" Julia growls as she engulfs me in a huge hug.

"I was scared. I'm sorry, and I'm so glad you're all are here," I sob. I'm yanked from her arms and straight into Sara's.

"Never do that shit again, do you hear me? We would

have never told anyone, you know this," Sara murmurs into my ear and holds me close to her.

"Give her to me, and then I want my nephew!" Ashley pulls me gently from Sara and wraps her arms around me.

"Yes, our nephew! I can't wait to see just how cute that bugger is!" Julia squeals.

"Since when do you use the word bugger? You've been hanging out with Eagle, haven't you?" My eyes narrow at her.

"No comment," she murmurs, and walks towards Marcus.

"What do you mean no comment? Julia, he has a girlfriend!" I harshly whisper to avoid disturbing Marcus. I forgot that he was sleeping when I saw the girls.

"He doesn't, actually. They broke up a month after you left. She didn't understand and hated that he was spending so much time trying to find you," she sadly tells me and gently runs her hand down Marcus's head.

"Speaking of your situation, we need to be filled in on what's going on," Ashley demands and sits on the bed.

"Wait, who told you where I was?" I ask.

It worries me because Steven's still out there, and I know he's been following them.

"Well, when Eagle didn't text or call me for a day now, I knew something was up. So I texted him saying we were coming down, which honestly, we were going to leave tomorrow anyway. He replied and said to be careful and keep an eye out on anything weird. He said that if we saw something off to pull over to the nearest stop and use a different phone to call him," Julia explains. "I knew something was up. After the girls and I talked, we headed down here. Nothing was out of the ordinary that we saw.

When we pulled in, the guys ran out and Dante is the one who ended up telling us."

"We demanded they tell us where you were and not to bother us for the night, because he had you for over a day now. It's our turn. We pulled the girl posse card," Sara states. She gazes down at Marcus who has ended up in Julia's arms.

"Oh, well, I'm really not wanting to discuss it. But I also know you three won't stop asking until I talk. So, get comfy, because this is going to take a while." I crawl up the bed, lean on the headboard, and just start pouring out everything.

Hours later, after lots of hugs and tears, I'm finished telling them what happened. I'm so emotionally drained and just want to go to sleep.

"Why don't we take Marcus so you can get some rest? You're tired, and he will be fine with us," Sara says, she stands up and walks over to the basinet.

"Yep, we got this. It's Aunty time!" Julia squeals.

Ashley is already packing things up in a bag for him.

I give him a kiss on his forehead and watch the girls walk with him out the door. I debate if I want to go find Dante, but decide that I just want sleep. I crawl back into bed and, the moment my head hits the pillow, I drift off into a deep sleep.

Twenty-Eight

DANTE

I HEAR FOOTSTEPS AND SEE the girls coming down the stairs.

"We got Marcus tonight because Len's drained," Ashley says as she puts down the bag she's carrying.

"Is she okay?" Neil asks.

I jump up from the table to head to the room to check on her.

"She's fine, just exhausted. She told us everything that happened. I want to kill that fucker. I can't believe that . . ." Her voice trails off behind me.

I take the stairs two at a time to get to Len. I slowly open the door and see a lump under the covers. Entering the room quietly, I begin to undress. I make my way to the bed and realize that I haven't talked to her since I went for my walk. I feel like a complete asshole that I haven't expressed that she really wasn't the reason I was pissed.

I gently get into bed and wrap my arms around her,

smiling at the slight snoring coming from her. I kiss the back of her neck and decide to let her get some sleep. It's been a difficult day for her, but come morning, she won't be leaving this room until I've told her just how much she means to me.

"Dante, help me! Please, HELP ME!" Len's screams have me jumping from the bed and rushing out the door.

I head in their direction and end up tripping over something. I glance down and see a body drenched in blood. Slowly and fearfully, I turn the body over and see it belongs to Ms. Cindy. With two fingers on her throat, I feel for a pulse, but can't find one. A cry sounds and I know it's Marcus.

"Len, where are you, *mio tutto*?" I yell out in the calmest voice I can muster.

Carefully, I scan the room, wondering where in the fuck the guys are. There is no way someone could get into the cabin with all of us here. I stand up and rush towards the stairs.

"Dante, please, he's going to kill us!" Len calls out as I hear a piercing scream coming from the back porch.

I rush towards the sliding door and see Adams there with a gun to Len's head. She's trying to shield our son, holding him close to her, and trying to sooth him.

I start to take a step to them, but stop when she looks at me. My breath hitches at the pure terror in her eyes.

"Take another step closer, and I end both of them," Adams threatens and makes my eyes snap back to him. "I told her she was mine, and I won't let her go. You can take the child though. I won't have him in our home with the children we're going to have. Len, put the baby down, or I will shoot him."

I watch her as she gently lays Marcus down on the porch and slowly turns towards Adams. My mind races, trying to figure out how to get Marcus to safety, and then get Len away from Adams. I begin to take a step towards Adams when she takes off running towards the woods. I hear a loud crack fill the air and see her fall to the ground. Adams turns the gun on himself and another sound fills the air. He falls off the side of the porch.

I run to Len's side, turn her over, and see blood pouring out of her.

"Dante, you're shaking." I barely hear the words coming out of her mouth.

I try to speak, but can't get anything to come out of my mouth. Why can't I talk to her? I need to tell her how much I love her, that I can't lose her. I close my eyes hoping I can get my words together.

"Dante, *amore*, come on open your eyes." Her voice is coming out stronger now and I try to open my them.

"Dante, please, you're scaring me." Her voice is full of panic which has me snapping my eyes open.

I'm covered in sweat. Wildly, I look around and spot that she's above me. Concerned is etched on her face as she gazes down at me searching my face to make sure I'm awake. I realize that I was having a nightmare.

I feel sick at the memories of my dream, seeing her bloody on the ground isn't something I ever want to think of. My heart feels like it is going to thump out of my chest, and my breath is coming out in heavy pants. I reach out and hug her to me, hoping it will calm my emotions down.

"What were you dreaming about, Dante? You kept screaming out my name, and it took me a while to wake you up," she murmurs in my ear.

"Just a nightmare, Len." I blow out a breath and hold her tighter. I'm not going to tell her about it.

She gives me a kiss below my ear, and I grow hard immediately. I need to make love to her to get that image out of my head. I pull her head back by her hair and begin kissing her gently on the lips. The moment I feel her melt into my chest, I gently turn us so I'm the one on top.

"Dante, are you sure? You just had a nightmare," she moans out as I nip her neck.

I don't answer her. I just decide to show her that I need this, that I just need her.

I slowly start undressing her from her sleep shirt and thong. I slowly make my way down her body and attack her sweet clit. Her body bows and she covers her face to hide her cries of pleasure. I love her taste and I can't get enough.

She reaches down and pulls on my hair trying to get me away from her. This makes me attack her harder. It isn't minutes before she's falling off the edge in a massive orgasm. I take one last lick and then crawl up her body nipping her flesh on my way up.

I reach for the pillow that's by her head and place it under her hips. I press my lips hard against her mouth. She moans at the taste of her on my lips which makes me even harder. I push softly into her, determined to take my time and show her just what she means to me. I stop once I'm fully inside her and wait for her to adjust to my size.

"*TI'mo, Len. Un'altra volta.* I can't live without you." I

glance down at her beautiful face.

"I love you too, Dante. One more time. I really need you to move already or did you forget how to fuck me?" she sasses to me with a smirk on her face.

"Oh, I haven't forgotten, *mio tutto*. Get ready!" I growl out and all thoughts of going slow are thrown out the window as I pull out and thrust back into her.

I use one of my hands to cover her mouth as she moans at the intrusion. I watch her face making sure I'm not hurting her and when she peeks up at me with lust shinning bright, I start pounding into her. I fuck her harder than I have ever fucked anyone before, and I let myself release the fear that I felt from the nightmare.

I feel her tighten around my cock, and I put my hand around her neck and just slightly squeeze. I watch her eyes light up, and she arches back when her orgasm takes over. I can't hold back. I thrust one final time and come deep inside of her.

I drop down on top of her, and her arms go around my neck.

"What the hell was that with my neck?" she groggily says into my ear.

"I know your neck is an erotic zone, and when you're right there on the edge it becomes even more sensitive. I'm not into breath play, but squeezing it slightly, I knew would trigger a bigger orgasm for you," I gasp, trying to catch my breath.

I slowly pull out of her and groan at the loss of her heat. As I roll over to the side, I pull her with me, situating her so she's laying on top of me.

"I'm sorry I didn't come up here sooner. I really meant

what I said a moment ago, Len. I can't live without you again. I got upset about you doing this sting operation because if something were to happen to you, it would kill me. I already lived without you for nine months. I refuse to let it happen again. Promise me that you'll be okay, that you will do exactly what we tell you to do," I whisper, staring in her eyes.

"I understand what you're saying, but you have to understand, I can't live in fear until he's caught. So if I can help the process. I will," she explains in her soft voice.

"I get it, I really do. I just want your word that you will do what we tell you and that you won't do anything unnecessary. If you sense any danger or you feel it isn't a good situation, then you get out of there immediately." I begin to get angry again because all I can see are the images of her bloody on the ground and the feeling of being powerless to help her.

"I will, Dante, I promise I will follow what you guys tell me. We don't even know what the plan is yet, but I won't let them set up anything that I don't feel right doing."

"Thanks, *mio tutto*. Now, let's get some more sleep." I kiss her head and hold her close as I drift back to sleep.

Twenty-Nine

Len

I RAISE MY COFFEE CUP to my lips as I watch Carlo feed Marcus with the milk I pumped the day before. It's quite a sight to see, because he's very scared of holding him. Marcus is squirming and whimpering while Carlo is trying hard to calm him down. The expression on his face shows just how much he's uncomfortable with what's happening. He looks so lost and just isn't sure what to do to get him to latch on to the nipple. I bite my bottom lip to try to hold in my laugh so I don't tip him that I'm watching. Just when I'm about to give in and go to relieve him, Nicoli walks over. Reaching down, he gently picks up Marcus, walks over to the recliner and calms him down enough to give him the bottle.

Shocked, I just stare in amazement at how natural he is with Marcus. I glance over to see Carlo staring as well.

"What the fuck? When did you learn so much about babies?" Carlo asks him, getting over his shock at seeing his twin brother handle Marcus like a seasoned pro.

"Friends," is all Nicoli says and smiles down at his nephew.

"Who?" he asks with narrowed eyes.

"None of your damn business," Nicoli grunts out.

"Look, dumb . . ." Carlo starts to say and I know I better step in.

"Hey, where is everyone?" I head into the room, making my presence known.

"Out front," Carlo murmurs still staring at his twin with confusion etched on his face. "Detectives are here to set up the plans, from what I overheard, so you might want to go wake up fuck face."

"Watch your mouth around my son and woman, Thing One," I hear from behind me, his arms wrapping around my waist. "Morning, *mio tutto*. You should have woken me up when you got out of bed. I needed my morning breakfast."

I turn bright red, because Nicoli and Carlo snap their heads our way. I turn quickly in his arms and give him a kiss to stop him from saying anything else.

"I'm out of here. I can't watch you two making out," Carlo mumbles and walks away.

"Come on, little man. I'm sure you don't want to see Mamma and Daddy make your little brother or sister," Nicoli says to Marcus which makes Dante laugh.

"Dante, you have to watch your mouth. Seriously, you can't do that!" I smack him on the arm and try to step back. This causes him to laugh harder and pull me tighter to him.

"Len, I did it on purpose so I could do this." His mouth comes crashing down on mine, and he devours me in a kiss that has everything melting away.

My body instantly lights up with desire, and I jump up

which makes him grab my ass as I wrap my legs around his waist. I'm just about to suggest we go back upstairs when I hear a clearing of a throat behind me. I immediately stop kissing Dante and shove my face in his neck.

"Can I help you, Walters?" Dante chuckles.

"Just wanting to know if you guys are ready to start the planning? I mean if you're busy we could always just come back." He laughs.

"I was just thinking of starting on Marcus's brother or . . . ump," he mumbles out the last word through my hand that I slapped over his mouth, and I glare at him with a look that says if you even try to say anymore I will kill you.

"Well, we'll be out back when you're ready." Walters laughs as he walks away.

"You can't tell people we're trying for another child, Dante!" I growl at him through my clenched teeth.

He removes his hand off his mouth and gives me a smirk.

"Too late, and why are you mad at me? Thing One gave me the idea. Why didn't you yell at him?" He bursts out laughing at the look on my face and nips my hand that he's still holding by his lips. "Besides, my baby could already be in there. We didn't use protection that first time."

Damn it. He's right, but I give him a death glare when, I'm feeling all kinds of happiness at the thought of being pregnant again. I hate that he missed the pregnancy with Marcus.

"Don't, *mio tutto*. No thinking of the past. Yeah, it guts me knowing I missed out on the last pregnancy, but I have you both in my arms and that's where you both will stay. So let's focus on the future, okay, Len?" He places a gentle kiss on my forehead at my nod and slowly lets me down. "Let's go get this over with."

Taking a deep breath, I link my fingers with his and we head out to the back deck to get the details all worked out.

We have been going around for hours on the best way to draw out Steven so they can catch him. So far the only thing we all agree on is that it should be done at the Nelson Atkins Art Museum, but outside near the shuttlecock sculptures. They explained it's because it's more open and they can have people around that he wouldn't recognize. They are planning on setting up base command inside the museum.

"I'm telling you that we also need to be outside somewhere. I refuse to let Marcus and her be out in the open without me being right there with them. I won't take a chance of losing them again," Dante demands yet again.

"He knows what all of you look like. Even if you wear a disguise, he will recognize you. We can have you at the door, ready to run out once we spot him. We not only have the cameras outside on the building, but we plan on adding them to the shuttlecock too," Walters huffs out, determined that this was the way it was going to happen.

"No! That's final! Do you think that stupid fucking piece of shit is going to believe that she took Marcus to a trip to the museum and that I would allow it knowing he's still out there?" he angrily explains which, honestly, he has a point.

"Tell me, Detectives, are you married with children?" Pops finally speaks up after listening to all the round and round that has been going on.

"I don't, but Edmonds is married with two little girls. What does that have to do with this?" Walters asks him with a sidelong glance.

"Edmonds, put yourself in Dante's shoes. Would you allow your wife and daughters to be put in this situation without at least one of us with her?" Edmonds shakes his head at Pops. "Then why are you asking us to do the same? I agree with Dante."

Pops holds up his hand at Walters when he goes to open his mouth. He looks at Dante and I can tell he's going to say something he might not like.

"I'm not finished. Now, Dante, I agree with the detectives that he isn't going to come up to them if we're around. We need him to get close enough for the camera to identify her. So, what I'm thinking is this, Tony or I will go with them so it looks like Grandpa is spending the day with them. Around lunch time, we will go out and set up a picnic by the shuttlecocks. When it's all set up, we can make it look like some kind of accident happens and it's necessary to take him into the museum. That should be enough to draw him out to go after her. Len already told us how much he doesn't like Marcus. So, I think it would be too tempting to not go after her seeing that Marcus will be out of the picture," Pops explains and I have to admit I like the way it sounds.

I look around the table and see the guys mulling it over.

"I actually think it's a great plan. I like it better because it means Marcus is out of danger if he has a gun or something," I finally speak up since it seemed that nobody else was going to.

"I still don't like the thought of you being alone, Len. I just don't have a good feeling about doing it. The last time I got that feeling . . ." Dante trails off, looks into my eyes and I can see the fear behind them.

"I understand, but what else is there to do? We both

283

know he won't come at me if you're there. I need this over, Dante," I whisper around a knot in my throat.

I can tell he understands that it has to be done and he nods.

"Okay, then the last thing we have to decide is when we're going to be doing this. I'm thinking the sooner the better," Edmonds says and writes in the notebook he has in front of him.

"We're scheduled to go home next weekend. If we come home sooner it might throw him off. I don't know if he checked into our business or not so knowing that it's best to stay here for the week then return home," Neil states from the other side of me.

"I don't like waiting but I guess that's what will have to happen. It will give us time to get everything set up at the museum," Walters says as he gathers up the paperwork in front of them.

"Call us when you are on your way back then." Edmonds tells us and nods at us then follows his partner around to the front of the house.

"Well, now that that's settled, let's enjoy this last week we're at the lake. Squirt, want to go cliff diving?" Neil chuckles and then cries out at the elbow that hits him in the ribs.

"I swear, I'm going to kill you in your sleep one day, Neil!" I growl.

Everyone cracks up laughing which makes a smile break out on my face. I look over at Dante, and he has a small smile on his face, but you can still see the worry in his eyes. I close the distance and give him a small kiss on his lips, letting him know it'll be okay. I decide right then that this week will be a good week for us to let go of the past.

And, for us to forget, just for a second, of the challenge that lies ahead.

Thirty

Len

WE'RE ALL AROUND THE CAMPFIRE talking and enjoying each other's company as we relax after the day we had with the detectives. I look to my left and spot Eagle sitting next to Julia. They're leaned in close and talking amongst themselves. I see the desire to be with each other so I wonder what's holding them back.

"Why won't they just get together already? And did you know about this?" I whisper over my shoulder to Dante who's holding me in his lap.

"I think your girl wants it, but Eagle's holding back. He has something from his past that he doesn't talk to any of us about. I'm sure that's what's holding him back from claiming her," Dante whispers back as he runs his nose down my neck.

"I'm going to have to keep an eye on that. I don't want Julia to get hurt." I melt into his arms and look over towards Neil.

He's sitting off to the side and staring into the fire. But, if you watch his eye movement you'd see that he is actually staring at Sara who's talking to the twins.

I glance to my left and see Sin, Doc, and Ashley are playing a game of cards. I smile because it seems Ashley's attracted to both by the way she's flirting. Ashley's always been one to plan things out before she settles on anything. I have a feeling she's testing the waters, so to speak, with them to figure out which one she wants more.

I snap my head towards the door and OPG stepping out on the deck. She glances around and when she spots me, she nods toward the water and holds up her poles. I grin because I know she wants to talk.

"OPG wants to go fishing. I'm going to spend time with her," I whisper over my shoulder.

I give Dante a kiss and then head towards OPG. I notice that Neil has also gotten up and grabbed the stuff from her hands along with the chairs. We walk silently down to the water's edge and get everything set up. Neil gives us both a hug and a kiss then walks back. I notice that we're in direct line of sight of the others.

"We haven't had alone time since that day in the cabin and with what's going to come up we need time together. So fill me in on what was decided once we return home." She's putting bait on both polls because she knows I won't touch it.

We cast out our lines, and I can't help the grin that pulls at my lips because of the memories flooding me of us doing this so many times. It dawns on me that we never catch anything because we end up forgetting our lines are in the water due to the time we spend talking and enjoying each other's company. It's then that I take those memories and store them in my heart because it means more to me than my OPG could ever know. Then again she's probably thinking the same thing.

I sit back and fill her in on all that was decided. We're both staring out over the water for what seems like forever when she finally speaks up.

"I can say that I'm not happy that you're putting yourself in danger. I already lost nine months without you, and it was the hardest thing I had to face. You're everything to me, and I'm not sure I can handle losing you." She holds up her hand when I go to speak. "That said, I understand why you're doing it. I would be doing the same thing. I just want your promise that you will make sure you're safe."

"Of course, and I'm not going anywhere again, OPG. I know there's more you're not telling me. What's going on?" I ask, because I can see it in her face that something isn't right.

"Don't worry, Len, it isn't something I want to discuss tonight." She gives me her signature look that says don't push it.

We settle into a quietness and just enjoy the time we have together at this moment. The next few days are going to be crazy with packing everything up here and heading home. Let's hope that everything goes smoothly so we can move on with our lives, because I'm ready for this to be over.

DANTE

Looking down at my watch, I see it's getting close to midnight and they're still by the water. I have been keeping an eye on them and, so far, it looks like they are just enjoying each other's company. I'm considering going to get them since we have a surprise for Len tomorrow, but I'm stopped when Neil sits down next to me.

"What's up, brother?" I quirk an eyebrow at him when he sighs.

"I don't know what to do with Sara." He's glancing back at her again. "I want her to open up to me and now that Len is here, I figured she would be more open with me, but she isn't. I want to run a check on her, but I have a feeling she will know that I did it."

"What do you think it is?"

"No fucking clue, but I know it's bad," he murmurs at me.

I turn back to Sara and see that she's relaxed, but there's a haunted gaze in her eyes that has been there since I met her years ago. I've always wondered what put it there, but I know from Len that she never talks to anyone about her past.

"What if you get her drunk and then kind of do an interrogation on her?" I suggest to him.

"Hmmm . . . that could work or it could backfire. Maybe once all this shit with Adams is done, I can talk with Len and we can figure out a way to get her to talk. I'm tired of waiting for her, three years of this is long enough," he murmurs as he stands up and walks over to her.

He bends down and whispers into her ear. She shakes her head at him and crosses her arms over her chest glaring up at him. A flicker of anger crosses his face before he gives her a smirk, and I know what he's about to do before he does it. He throws her over his shoulder then storms towards the house.

She's yelling at him to put her down as she beats on his

back. Sin steps in front of him. I can't hear what is said but I watch as Sin steps behind Lucky and speaks to Sara. She slowly shakes her head at what he says and then slaps Lucky on his ass. Laughter fills the air as Lucky storms into the house with Sara still on his shoulder. I have a feeling we'll be staying outside for longer than we thought we were going to.

I feel a hand on my shoulder and turn to see Len standing there giggling at what Lucky just did. I stand and grab her by the waist to haul her in for a kiss.

"Wait, before you kiss me. Can you get the stuff from the shoreline for us?" she whispers quietly against my lips.

I press my lips against her then pull back to go get the items they left. I notice that OPG isn't there and wonder where she went. I feel a hand at my back and turn around to see Len standing there.

"Where's OPG?"

"Ms. Cindy came and got her. No need to worry, sexy sailor." She giggles.

I drop the items and then pick her up over my shoulder like Neil had done with Sara. This causes her to giggle, so I smack her ass.

"I'm going to show you sexy sailor, *mio tutto*. Sin, will you get the stuff from the shore? I have something to take care of," I yell at him while carrying her to the house.

We're almost to the bedroom door when we hear moans coming from the room down from us. I start to walk faster, but what we hear next has me stopping in my tracks.

"If you don't stop those noises I'm going to gag you, Sara," Lucky growls.

I start laughing and run into our bedroom. I barely make out snickers coming from Lucky's door as I shut the door to our room. I pull Len from my shoulder and place her on her feet.

Oh, tomorrow's going to be very interesting to say the least.

"God, that's so not something I ever want to hear my brother say again," Len says and wipes the tears off her face.

I slowly walk up to her and lust fills her eyes the moment she realizes that I'm about to ravage her. She's taking steps backwards until her legs hit the bed and ends up falling onto it. I crawl up her body and make my way to her ear. I nip the lobe and it makes her moan out. Not being able to help myself I move my lips to her ear and whisper into it, "If you don't stop those noises I'm going to gag you, Len." I start silently laughing as she burst out laughing.

"Damn it, Dante, that just ruined the moment." She giggles.

"Let's see if I can make you want me again."

I go about worshiping her body which makes her have to hide her head in the pillow to scream out her release.

Thirty-One

Len

"IS SHE ALIVE?" I HEAR whispering from a voice I know but can't place because I haven't had my morning coffee.

"I bet he fucked her to death, I mean, shit, if I were straight, I'd be doing the same," the voice murmurs, and I slowly start waking up.

"You better watch your mouth around my woman before I knock the fuck out of you. What the hell are you two doing in our room anyway?" Dante growls as he grabs me tighter to him. Thank God he pulled the covers over us last night after we finished.

"You're the one who called and told us to get our ass here because we needed to spend girl time with our girl. So you can kiss my ass and leave now. Wait, are you dressed under there, sexy sailor?" The question was purred out and it makes me crack up laughing.

"You're fucking lucky Len likes you, dipshit, or I would kill you already. Get the fuck out so we can get dressed," he growls between clenched teeth.

"Well, where would be the fun in that? I've been trying to get a peek at what you're packing for months now. Come on, sexy sailor, give us a little peek." I realize who is in the room with us, open my eyes, and spot Andy and Chris on my side of the bed.

"Well, hello, Len, about time you got your ass found. He's been a spastic cum butler," Andy pipes up.

"Oh, my God! You're here," I yell and try to get off the bed.

"Len, you're not getting up. Your naked under here, and I don't give a fuck if they're gay, they aren't seeing you like that." Dante squeezes me even harder holding me in my spot. "Get out, boys. We'll meet you down stairs."

I blow Chris and Andy a kiss as they walk out the door. I turn and hug Dante close for bringing me my other two best friends because I know he set this up.

"Thank you, Dante," I murmur.

"*Mio tutto*, I just want you to have one night with your friends before we have to go back home and face what lies ahead of us," he murmurs in my ear then turns my head and kisses me deeply.

"Come on you two! No fucking allowed. It is our turn with our girl!" I hear Andy yell through the door.

I bust up laughing which ends the kiss Dante was giving me.

"I swear to God I will end up killing Andy before the day is over. What the fuck was I really thinking?" Dante grumbles and gets up to get dressed.

Even though he grumbles about it, I know he wouldn't hurt them. I jump up and hurry through my morning routine so I can go and spend time with my other two favorite guys.

I have tears running down my face due to the horrified expression that's on Eagle, Sin, and Doc's face. I glance over at Dante and Lucky, and it isn't any better. Andy pulls out a box full of cinnamon Tic Tacs, and that makes me laugh even harder.

"Seriously, we're doing research here. Since you men don't know how many pills you can swallow at one time, I figured Tic Tacs would be the best thing to use. I mean, we don't want you overdosing on pills. However, we could do placebo pills that actually might be better. Hey, Len, how can we go about getting them?" he asks me with a straight face, but I see the humor behind them.

"No," is all Chris says with a glare at his husband, telling him that he won't let him go that far.

It hurt to find out they had gotten married while I'd been kidnapped, but I'm so happy for them. Chris is the laid back one of the two, whereas Andy is the flamboyant, funny, and in your face one.

"But, baby, seriously, Tic Tacs are smaller than pills so, the results would be so much better with placebos." He crosses his arms and stares at him with narrowed eyes.

"I told you before that it wasn't happening so don't ask again unless you want a punishment," Chris growls and it makes all of us crack up, laughing louder.

"Maybe that's what I'm wanting." He leans over and gives his husband a kiss on the lips.

"Okay, explain this logic again because it's just too awesome not to hear it for a second time," I rasp out between fits of laughter which causes the guys to moan in frustration again.

"Okay, so I was talking to my neighbor who said she takes, like, thirteen pills once. I thought that was impressive, and we discussed how most men can't do that. Their count is, maybe, two pills. Anyway, it hit me that it has to be because women give head, and that means deep throating. So, that has to be training the throat to do that shit. Then, I was like, well hell, if that's true with women then it has to be true for gay men. So, I decided that it should be tested, but again, I don't want people dying for research purposes. So, cinnamon Tic Tacs it is, and I chose that flavor because it has to be better for burping up than mint," Andy explains with a huge smile on his face as we yet again go into a fit of laughter.

"Fuck me, I can't believe this guy is serious. I need to get the hell out of here," Doc stays, he gets up, and runs out the back door.

"Right behind you," Lucky murmurs which leads to the rest of the guys, including Chris, following behind him.

"Good, now that I cleared the room! Let's talk about girl time. You're leaving tomorrow to head home and we still have to pack up the cabin. So, here is my suggestion, let's go do that, then get back here so we can get our drink on and girl time." Andy declares and stands up. "I will just leave these here so the guys can do the swallow challenge for my research."

This makes us all squeal out in giggles as we follow him out the front door.

Thirty-Two

DANTE

LAUGHTER FILLS THE AIR AS the girls head to the cabin, to, I assume, pack it up. I look over at Chris and shake my head. I swear he puts up with some shit from his husband. I'm totally straight and I honestly don't understand the whole being gay thing, however, I believe that you can't help who you fall in love with and, as long as you're true to the person who has your soul, then it isn't my business.

"How in the fuck you can put up with Andy's shenanigans is beyond me, dude," Sin murmurs and I grunt in agreement.

"Same way Dante deals with Len's, same way you will deal with yours one day. Just because we're gay, it doesn't change the dynamics of a relationship," Chris murmurs quietly.

"I didn't mean any offense, dude, and wasn't commenting on you being gay. It was a true question like I would ask anyone." Sin stops and turns to Chris.

"You'll find we aren't judgmental people. Look, I'm a Christian but that doesn't mean I'll judge you. Anyone who does judge people isn't right. Nothing in the Bible says that, since you're gay, I can't be your friend, hang out with you, and have dinner," Eagle pipes up from beside me.

Chris glances at all of us and then gazes down as he absorbs what we just said. He finally looks up, grins at us, and holds his hand out to Eagle.

"Thanks, I'm just used to people judging me for my lifestyle and it pisses me off. I've honestly never met a Christian who wasn't judgmental."

Eagle grabs his hand and give him a guy one handed back slap. We head down to the river to fish and have some man time.

I feel hands on my shoulders and take a deep breath of amazing scent that's my girl. I reach up and grab her hand and bring it to my lips for a kiss on her palm. I've learned that's a trigger to her and I feel her shiver at my lips there which causes me to smirk into her hand.

"We got everything cleared up. The bags are all in the truck and ready to go. I just finished feeding Marcus and pumped for the night since the parents are keeping him with them. They are staying the night with Ms. Cindy so we have the cabin to ourselves. We're starving so you men need to get on it and get the grill fired up," she murmurs in my ear before nipping the lobe.

I pull her around to the front of me into my lap and kiss the fuck out of her. After whistles and moans of frustration, I finally pull away and look into her eyes.

"Okay, *mio tutto*, let's get you fed and then we can have one more night of fun before real life has to happen." I kiss her forehead and we gather everything up then head to the house to get the grill going.

Len

I realize that I'm slightly tipsy from the two drinks I've had. I gaze over and spot Sara on Neil's lap, and he's whispering in her ear which is making her squirm. Julia and Eagle are leaned in close talking in hushed tones. Sin, Ashley, and Doc are all laughing at something Andy's telling them. Chris's sitting behind Andy with his hands on his hips shaking his head at his husband.

"What are you thinking, Len?" Dante whispers into my ear as he pulls me closer to him.

"Just thinking about how lucky I am to have such an amazing family. Also seeing the relationships of our friends is kind of cool and sad since I missed the beginning of it," I whisper, he's nipping at my neck.

"No sadness tonight, *mio tutto*. We're celebrating you being back and Marcus being here, too. I'm about to say fuck it, and drag your ass into the house because I need you," he growls and bites where my neck and shoulder meets. He pulls back for a second, "Len, where's your necklace?"

It takes me a moment to register his question.

"Shit, I forgot it back at the cabin. The chain broke, so I put it on the counter since I didn't have pockets." I wiggle out of his arms and stand up. "Stay here. I'm going to run over there really quick."

"Not by yourself."

"I'm going to get Andy to walk with me," I tell him after giving him a quick kiss and heading that way.

"Hey, can you walk with me to the cabin? I forgot something," I ask Andy when I walk up to the group.

He nods his head and jumps up.

"Be back in a second, Dr. Sexy Ass," he says after leaning down and giving Chris a kiss on the lips.

"That's it, Andy, you're going to get it when you get back," he grunts.

It takes five minutes to get to the cabin and get inside. I run into the bathroom and look around for my necklace.

"Where is it?" I murmur to myself.

I search on the floor thinking it might have fallen off the counter when I hear a loud thud, and it brings me out of my thoughts. I walk out of the bathroom and see Andy laying on the ground.

"Oh, my God! What happened, Andy?" I yell and run to his side. There's a small cut on his head so I turn him over, check for a pulse, and exhale when I find one.

I reach out to shake him when I feel a prick at my neck and memories flood back to me. I look to my side, and my heart begins to race.

"Hey, Linda, you thought you could get away from me, love? Such a shame that you did what you did. Now, I will have to punish you." That's the last thing I hear before sleep claims me.

Thirty-Three

DANTE

I'M KICKING MYSELF IN THE ass for letting Len and Andy go by themselves. I might be overprotective, but I just don't trust anyone with Len, but me, and maybe Neil. I gave them about five minutes to make it to the house then started after them.

I get close to the cabin when I hear her yell, but I'm still far enough away that I can't make it out. I start to run towards the house, and once I reach the porch I slow down so I don't make any noises.

I peek through the sliding door, the sight that's in front of me makes anger go through my veins; Adams has Len in his arms and is walking towards the bed. She's limp in his arms, and it takes everything in me to not rush in there. I slowly move to the side and text Neil to get his ass here now.

I watch through the glass waiting for the right time to get into the house. I spot Andy on the floor out cold. I know then that that's what Len was yelling about.

I turn towards the wood and spot Neil. I motion him to check his phone because I texted him about what's going on inside the cabin. He nods, reaches behind him, and pull out two guns. He starts making his way over to me, hands me one of the firearms, and goes off to the front. I peek in again and Adams is standing over Andy. I turn back to the bed and Len has been tied to the bed.

"You fucking faggot!" he screams, then kicks Andy in the ribs. "You will pay for being near my Linda! I don't want your dirt to rub off on her, and since you spent the day with her, I will have to make sure to end you for that."

My phone vibrates and its Lucky telling me he doesn't have an open shot. I curse under my breath and tell him I'm going in. I take a deep breath, flip my safety off, and start making my way through the sliding door.

"What's going on?" Andy moans from the floor, as Adams pull out a gun. He aims right at Andy and then kicks his leg.

"Steven, what are you doing?" Andy whispers.

"I came to get Linda. I've been watching the houses of the family, but found out through calling Seal Security that they went on a family vacation. The person on the phone wouldn't tell me where and by the time I got to Sara, Ashley, and Julia's home, I was too late. They'd already left," he sighs. "So, my next step was to watch you and that faggot of a doctor that wants my Linda. When you both left early this morning, I followed you here."

"You followed us?" Andy murmurs.

"Yep, and now, you must die because I can't have your filth touching my Linda." He raises up his gun.

"Stop!" Len groggily says from the bed which makes

Adams turn suddenly towards her.

"Linda, it has to be done. Now, be a good girl and your punishment won't be so bad," Adams says and starts to turn back to Andy.

"Don't. Please don't kill my friend," she sobs.

"Say bye, Linda."

He raises his gun, and I know I have to stop this. I raise my gun, aim for his shoulder, and pull the trigger.

I hear screams, and Lucky storms in the front door. I run over to unite her from the bed, and hold her close, murmuring into her ear for her to calm down. Lucky's talking to Andy to see if he's okay. Once he helps him to stand, he starts walking him to the couch. Adams howls in pain as he lays on the floor holding his shoulder. I spot his gun over by the couch and relax a little knowing it's by Lucky.

After what seems like forever, but I know is only moments, I push Len back and check her over to make sure she's okay. I'm about to ask her if she was feeling all right when she begins to pale even more than she already is and a horrified expression crosses her face. I follow her line of sight and know she's staring at something behind me.

Without a second thought, I turn raising my gun along with my movement and come face to face with Adams holding a gun at Len. He had to of had a second one on him.

"Drop it!" I yell which causes Lucky to run in from the porch.

"If I can't have her, nobody will have her!" he screams and I see his finger start to move.

I hear two gun shots, and Adams falls to the floor. Blood pours from his head, and I know he's gone. I hear a gasp from behind me, I snap my head towards Len, and she's sitting there staring right at Adams.

I run to her side and hold her close, murmuring words into her ear. I realize she's starting to go into shock and I can't get through to her. I hear footsteps coming up the steps and watch the guys rush into the house. Eagle's on the phone with, I'm assuming, the police and stops when he sees what Lucky is staring at.

"Oh . . . my . . . God . . . Dante . . . he . . . he . . ." Len starts saying to me. "He's dead. You guys killed him. Oh, my God, Dante, you killed him!"

She begins to hyperventilate and next thing I know Lucky's on the other side of her, trying to calm her down. I know this is going to take time to get her through this, but now that Adams is gone, we have nothing but time on our side.

Len

Two months later...

I stare out of the window of my bedroom lost in thought. I've been going to therapy once a week, and there are times I'm still struggling with what I went through. I'm realizing that I'll always battle the past but with time I'll be able to work through the memories.

The major problem is that I can't get the image of Steven laying there, dead with blood pooling around him, out of my mind. I just want something to wash my brain clean of the images that flood my mind now when I close my eyes.

I jump when I feel arms wrap around my waist and lips

at my neck. I lean back into Dante's arms, but still don't say a word.

"Len, talk to me, *mio tutto*," he says so quietly that I almost miss it.

"Nothing to talk about Dante. I just want the images gone," I whisper out.

"You had another nightmare last night. You need to make sure you talk to Dr. Pickett about it tomorrow when you see him." He slides his hand up the front of my stomach and rubs in circles.

I nod because there isn't anything I want to say about what I dreamed of last night.

"Len, I need you to do me a favor. Can you go and take this test for me?" He holds something in front of my face and it takes me a minute to register what he's showing me.

"You're late and I know stress can cause it, but I think you should take it just to make sure," He says against my neck.

I know I'm late but I'm pretty sure it's due to all the shit we have been through. However, there's a chance I might be pregnant.

I grab the stick and head to the bathroom.

I lay the test on the counter and head back to where Dante is waiting for me by the bed.

"Do you think I might be pregnant?" I ask walking into his arms.

"I don't know. I know that I'm hoping it's positive, but if it isn't then we can discuss when a right time would be for us to start trying again." He murmurs into my hair.

We just stand here, content with holding each other, while we wait for the timer to go off. Finally, the alarm sounds, I take a deep breath moving out from Dante's arms, and head to the bathroom. I pick up the test and flip it over to get the results.

Positive.

Dante wraps his arms around me, and I can tell the moment he sees it. His arms tighten around me and he buries his face into the side of my neck. His body starts shaking against mine and I can't hold back the tears any longer.

"I'm going to be here this time, *mio tutto.* I'm so happy," he whispers and that's then that I feel the wetness on my neck.

I start sobbing and turn around and cling to him. I pull back and glance into his face and see the streaks of tears on his cheeks.

"You're crying," I whisper.

"Len, I would've reacted the same way with Marcus. I'm so happy. I get to see you round with my child and I'm so blessed for that," he chokes and bury his head into my shoulder.

I stand there, holding him and let the happiness fill my heart because I know our future is going to be amazing.

"*TI'mo, Dante. Un'altra Volta.*"

"*TI'mo, Len. Un'altra Volta.*"

Epilogue

DANTE

Four months later...

I GLANCE AROUND AND A grin pulls at my lips at hearing the laughter that fills the air. I turn my head and kiss my wife on her temple. She gazes up and smiles at me before she continues her talk with Andy.

Currently, our yard is filled with family and friends as we have a baby shower for Len. She's five months pregnant and Andy demanded that we have a co-ed baby shower. I was against it until she turned her big, blue eyes on me and I saw tears in them. I was done and immediately told her she could have whatever she wanted. I was called a pussy for months, and I told them that, when it comes to her, I would be the biggest pussy there was if it meant no tears.

Andy decided that we would have a gender reveal party, whatever the fuck that is. Len said that's when it's revealed at the party what the sex of the baby is. She had the doctor put it in an envelope and then handed it over to Andy to take care of the rest. However, there was something that showed up during that scan that was a shock. I can't wait to see their faces when they find out, not only the sex, but the surprise that shocked us to our core.

"Okay, Daddy, hand me the brother and let's get this box open to show everyone what we're having!" Andy claps his hands together, then jumps up and down before he grabs Marcus away from me. This causes him to giggle out and slap Andy on his face.

"Little man, don't hit your Uncle Andy. That isn't nice," Len scolds him.

We walk over to the huge ass box that's in the center of our yard and everyone crowds around us.

"Open it already! We only have three months to shop!" Ashley screams at us which causes all the women to agree and the men to moan, because we know we're going to be dragged into this.

Len grins really big then takes the ribbon off the top and pulls up. Pink and blue balloons pour out and float into the sky which makes Len squeal in excitement. I pull her into me and can't help the huge grin that I'm sporting at the fact that we're having a boy and a girl. The confused expression that's on everyone's face has me chuckling because you can see them trying figure out what the hell just happened.

"We're having twins!" Andy screams to everyone.

"You're not having anything, dipshit! *We* are having twins!" I growl at him which causes Len to burst into a fit of giggles.

"Why are you cracking up? It's true he isn't having anything!" I explain to her with a huff and this causes her to laugh so hard she ends up leaning into me for support.

"I'm going to pee if you don't stop!" she howls at me.

"What the fuck is so damn funny?"

"Well, *dipshit*," Andy does finger quotes on the word dipshit which causes me to grunt at him and Len to double over from her fit. "You're not having anything, either. Len, is the one who will be delivering your spawns."

"Whatever," I mutter, rolling my eyes at him and that makes Len jerk from my arms and rush towards the house, screaming she's going to pee her pants between peals of laughter.

I hear a phone ringing and glance over towards the sound. Sara's staring at the phone in her hand with fear forming all over her face. I turn to Lucky who is watching her and from what I can tell he spots the same thing because he stops what he's doing and rushes to her side.

"*Habibi*, you okay?" I hear him ask.

Since we returned from the lake, they've been skirting around their feelings. I don't know what's going on with that, but I've been keeping an eye out on her when he isn't around. Len said she has been pulling away from everyone and was worried something bad is going on with her.

"I have to take this," she says and walks away to answer the phone.

I stop Lucky from following too closely but understand his need to make sure she's okay.

She turns around to spots us standing there and my body tenses at the sight of her expression. Her face is ghost white, her eyes are empty and her body is starting to shake from the terror that's coursing through it.

"I have to go. Please tell Len I'll call her later," she rushes out then turns and runs to the front of the house which has Lucky following after her yelling her name.

"What's going on?" I turn to my left and Len's standing there with worried expression.

"I don't know, but Sara said she'll call you later. She got a phone call and had to go," I tell her, pulling her into my side, which at that moment, I feel a kick against me.

I fall to my knees and place my lips to where the kick was and give her belly a kiss. Her hands go into my hair and she looks down at me as I gaze up at her.

"Daddy loves you both so very much. Take it easy on Mamma, okay?" At that I feel another kick and it causes Len to giggle.

I take a moment to stare into the eyes of the one woman who has had my heart since I was eighteen. I say a quick prayer of thanks to God for giving me her and it makes me appreciate our saying that much more.

"*TI'mo Len. Un'altra Volta,*" I murmur to her and then close my eyes and relish the words being said back to me.

I look over and spot Lucky walking back with worry in his eyes. I say a quick prayer that whatever is going on with Sara doesn't stop the love I know they both could have.

More Than Anything
More Series Book 2
Neil and Sara now avaiable

Continue reading for a special bonus chapter that has notes between Dante and Len during his time in the Navy. As well as, a sneak peek at Book Two.

Bonus Chapter

Note: these are letters between Dante and Len that span over the years of his time in the Navy. I didn't write each letter. I just decided to give you a small taste of the joking around they did with each other during this time. I hope you enjoy this bonus chapter.

January 6, 2008

Dante,

I'm hoping all is well in your part of the world. Neil told me that you all are leaving on your first mission soon. I won't lie and say I'm not scared because I am. Promise me that you will be safe and watch each other's back. I want to make sure you both come back home safely. Whether you believe this or not, you're needed in my world.

I'm sorry I missed your graduation from Seal school. I had finals and there was only one professor who wouldn't let me take my final early. I tried, and I hope you received my gift. I saw the pictures that our moms took. They looked great, and both Neil and you have changed a lot. I was shocked at how much muscle you both put on. But I wanted to say I'm proud of you both so much.

I start classes again on Monday, and I'm really enjoying college life. There's a major difference between ages though. I'm finding it tough to relate to my classmates because of it. However, Sara and I hang out often and get along well. She was the girl I told everyone about that night after my introduction night at Gates N Sons.

The twins, or as you call them Thing One and Thing Two, are still being their crazy selves. They each have a girlfriend now. The girls don't like me much; they don't really understand that we're like family. Hopefully, that will calm down a bit.

Thanks for the package you sent me. I loved the journal. The picture on it makes me want to take a trip just to relax and watch the waves roll in. Is that the same beach that you did your training on?

Here's a box of goodies for you. Share this time! I think I made enough for everyone on your team. If not, then between both Neil and your boxes, you should have enough. I will send another box once I get word on where to ship to.

Be Safe and write back soon!

Len

P.S. Just because I love learning doesn't make me a nerd.

P.P.S. One more time!!!

9th June 2008

Len,

How's summer break? Or did you decide to take some

summer classes? I'm thinking you picked the latter because it's the nerdy thing to do. And, before you can say it, one more time!

Things are going great here, now that we're finally back. It's strange being on U.S. soil after being gone for six months. I've included a few things from that mission we went on. Most are things I found and thought you might enjoy. But a few are things that I purchased after the mission was complete, before we headed home.

How are the twins now? I heard they broke up with their girlfriends. Care to tell me the real reason why? They just said the girls weren't who they wanted in a relationship. I'm assuming they didn't get use to the dynamics of your relationship with them. If that's the case, it's their loss because you're an amazing person, and they have no clue what they would've gained by being your friend.

Your birthday's coming up, and I won't be able to attend. I'm sure that Neil filled you in on our training that's required of us. I'll be sending you a package though, so keep an eye out for that.

There really isn't much more to update you on. I'm looking forward to hearing from you again soon.

Waiting for the next letter,

Dante

December 3rd, 2010

Dante,

Mom just informed me that you aren't coming for Christmas this year again. I was hoping I was going to finally see you. You do realize it has been over two years now. But I understand that you have things that are keeping you there. It just sucks. I'm also happy to know that your family is flying out there to see you.

How is California? It's cold here in Kansas City. It was fifteen degrees and we got a foot of snow. They closed all the schools so I was able to snuggle in front of the fire with hot chocolate and a blanket. I read the Twilight series again. I'm sure you're rolling your eyes at me and thinking what a silly girl I am for it. Just remember, one more time.

Thanks for the amazing perfume. I love the scent of it. I wear it daily and get compliments on it all the time. Julia and Sara tried to swipe it from my dresser and I told them think about doing it again, and I won't hesitate to cut a bitch. Okay, we both know they just laughed at me.

The families are doing great and things are just moving right along. However, I won't deny there is still two empty spots when we're all together. We all miss yours and Neil's presence when we're doing things.

Anyway, here are your gifts for Christmas. *DO NOT OPEN BEFORE CHRISTMAS*! I mean it! I hope you're doing ok and looking forward to seeing pictures that your mom takes when she returns from her visit.

Write soon!

Len

23rd December 2010

Len,

Really? Empty boxes? That wasn't very nice, and now

you know I opened them as soon as the packaged arrived. Neil died laughing and said he knew you were going to do that. He also said the real presents are coming with Mamma. I'll hound her until she gives them over.

Nothing much has been going on lately. A few missions here or there but normally they're only a week or so long. We do have another one coming up. We're not sure when but we'll keep you posted.

I'm glad you liked the perfume and yeah you won't cut a bitch. At least not your friends. What about surgery? What if your patient's a pure evil bitch? Would you cut her? Yep, that's pure logic right there. Words to think about, huh? Don't even think about calling me an idiot because you know you laughed out loud at my thought process. I'm way beyond smart in that realm. Oh, one more time on the smarts.

Anyway, I know this is short but the parents will be here in an hour. I hope you have a great winter vacation and please for the love of everything holy. Don't study on your break!

Merry Christmas Len!

Dante

June 16th, 2015

Dante,

I'm sitting here scared watching the news. There has been no word if you guys are okay. Everyone is on pins and needles waiting to hear what happened. All we know is that Neil and you were involved in a failed mission and are currently in the hospital. I hope we hear soon because I'm not sure how much longer we can wait. Please don't give up and come home.

Len

10th December 2015

Len,

No more tears and no more worries. We're coming home. We should be back by summer.

Dante

Acknowledgements

Wow, there is so many people I need to think for this amazing journey. I know I'll end up forgetting someone so in advance if I forget you, I'm sorry. I didn't do it intentionally!

First and always will be **God**. Without him in my life, I am nothing.

Lee aka My Ghost: You've been my biggest cheer leader and I'm grateful for everything you have pushed me to do. Thank you for the love and support, along with the frustration that came with me writing this book. You're the love of my life and I can't imagine my life without you. Thank you for everything you do for our family. I love you, One More Time xoxo

My kids: Thanks for making me laugh and for keeping me on my toes. Also, thanks for the times you allowed me to get lost in this book and entertained yourselves. I have a plan to take you each on a day of fun...

your choice of what we do. I love you both beyond words. Thanks for being the best teenagers a Mom could ask for.

My Family: Thank you for everything you have done in my life. I love you all.

Mari: The friendship we have wasn't one I was expecting. What started off as bonding over being writers and Military wives now has turned into something much more. I can't thank or tell you enough how much you mean to me. I can't wait until I can see you in person finally. I don't know what Germany or Italy is going to do once we finally meet!

Lynne aka My Sister/Friend/HLM4L: I'm beginning to think our friendship defies the odds of what's normal. I haven't ever heard of two people who never met in person, and live thousands of miles away from each other, be as close as we are. I can't go a day without hearing from you in some way. You're the most amazing person I know. You're also the most selfless person there is in this author world. I can't thank you enough for all you have done for me. But more importantly, you accepting me the way I am, means more than you will ever know. You're stuck with me for life. I love you and little man, tons and bunches.

Jane aka My Soul Mated Lover: You have supported me from the moment you spoke to me and I can't thank you enough. I miss our talks and text. I'm so grateful this book is done so we can get back to having fun! Thanks for all the advice, help, countless reads you have done and just being the best supporting person I know!

Kacey: From the first moment I messaged you saying, "I'm thinking of writing. Do you have any advice?" You jumped in telling me everything you can think of. I can't believe that was well over a year ago, but you still haven't wavered and still encourage me to keep going. Thank you for everything you have done. I honestly can say that, without you and your support, I would not be here right now. Thanks for giving me that push I needed. And be ready for when I finally meet you and be able to get to give you a huge hug and probably get some squealing in your ear.

Keshia: Thank you for the support and the advice that you post daily. You have a huge heart and are always quick to share whatever you can to help others succeed. That speaks numbers about the type of person you are. I can't wait until I can finally meet you one day. Don't be surprised if I fangirl all over the place and hug you to death.

Beef: I never imagined that I would run into someone who struggles with having a child that has challenges, as well as writing stories. I can't tell you just how much I adore talking with you daily and laughing at the crazy people out there. Also, your friendship you give me is one that I wouldn't ever take for granted. Thank you for being so amazing. I look forward to many more years of our daily chats.

My Crazy Beta's: Lucy, January, MaryAnn, and Diane: Thank you for all your advice, support and laughs you gave me with this book. I couldn't have made it as good as it has turned out without your help. I hope you all are ready for book two... because it's coming sooner than I thought!

Travis: You're an amazing photographer and an even more amazing person. Thanks for helping me find the perfect cover for my book! I hope I did it justice.

Meghan: You're the perfect image for my Len! Thank you for being the model for my book.

Personal Friends: Thank you for the support you gave me through this. Even if you never read it, know that I appreciate the help you gave me along the way.

Princesa, Eve, and Krystal: I still say that if anyone sees our conversations that we have... it would make people think we're truly nuts at times. Thanks for the laughs, support and the truth when I needed to hear it. I'm grateful to not only call you authors I love to read but also my friends.

Layla: Thank you for reading it and for all the amazing help you did with this book! The idea you had made it so much better and I can't thank you enough. Now, time for jello shots!

Readers: Thank you for taking a chance on a new author. I can't tell you enough how much I appreciate you reading my book. I hope you enjoyed it.

About The Author

S. Van Horne was born and raised in the small town of Belton, Missouri, which is a part of the Kansas City metropolitan area. She's from a very large family and is the oldest of six. Growing up, she didn't have the easiest life. She learned quickly that family means everything, even if it's the type that you get to pick for yourself.

She met the love of her life at the early age of twenty and was married just after nine months of meeting him. Shortly after marriage, her husband rejoined the U.S. Navy and they moved from Kansas City and started their journey together. Currently they have two amazing children, a boy and a girl, and are still enjoying the Navy life.

She spends her days being a wife, mom, reading books, writing her latest novel, watching her beloved Kansas City Chiefs or Kansas City Royals, watching movies, hanging out with family and friends and having girls' day at least once a month.

CONTACT:

FACEBOOK: S. Van Horne
FACEBOOK LIKE PAGE: Author S Van Horne
FACEBOOK GROUP: Devils Who Wear Halos
GOODREADS: Author S Van Horne
TWITTER: @smvh79
INSTAGRAM: @authorsvan
EMAIL: svanhorne@authorsvanhorne.com
WEBSITE: www.authorsvanhorne.com

Tic Tac Challenge

Hello everyone! Andy here and I needed to let you know that the website **http://www.hmttcys.com** is a real site that I created. This website is mentioned in book two. This is where you can now go and tell me just how many Tic Tacs you can swallow if you're up for the challenge. If you're not sure what the challenge is, then make sure you check out S. Van Horne's first book, One More Time. This challenge will now be in each book.

She will also have custom made Tic Tacs that will have this on it as well. There will be a section on the site soon that will also allow you to ask me questions and interact with me. I hope to see your answer soon!

-Andy

Other Books by S.

More Series:
One More Time – Book One
More Than Anything – Book Two
More To Me –Book Three – (Current WIP)
More Than Enough – Book Four (Coming Winter 2017)
Worth Much More – Book Five (Coming Summer 2018)
More Than Air – Book Six (Coming Winter 2018)
More Than Forever – Book Seven (Coming Summer 2019)

More Series Novellas:
More Than Falling – Part of the Passion, Vows and Babies Kindle World (Current WIP)
More Than Life (Coming 2018)
More Than Us (Coming 2019)

The Vow Series:
The Vow: Leaving Home– Prequel
The Vow: Jess – Book One – (Current WIP)
The Vow: Shania – Book Two (Spring 2018)
The Vow: Talina – Book Three (Winter 2018)
The Vow: Megan – Book Four (Spring 2019)
The Vow: Cassia – Book Five (Winter 2019)
The Vow: Returning Home (Spring 2020)

Anthologies:
Meat Market Anthology – KC Strip

More Than Anything

⁂

More Than Anything – More Series Book Two – Neil and Sara - Subject to change

Sara

I GLANCE AROUND LEN'S BACKYARD and smile at the happiness that fills the air. I've always wanted a family that could come together and celebrate the small joys that life brings. I almost had that at one point in my life, but it was ripped from my hands before I could even grasp it. A pain of sadness and fear flood my body, but I push it away not wanting it to take over this brief moment of happiness.

I peek out of the corner of my eye to the left and see Neil watching me. He's the hottest guy I've ever laid eyes on. The moment I met him three years ago, I thought I would faint from just how damn good looking he was. He seemed like a stuck up asshole because he really wouldn't say shit to me.

All he did was glare at me like I took the prize out of his cereal box on Sunday morning while changing the channel from his favorite cartoons.

But it slowly started changing, and I realized that he just wasn't interested in me and was just protective of his sister. I'm not one to open up and tell people my problems, as a matter of fact, nobody knows about my problems right now. I'm afraid of bringing it up and them finding out just how much trouble I can bring to their family.

I know I should be more open about it, but the detectives assured me that my file is closed tight, and that it couldn't be tapered with. That's the only thing saving me right now from Neil finding out about my past. At first, I was scared that he would find out when he did my background check for Seal Security. But nothing came up and that was a sigh of relief.

Then, there was that one night at the lake that I can't get out of my mind. It was the best night of my life, and I want to reach out and grab what Neil was offering with both hands. But my past stops me from doing that. So, for now I live though my memories and try to keep him at arms length even though he's doing everything in his power to change that.

The sound of laughter snaps me back into the present, and I see pink and blue balloons rising in the air. I'm confused for a brief moment until I hear the word twins. A huge grin spreads across my face at that thought of Dante having three kids in diapers, one of which is a girl.

That man is an alpha to the max at times, so I know that little one is going to end up hating her daddy when she gets older due to his overprotectiveness.

The sound of a phone catches me off guard, and I realize it is mine. I reach in my purse and pull out my phone to see who could be calling me. Everyone that would call me is here so it has to be the call service for Seal Security. With me as the main admin for the front all calls come to me when we aren't in the office.

I glance at the screen and freeze once I see the name and number.

This can't be happening.

He said he wouldn't call unless it's an emergency. I'm not sure if I want to answer it.

"*Habibi*, you ok?" Neil asks coming up to me.

"I need to take this," I say and rush off to the side of the house to answer the phone in private.

"Hello," my voice trembling softly afraid of what he might say.

"Sara?" a voice I know so well on the other end questions.

"Yes, this is her."

"They know, Sara. I need you to get here as soon as you can. We've got to get you to safety." I close my eyes at the words; one of my biggest fears becoming reality.

After gathering enough strength, I make my way back and spot Neil and Dante. "I have to go. Please tell Len I will call her later." I rush out before turning and running to the front of the house. Neil runs after me, shouting my name, but I quickly say something over my shoulder without stopping.

The life I know, the life I've come to build is no more. All I can do; all I *must* do is leave. They have found me, and in order to keep those I love safe, I must run without turning back.

NEIL

I glance, yet again, at the redheaded goddess that has been on my mind from the moment we met three years ago. That first meeting, I didn't mean to glare at her the whole time, but I was trying to figure out why I wanted to pick her up, throw her over my shoulder, and never share her with the world. It bothered me that she had that much power over me.

Then, I realized that the only reason I would feel that with her was because she was my one. After that, I tried everything to get her to notice me, short of just announcing that I liked her and wanted her. Nothing was seemed to work, and right when I was about to just take that plunge, my sister came up missing, and that stopped everything.

It isn't a secret that I'm a protective ass when it comes to my sister. So when she vanished the night of my company party, I felt like I failed her. After a few weeks of her missing, I knew then that after she was found, only then was I going after Sara. And, nothing was stopping me from having her.

That night at the lake was the most amazing night of my life. I had never felt perfection like I did when I made love to her for the first time or the times that followed. . But the following morning, I woke to an empty bed; abandoned and furious. When I stormed downstairs, she acted like she didn't even know me, and that made me even angrier. I'm not one to blow up in public, so I bit my lip and decided to wait until we had a second alone.

But, that second never came.

After Adams was killed, it took a while to get things back to normal, and by then I was over the anger. Now, I'm trying everything to get back to that one night we had. So far, I haven't made much leeway.

The sound of Sara's phone snaps me out of my thoughts. When she glances down to look at her screen, she turns pale, and I immediately rush over to her side.

"*Habibi*, you okay?"

"I need to take this," she states her voice trembling with fear and rushes off to the side of the house. Before I can follow, Dante steps up besides me and stops me from intruding on her call.

As he holds me back, I see her listening intently to the person on the phone. Whatever they say has her turning even palier. I swear I can feel her fear radiating from her body. I don't know who is on the other line, but I'm about to march over there and snatch the phone from her to find out who the fuck it is, when she hangs up and glances over at us. She quickly makes her way to us, her eyes show nothing but pure unadulterated fear.

"I have to go. Please tell Len I will call her later," she states in a whisper and then turns and rushes to her car.

It takes me a moment to process her words before I'm hot on her tail, chasing her.

"Sara, wait a minute. What the fuck is going on," I yell.

"I don't have time explain, Neil. I have an emergency. I'll call later," she tosses over her shoulder, without stopping.

She reaches her car and has it started before I can reach her. Just as I get close enough, she glances towards me with tears streaming down her face. So much hurt is coming through her beautiful eyes, that I stop in my tracks, something preventing me from opening her car door. Instead, my chest rising and falling fast, and my eyes silently begging her to come to me.

"I'm sorry, Neil. I never wanted you to know. Please, let me go," she whispers out of her window that's barely down.

"Never," I growl out between clenched teeth. Before I can open her door, she flips the lock and shakes her head sadly.

"Goodbye, Neil. If you remember anything, remember this, you always made me feel as if I was so much more than what I thought I would ever be," she states with a soft smile as the tears just keep streaming down. Then, she pulls out of the driveway without a backwards glance.

I stand there, shocked at the words she just spoke, watching as her car fades down the road. I vow in that moment that she isn't getting away from me that easily.

Furious, hurt, and determined, I turn and storm back into the house to let the others know that I have to go. I have to find Sara and get to the bottom of this once and for all.

It's time she sees the beast within me. The beast that will weather any storm her past can bring. Because nothing will stop me from showing her just how much more she really is to me.

Preview Leap Of Faith

Leap of Faith

Book One - La Flor Series

Copyrighted © 2015

I return to the present as I reach the stoplight. I stop and shake my head. All those memories—so haunting and beautiful. How will I ever be able to let go? When will I be able to move on? Miranda Lambert's "Over You" plays on my stereo as I wait for the light to turn.

I listen to the lyrics and realize how true they are. He went away, leaving me alone—how dare he? I know he didn't mean to leave, but he did. He went away and now I'm here raising our daughters. Alone. God, why did you have to take him from us? Why . . .

I've gone through the stages of grief but nothing takes away the pain, the loss of him. After hearing the news, I pretended he was deployed and just couldn't call me. When I couldn't pretend anymore, I became so angry—angry at the person responsible and angry that Jake would never meet our unborn child. I was angry at everything he'd miss. I also turned my anger and blame to the job he loved and the responsibilities he held. Later, I just wanted to wake from the nightmare of reality. I prayed for the nightmare to go away and I lost myself in a sea of "what ifs" and "only ifs." The only things keeping me from going into a full and dark depression were our children: Rylee and our new little miracle. I needed to be strong for them. And then, there was Phoenix. I couldn't let Jake's dream die with him. I had to toughen up and take charge. Julia was going through her own loss, so my pregnancy not only gave me strength, but it also helped bring back my best friend.

Finally, I pulled myself together and came to accept the loss of my husband. I began to live my life for our children and his dream. I existed, but I didn't *live*. My smile never reached my eyes, but I made sure to put on a strong face for my loved ones. I lived during the days and I cried myself to sleep at night. I had to learn how to live without him—I've accepted his loss but I don't like it. At times, with everything that occurred, I wonder if there was a higher power at work—guiding us, giving us strength, and making things happen.

In the distance, I hear the roar of a motorcycle, getting louder as it nears. I hear it stop beside me. I turn to my left and see this huge, beautiful black-and-chrome motorcycle. I think to myself how much Jake would like that bike and would totally want it.

My eyes leave the bike and move up to its rider. I see the side profile of a man wearing sunglasses and one of those black helmets without a visor. He looks handsome, I think, surprising myself—I haven't looked at another man since Jake. He's dressed in black from head to boots, his shirt molded to his muscular chest and his pants covering amazing-looking thighs—a work of art. I stare at him for what seems like an eternity. I know I need to stop, but for some strange reason, I can't bring myself to look away.

He must feel my stare because he turns toward me. We stare at each other. I can't turn away and I can't see his eyes. I feel a strange force refusing to let go. His right hand slowly comes up and he removes his glasses.

I gasp.

I feel that jolt, like lightning.

Oh my . . . his eyes—can they be?

From our short distance, I'm mesmerized. I've never seen eyes that color in person. So unique and beautiful. They hold me captive—I stare and get my fill. And his face . . .

Holy freaking crap!

He looks like a model. His skin is tan, his eyebrows are perfectly arched, his cheekbones are high and defined, his nose looks slightly crooked (like it was broken at one time—so he can't be a model), his lips are full but not feminine, and he's grinning.

He knows his effect on women. He's a walking dream—all deliciousness on a stick. But it's his eyes that hold me captive. They're unique to the point of being strange, and yet amazing. I can only describe them as violet. His eyes are freaking purple!

By now, I'm almost drooling, but also uncomfortable. It's been years since I've been affected by the opposite sex, and I don't know how I feel about it.

I may be drooling and staring, but so is he. I mean, he's

staring back at me. He gives me a wink and that cool-man chin raise I always thought was so sexy when Jake did it. As soon as Jake comes to mind, I feel like cold water has been thrown on me and I'm quickly pulled out of my daze.

What in the world, Faith?

I'm so engrossed, I don't notice the light has turned green until I hear a loud honk behind me. I immediately turn away and start pressing the gas to move forward. I hear him rev his engine. I take a quick glance at him one last time and notice his eyes are still on me. I think he wants me to put my window down, but I quickly look away and start moving forward. As I'm speeding away, I look into my rearview mirror and see him still in the same spot, watching my Jeep drive away.

Finally, I hear him accelerate and see him turn left. Thank goodness he went in another direction. I feel weird and unsettled. I try to shake those feelings off and keep driving. I speed away from that beautiful and electrifying man and make my way to Jake. Right now, I need to be near him and I need to share this day with him.

No matter how much I try, I just can't help but feel like my world is about to change—that it's about to be flipped upside down once again.

Preview Of Forever Mine

Forever Mine

Book One – Providence Series

Copyrighted © 2016

Ren

Jaysus, but it was hot out. I'd been guilted into spending the day helping Dad out on the family ranch instead of working in the garage that I owned in town, and if I had been in there today like normal, I wouldn't have been sweating my ass off in ninety degrees of heat and sun. Why had I said yes? Oh yeah, because of my mom. None of us could ever say no to her. With four boys and a girl under her belt, she pretty much had the entire family wrapped around her little finger.

At least it was Friday, so I could head into town tonight to get rid of this tension that felt like it was suffocating me. A couple of days ago, I'd seen a dark blonde in Cooper's while I was picking up some groceries. It had been her hair that had initially grabbed my attention because it was so unfamiliar, and between my brothers and me, we pretty much knew all of the females in the county. I'd stared, waiting for her to turn around, because if the back was that amazing, then God would be a cruel man to make the front less than the back. When she turned and started walking in my direction, I'd been floored—who the fuck was this beauty? Was she passing through or staying in the area?

She'd turned just then, and I remembered struggling to breathe for the second that we'd looked at each other for, until Grandad had suddenly stuck his face in mine, scaring the shit out of me!

"Ren, boy! I was beginning to think you'd skipped the county. Where the hell you been, and what are we staring at?"

By that point, I had been twisting and trying to look around him back at the angel, but the old bastard had been deliberately blocking my view, and when he'd finally moved, she had disappeared. For the last three days, all I could think about was her. Seriously, seeing was believing when it came to how beautiful she'd been. The problem was I'd been back to town every day since and had gone into Cooper's and hung around the area, and there was no sign of her. I thought at one point that I saw her driving a new black Escalade around, but it turned out to be George Montgomery's, which I learned because he'd driven it into my garage yesterday saying that there was an electrical fault in the driver door that needed to be dealt with. Who was she? Was she gone now? I rubbed a hand down my face and decided I needed to get laid tonight to get my man card back, because I was obsessing over this girl like chicks did over guys.

"Hey, sweetie," Mom said as I walked in. She walked up and handed me a cold, damp cloth to wipe my face and neck down. She then passed me a huge glass of iced tea.

"Hey, Ma," my younger brother Cole yelled as he walked in before I could thank her. I watched as she gave him the exact same, but that was just so he didn't get jealous. Like she could tell what I was thinking, she caught my eye and winked at me. I was so her favorite!

"Now don't y'all forget that the interior designer is coming to look at y'all's houses, okay?" she said, hands on hips.

Mom had organized this weeks ago when she'd found out that someone's niece was moving here and that she was an interior designer. Our parents had built us our own homes on the property on our 18th birthdays. Obviously, it takes a while for houses to be built and all, so we moved in when we were 19 or 20 when they were completed, but on our 18ths, we had sat down with an architect, a plan had been decided, and we'd been allowed to choose where we wanted them to be on the land the family owned. I'd been living in mine for seven years, and in all that time I hadn't really lifted a finger to change the place or decorate it aside from hanging some pictures or shelves or shit like that. My excuse was I didn't ever have the time, but the truth was I didn't know what the fuck to do with it. Then Mom had come in with this curveball, and now I was feeling a bit protective of my home, not really trusting a stranger to decorate it. I mean, they didn't know me and what I liked, and they didn't live there, so how would they decorate it for me?

"Shit, Ma, we know. You've been going on about it for weeks now. What's wrong with how they look?" Cole whined. He was such a little bitch. Even my baby sister, Layla, didn't whine as much as he did.

"Y'all haven't done one thing to those houses since they were built. The walls are still covered in white primer, and the floors are bare wood, for the love of God," she said, throwing her hands up in the air.

"Now, Ma, you taught us better than to leave our wood bare," Cole replied with a smirk on his face just as I took a gulp of my iced tea, which I sprayed all over the kitchen floor.

"Cole Jessop Townsend! That is...you are...I don't even know what to say back to that comment, apart from the fact that you will eat your words the day you meet the girl who is yours, and you'll regret your tomcatting when she finds out about it and you see the look on her face. Now get your mind outta the gutter and start thinking about what you're gonna ask her to do to your home. And you, Renwick Samuel Townsend, go get a cloth and clean your mess off the floor. I swear, I raised y'all better than this. You get this from your father's family." She walked away to the pantry, still muttering under her breath.

"Speaking of which, last night at Jilly's, I saw the most beautiful girl I've ever seen in my life. I've never seen her around here before, but she walked in with the Montgomerys, and hand to God she has unrivaled beauty in these parts," Cole told me as I mopped my spit and tea off the floor while laughing at him for using the term 'unrivaled beauty.' He'd obviously been lifting Mom's Harlequin books again which he'd done since he was twelve. Any other pubescent teen would have hit Playboy or gone online, but not Cole—he'd always loved a 'happy' ending to his fantasies. Then again, didn't all teenage boys want a happy ending to their fantasies? But Cole hadn't thought outside the box, and had instead stolen Mom's books one by one until she'd found them in his closet. Of course, we had never let him live it down since we'd found out.

"Really? Did you talk to her? What was she like?" Mom was suddenly full of interest.

"She was quite tall, say to here," he said, pointing at the bottom of his neck, "with long, curly blondish hair and these eyes that—"

My head snapped up at the description of my angel from Cooper's. "She was with the Montgomerys?"

"Yeah! All I know is she's just moved here to work or some shit and has just rented the Twyman house outside of town. Jaysus, she's beautiful, man! I'm gonna head back into town tonight and ask her out." He wiggled his eyebrows, not realizing that he was now closer to death than he'd ever been in his life.

"The fuck you..." I started just as there was a knock at the front door.

My mom clapped her hands loudly. "That'll be Maya. Y'all stop your arguing and get ready to meet the designer."

Still in the kitchen with my brother, I put my face in his. "You won't be asking her out, Cole. She's mine, and don't you forget that."

Before I could threaten him further, Mom walked into the kitchen with her guest. "Ren, Cole, this is Maya Price, the designer. Maya, these are two of my troublemaking boys, Cole on the left and Ren on the right."

Cole and I turned around, and I damn near choked all over again. There, standing in the doorway, was my beauty from Cooper's, who was now my interior designer. All of a sudden, I felt a healthy interest in decorating my home come on, and judging by the gulp I heard from beside me, I'd say my shithead of a little brother was thinking the same thing. The only difference between his thoughts and mine was that I knew in reality she would soon be mine, whereas for him it would always just be a pipe dream.

Preview Of Caught

Caught Breaking the Law
Book Five in the Caught Series
C.M. Steele
Copyrighted © 2016

Chapter 1

"I'm investigating the death of Veronica Mason," I said, showing my private investigator's badge to the receptionist at the District Attorney's office in Phoenix, Arizona. My friend asked for a favor and well there wasn't anything I wouldn't do for a buddy of mine. Trent was a good hardworking man and he needed me to do him a solid, so I said yes without hesitation. Besides it was cold back home. Here the weather was sweet.

"I'm sorry sir, but the DA is presently out to lunch with his intern," she replied with a smile. I bet he was. I twisted my lips thinking he was probably a fucking sleaze ball. Hell, what I found out took a couple of days, he had a fucking decade to figure it out, but was too busy to deal with it apparently. "But if you like I can schedule an appointment with them sometime this week." She started looking down at a large planner. Typical bullshit. Something I didn't have time for.

I immediately placed my hand over the planner, stopping her in her tracks. "I don't have time for that. I have to be back in Seattle soon." My tone wasn't harsh or anything intimidating, but she got my point. I heard the ping of the elevator behind me and the snooty receptionist look up.

"I'll see...oh they just walked in." She stood up and looked around me. I followed her gaze and fell in love on the fucking spot. Before me was a voluptuous brunette with a DA who was standing a little too close to her. I let out a low growl, that I don't think she heard, but her eyes smiled up at us. She was going to be mine. I had to bide my time until the Mason case was dealt with, but as far as I was concerned she was my woman.

"Sir. This gentleman wants to look into the case that Lily Mason keeps calling about." So Trent's woman was trying to get real answers, but that was what Trent asked me to do. It was time for the professional to make things happen and I was that guy. I had this all wrapped up and ready to gift the DA. I hoped as a reward the beauty would just fall into my lap.

"Really?" He scrunched his eyebrows at me with a suspicious gaze, then addressed me, "Give me a few minutes we'll take a look into it together."

"Miranda, can you set up conference room B?" he asked my woman. I didn't like the him calling her by name.

"Yes, sir," Miranda said, walking past me and down the hall. Tilting my head, I watched her walk away from behind. Fuck, her ass was round as hell. I wondered if she spent time in the gym or was she naturally hot. Either way, I'd learn one way or another. Too busy, ogling her curves, I forgot to scope out her ring finger. Damn it.

I heard a cough behind me. Oops, I'd forgotten the DA was standing there and that he could be hitting it. "She's not available to you. You're lucky I want this case solved sometime before I retire," he grumbled at me.

"Yeah, well you looked awfully close to your intern," I challenged, my jealousy showing.

I heard a giggle coming from the receptionist that stopped short with a glare from the DA. Then the old pervert responded, "She's my daughter."

I pursed my lips in a 'oops, my bad,' kind of way, then I apologized, "I'm sorry. It was wrong of me." I didn't tell him that I was leaving her be because that wasn't going to happen, but I needed to get the case handled, so I had to be on my best behavior. Normally, I wouldn't have done a double take on any woman, but something in Miranda's smile hit me straight in the chest.

"The conference room is ready," Miranda said, walking into the reception area. "I pulled the file and set it up for you." She also handed him another file and his glasses. He was lucky that was his daughter because I wanted to be taken care of like that and it irked me that she was catering to him.

I followed behind them, hoping to get another glimpse of her ass. The damn DA was blocking my view. I tried to get my shit together. It would be okay; I would manage to control my lust. I was going to find a way to get her alone and in my arms.

"So Mr. Wyatt, what's your role in this?"

"I was hired by Lilly Mason's fiancé to look into the matter. He doesn't like that she's still living with the uncertainty and that she probably lived with her mother's killer all these years."

"Are you saying you believe her father had something to do with it?"

"I know he did." I opened my satchel and tossed the case folder across the table, before turning to give Miranda a wink. DA Russell opened the file and his eyes popped open in surprise. "This is information you couldn't get without a warrant, but it's all the proof you need to focus on him as the prime suspect."

"We can't use this in court," he reminded me, sliding the file back toward me, but I just slid it back.

"No shit. I'm just telling you so you could go after Mason. Just so you know, he's believed to have something to do with the explosion that happened at his house up north in Lake Oswego. Lily was the only one in the house at the time." Miranda gasped, with her hand on her mouth. I reached over and patted her other hand. "Don't worry, she wasn't seriously injured," I responded with a smile.

"So tell me, Mr. Wyatt. How did you get this information?" he interrupted, giving me that stare that he bestowed on me since I eyed his daughter.

"I looked," I replied coldly. "Something your people didn't even bother to do. All searches stopped at his bank records. If you all had dug deeper than you would have found this back in the day."

"After his financials were cleared we didn't think we had to dig into his company records," he justified, clearly unhappy with their lack of conviction on the husband.

"Well now you have it. I want this solved because there are other things I have to work on," I said, giving Miranda another wink.

"Thanks for your time and this information. We'll look into both this Jerry Kroll and Mason."

"I'll be following up with you." I stood up and shook his hand and then reached for hers. Once she gave it to me I kissed it. My eyes made contact with hers briefly and I saw the attraction. We could burn down the building with the molten energy passing between us. If her fucking father wasn't coughing again, I'd close the distance and pull her close enough to kiss her.

Leaving the office, I had lots of regrets. I wanted to go back in there and take her back to my hotel. Reminding myself that I was trying to help those who needed me. I couldn't be selfish.

Going back to my hotel, I thought about how I was going to win the smart, up-and-coming lawyer. I thought about her all night, even though I shouldn't have. Trent was counting on me to find out the truth. I closed my eyes and with everything I had in me I pushed Miranda from my thoughts. I came up with my plan in a matter of a minute. First thing in the morning, I was going to visit Jerry. Now, I went back to thinking about my Miranda. Damn that ass. A cold shower was calling my name, but something about her squashed that idea and I took my cock in hand, then slept like a baby.

Preview Of Sugar Baby

SUGAR BABY by Eve Montelibano
Copyrighted © 2016
Coming Soon to Amazon...
THE GAME IS ON...

I feel my pussy gushing more fluids after that brief conversation. I stare at my phone in frustration. He sounded so cold and impersonal. Like he's too busy to be bothered by me.

While you're waiting for him here like his personal whore, excited to feel his touch again. Craving to feel him fill you again. Poor bitch. Where's you game going, I wonder?

I make an unintelligible sound, choking my bitch of a conscience to silence. I don't need to be reminded of that. My swollen, pulsating-with-need kitty is proof enough.

God, three days and I'm craving for him like a druggie. This is the first time he's left me on a business trip for days.

I've been ensconced in his penthouse suite with him most of the month, exploring the joys of carnal ecstasy. I didn't know I already got addicted to his lovemaking. To him. All of him. It happened so quickly and I fully realized it when he left three days ago for Texas.

I hate it. I'm not supposed to feel like this for him. I hate him with every fiber of my being for what he's doing to my father and our family. But I must endure it.

I must be with him for as long as he wishes, until he decides to show mercy and spare my father from going to prison. I'm the sacrificial lamb in an age-old practice of commerce. A bargaining chip.

I have to be thankful the bastard liked me the first time he saw me. I was desperate, grasping at straws.

Two days later, he claimed my virginity. And here I am now, still trying to change his mind.

There's some development though. Dad's trial has been postponed for another three months. Enough for his lawyers to regroup and find other ways to work on a plea bargain.

I knew Josh had something to do with the postponement. I felt it. Nobody can move the trial except the one pushing for it.

I have to build on that hope.

I know I can get my father out of this. I sigh and send Josh another picture.

My phone vibrates.

A message comes in from her again.

I open it and I see her little hand trapped between her tightly crossed legs with the caption: "If you don't come home to scratch this right now, I'll scratch it myself. I've learned new tricks from Xtube. Soon, I won't be needing your cock or any part of you to get me off."

I curse loudly just as the stewardess comes over to tell me the door's open.

I nod at her politely, ignoring the inviting smile on her face, another female willing to be with me for opportunities. I have ceased to believe in the power of my own physical appeal towards the opposite sex since my billions entered the two-digit category. You can't just trust anybody these days.

Whenever a woman approaches me, no matter how decorated her resume is, I'd get a serious case of commitment allergy. I can't help but remember what happened to my buddy Eric when he split with his wife a few years ago. The bitch took half of Eric's hard-earned fortune because the stupid fuck believed in true fucking love he didn't draw a prenup. Talk about blind faith. Even Jesus got betrayed by his disciple and a woman is far from a disciple. I'll never commit that stupid mistake.

I have another great example of that colossal lack of keen character judgment. My grandfather married thrice and all three ended in disaster, the second one nearly bankrupting the Landis coffers as the old man, like Eric, dared to believe in true love. Good thing my father was a genius in numbers and the Landis fortune got replenished over time. Now my father is happily married to his third wife too, but Joshua Junior was wise enough to protect the Landis interests. By the time I was ready to inherit, it has been well inculcated in my skull that marriage is a business deal. It must have an airtight contract attached to it and it must protect my interests first and foremost. Otherwise, no fucking deal.

Now here's the kicker. As much as I hate the idea of shackling myself in matrimony, I'd need one sooner or later to produce a legitimate heir to my fortune. That little brat would serve the purpose as I can demand anything from her

S. VAN HORNE

and she won't have a choice but to agree or I'll pull the trigger on her father and—

Wow. Seriously?

Shit. That brat makes me think of the stuff I dread like the fucking plague.

Grabbing my attaché case from the nearby seat, I walk towards the exit. The pilot comes out of the cockpit to shake my hand.

"I hope you were able to rest even for a bit during the flight, Mr. Landis," the pilot said with a smile.

"I sure did. Great flying, Grayson. Take a break. Visit your family. I won't be needing you until next week."

"Thank you, Mr. Landis."

I descend the stairs.

My chauffeur is waiting for me a few meters away with the stretch limo.

"Welcome back, Mr. Landis," Floyd, my loyal chauffeur greets me with a slight bow of his capped head.

"Thank you, Floyd. How's everything?"

"All's well and good, sir." I nod.

"Good. Why the limo? I'm alone."

"You might want to relax and take a snooze while we drive towards the city, sir. I stocked the cooler with your favorite drinks and Linda prepared a light snack in there. She figured you'd be hungry by the time you get here. She knows you don't eat on the plane." I smile.

Linda is Floyd's wife and the couple have been in my employ for ages. They're like family to me, some of the very few people whose loyalty to me has been tested by time.

"I see. Linda knows me too well."

"She sure does. Where to, sir?"

My cock screams home. Now!

"The JL Tower."

I regret it instantly but I won't take it back. My cock must know who's the fucking boss and it's not that fucking pussy.

Floyd nods and opens the limo's door for me. Before I get in, I nod at Reno, my personal bodyguard standing beside a black 4-Runner some meters away, silent as a ghost but deadly.

Reno gave me a salute and boarded the SUV. He will be tailing us, as he does every day if I'm not riding with him.

I enter the limo. Just as Floyd shut the door, a familiar scent attacks my senses like a blitzkrieg. Right there, reclining like a wanton goddess on the black leather seat is my little sexpot.

Clad in an outfit that could have been her old school uniform of white long-sleeved shirt with buttons at the front and a plaid skirt in red and green, her long, honey blond hair in pigtails, she greets me with the kind of smile that has driven men to madness since time immemorial.

"Welcome back, Joshua Landis the Third."

"Cressida, what the fuck are you doing here?"

She craws like a feline on the floor towards me.

"I'm here to welcome you back."

It's obvious, the little brat has taken over my household staff, including my hardcore bodyguard as they all seem to indulge her little whims.

I should send her to the other car, so Reno can drive her back to my apartment and wait for me there like I instructed her to do, but when she puts her hands on my knees and kneels between my legs, I lose the battle with my cock.

I feel myself leaking and I don't think I can attend a meeting in such condition. I wouldn't be able to think straight.

"I told you to wait for me at the apartment."

She makes this little purring sound, like a kitten snuggling closer, seeking body heat. My body heat.

"But I was so sad."

"Why?"

"Because you left me all by my lonesome there."

"I was on a business trip. Besides, you can't miss your classes."

"I was bored out of my panties."

I couldn't hide my smile. The little witch can be funny as shit.

"Bored shopping? Never heard of a female say that."

"You're looking at one."

Her hands creep to my chest, deliberately bypassing my bulging fly. She already knows how to tease me.

"I missed you. The penthouse was so empty without you. Your bed is so huge it made me miss you more."

My cock expands even more, if that's still possible. That girlish lilt in her voice is so sexy and alluring, like a potent drug enhancing my want and need of her.

"Oh Josh, I need you." She breathes, her palms framing my face. They're warm, adding heat to my already over-heating skin.

"Yeah? How much?" I remain calm.

The witch must not know how much I'm dying to bang her right now, like she's the very air that I breathe. She smiles naughtily and her hand dives between her legs and then comes back to my lips.

"Here. Taste how much I want you."

Jesus H! The scent of her arousal invades my nostrils like a snort of coke. Highly addictive shit. My calm goes flying out the window.

More Authors To Check Out

These are just a few of my favorite authors, that are automatic one click for me, for you to check out.

ML Rodriguez
Mary B Moore
Elena M. Reyes
Eve Monte
Cassia Brightmore
Sarah Curtis
Winter Travers
M.R. Leahy
Brynne Ashers
Layla Frost
Jess Eeps
Sarah O'Rourke
Trinity Rose

Made in the USA
Columbia, SC
04 September 2017